A Demon's Book of Shadows

Amanda Casey

Book Cover by 100 Covers

1st edition 2024

Also By Amanda Casey

Ocean Apothecary Series

Blue Mermaid Memories

Blue Reflections

Tidal Ancestry

Ocean Origins

Join Amanda's newsletter to receive a free novella!

amandacaseybooks.com

For those who find magic in books.

Content Warning

This book contains situations and themes that include language, blood and violence, alcoholism, loss and grief, and explicit sexual intimacy.

Prologue

I had been called against my will into the dank, underworld-equivalent layer of existence known as the Summoning. A demon far more powerful than I lived between the world of the living and the dead, where familiars had tunneled through the ground in an effort to form a barrier between witches and demons with their earth magic.

The tangy scent of decomposition burned my nose as my boots scuffed against damp soil. Water trickled through stones lining the tunnel I had no choice of running from. Any entrance or exit to this place led into a dense forest full of ebony-barked trees planted by familiars long ago. The very roots of those trees, hollowed out by eons of wind, water, and an occasional wildfire, had eroded into what today was known as the shadow archives.

My foot caught in a root cluster, forcing me to slow. Finger bones gripped the gritty threads that wove themselves over my boot. As the fingers retreated, so did the earth. Down I went, further into the pockets of clay, sand, and soil. Hollow ground always seemed to argue with itself.

Voices filled the tunnel. The demon council had already called to order.

Shit. I hoped Dad wasn't here. If he was, I'd have some explaining to do as to why I hadn't yet. . .

"Amon."

A voice rumbled like a great terrible thunder as I entered the hearing chamber. As I descended, the voices went quiet. Only my muffled footsteps echoed off the walls, which dripped with something far too sticky and green to be water.

An ancient demon sat atop a gnarled wooden stump of a spirit tree. Long, bony arms covered in dark gray skin stretched like a sickly animal to his sides. His arms were made for digging. His mouth, devouring.

The Bone Threader was a wendigo with an insatiable hunger for magic abused, unused, or otherwise, suppressed by demons and witches alike. Just the sight of him made my shadows quiver in fear. The black bands on my arms retreated, where I felt them huddle against my ribs.

The demons present in the chamber had all but retreated against the walls. Their disheveled expressions flexed and morphed with looks of horror. Striations of their auras offset the magical tomb where dreams went to die, and spirits never rested.

"Amon, firstborn son of Eugene Ravenblood. How nice of you to answer my call," the Bone Threader said with a gnash of his teeth. His face was covered by a bone-white mask without eye holes. He was hiding his identity from me today. A wendigo could take on the form of the magic abandoned by spirits he devoured.

Over the past few centuries, he'd grown stronger. As my father and brothers shifted from town to town, I thought we had escaped him forever.

"What is it that you want?" I asked, not taking my eyes off his wriggling hands.

He grinned nastily. "To discuss a grimoire."

I dug my heels into soggy earth. It was always back to the shadow archives. He'd wanted to devour the magic there ever since I was a boy. Back when mom was alive, I spent my days down by the river with her, learning about the magical shadow symbols that lived inside the grimoires.

The tang of rot stung my nose as the earth cracked and folded. His horrid breath caused my shadows to wither.

The Bone Threader dragged his massive claws across the ground. "Rumor has it that you are missing a piece of yourself."

My shadows gripped my ribs so tightly, I struggled to breathe. "I'm not admitting to anything," I barked, the sinew of my shadows aching to rip out of me. They wouldn't tolerate threats, especially from a demon who would gladly rip them to pieces.

A low, rumbling laugh filled the chamber, dislodging clumps of dirt from the ceiling. "Three hundred years ago, a witch died at the entrance to the shadow archives. When she harassed you, confused at the cause of her death, your father locked her spirit into a grimoire." He flexed his greedy fingers. "I have learned that this grimoire, along with one of your shadows, has also gone missing."

I shivered. My father had lost the grimoire shortly after he'd trapped Melrose's vengeful spirit.

The Bone Threader ground his jaw, creating a horrible cracking sound. "Your father has not done his job, nor has his sons. You must find me the grimoire, or I will devour what shadow magic remains of the Ravenblood family bloodline within the shadow archives."

"You can't punish my family like this," I bit out, exhaling every ounce of rage I had toward him.

His sinister laugh followed. "Oh, but I can. Since your mother died, your demon bloodline has fallen into my hands." He flexed his fingers, making his bones twist and crack. "Your fate is bound to the grimoire, Hidden One. You know what happens to a demon when he's missing one of his shadows."

The tattoos on my forearms burned. I knew my shadows heard what he said. The Bone Threader was right. For over three hundred years, I had not been whole.

The Summoning faded as the Bone Threader released me to the small Midwestern town of Midhaven. Cool crisp air enveloped my senses as the asphalt in the streets shimmered with dew. A small creature scurried across the street, too scared of the demon who had no place to run.

A flickering lamp illuminated a sign on a brick building:

Midhaven Public Library

1
Lucy

October 30th

A chill worked its way up my neck, cramping the base of my skull. I'd been experiencing waves of this strange energy ever since I entered the library this afternoon. Then again, I usually felt the presence of spirits more often as we approached Halloween.

I rolled my book cart toward the stacks. Working at the public library had long been my therapy. Books housed worlds that we could escape into. After the emotional turmoil that I'd been through over the past month, I would do anything to escape my personal life.

After I parked the cart by the juvenile readers, I settled in for my favorite librarian duties—shelving. Words became friends, and enemies. Some words triggered not so distant memories.

Junie B. Jones, Cheater Pants easily brought me back to life only a month ago. Memories of Jason cheating on me still festered. The wounds were still bone-deep, threatening to burn holes in my magic.

I stood by the choice I made a month ago—no other man would witness my magical talents.

My sisters did their part in helping me put my disaster of a dating life behind me. They'd gone and conjured up spells and all kinds of hexes I was sure, so that I wouldn't bump into my ex.

I worked my fingers into my favorite genre of books—fantasy. The red spine of a book with a shimmering foil title caught my eye. I grabbed the book, reading over the title. *The Devil's Desire: A Witchy Erotica Novel*

Whoops. Definitely not reading material that was appropriate for children. I flipped through the pages, catching phrases like, "*The towering wall of dark muscle pins me against the wall,*" and, "*His cock feels like ribbed silk against my—*"

I closed the book. I was no virgin, but there were absolutely some sexual fantasies I had yet to explore. In the twenty-seven years I'd been on this earth, I was likely only to find them in one of my sister's smutty romance novels.

I set the scandalous title on my book cart, returning to the shelf. One day, I'd find some hot guy found in paranormal romance books, minus the vampires. I was more of a demon girlie, anyway. Their horns were wickedly sexy. Bat wings had never been my thing, although feathers weren't all out. The book market was flooded with dark romance about fae and vampires, which I wasn't infatuated with like every other twenty-seven year old female was.

My phone chimed. I retrieved it from my purple cardigan pocket and jabbed my thumb onto the screen.

Alyssa texted me.

OMFG. Have you gotten to chapter 55 in ACOMAF?!?

No. I had not been enchanted with another spicy fantasy romance novel, which was all the new fad in the bookish world. As much as I would like to be whisked away from my Midwestern town at times, becoming trapped in a fae kingdom was not one of my fantasies.

I wedged my fingers into the spine of a children's title. The pages were grimy with fingerprints, a few ripped pages, and oh look—a drawing. The chalky scent of ink on paper that had started to yellow dictated this book was old, probably published well before the library in the quiet Midwestern town of Midhaven was built.

A ripped piece of paper with a drawing stuck out from the pages. I tugged out the drawing. The paper was thick with the waxy texture of crayon. An image of a woman with glasses appeared alongside a ghost—a shadow I'd seen drifting in and out of the stacks every evening.

I knew these doodles were made by the demon who had an unusual artistic streak. This shadowy figure had been the bane of my existence for the past week.

My shoulders tensed. This was probably the *twentieth* book I'd seen him completely vandalize. I set the stack of books aside, finding a fallen leaf. It was autumn, and Grace's dragon tree sitting atop the bookshelf was losing its foliage at an alarming rate. My youngest sister had recently convinced me of rehousing one of her plants in my work environment. Who wouldn't want a Dr. Seuss tree decorating the children's department?

A crunching noise sounded from the bookshelf. I pressed my ear to one of the books. The munching sound of a certain creature echoed against my eardrums. This creature loved books as much as I did, however, he could devour an entire shelf of them in an instant.

I grabbed the book and flipped it over so the pages opened toward the floor. The munching continued. I gave the book a shake, peeling it open to remove the dust jacket from the binding. A tiny pin-prick of a hole was present along the book's spine.

"Grubs, I know you are in there," I said, lowering my voice to the tone I knew he couldn't ignore.

The munching stopped. It took all of my strength not to fling the book across the room, forcing him out of his camouflage spell. Familiars possessed a magic all of their own, mostly allowing them to hide when they felt threatened.

"*You are lying. You can't see, or hear me,*" his grubby little thoughts came inching their way into my mind. He began his happy-go-lucky tune, which he often sang to himself as he ate holes in my books.

"*Gimme dem grubs. Gimme dem grubs. Eat them up, until they're nothing but nubs.*"

I pressed my ear to the furthest book on the shelf I assumed he was hiding in.

"*Ho hum, ho hum, don't ever think I'm dumb. I'll eat you up and spit you out ho hum, and next I'll bite your thumb.*"

I'd located the bookworm I had since I was approximately five years old. Grubs loved to spend his afternoons tunneling through the stacks while I shelved books.

He was my shelving assistant, often taking a bite out of each book as I tried to return them to their proper home.

"*Hey, books have flavor, didn't you know*?"

I shook my head. Good thing familiars had their own kind of reparative magic. Today, he was feeling rather destructive. I grabbed the book I was certain he was feasting on. He was no longer inside of it, having discarded his first snack and started somewhere on another one. "Apparently *The Very Hungry Caterpillar* wasn't your thing today?"

"*You haven't looked inside yet.*"

I flipped the book over. "You tunneled through the spine? Are you *kidding*?

"*I was hungry.*"

"No shit you were hungry." I flipped the book upside down, bending it at the spine. "Look at this. I can't keep this on the shelf," I sighed, setting the book my familiar had destroyed on the cart. It would be at least a day before his magic patched the holes and the book returned to its prior state. "You'll have a gut full of binding glue before the day is over."

"*At least I'm not eating all of the crap Jason did.*"

Ever since I moved out of Jason's apartment, my familiar's appetite had gone haywire.

"*I knew Janky Jason was no good. The guy ate a thousand pounds of Italian food a day, and fed me leftover tortillas. How does that happen in the same meal? Who mixes Mexican with Italian*?"

"Somebody who doesn't know what they want," I said, realizing why he was always ordering take-out from three different restaurants so he could satisfy his hook-ups. Note to self—never date a body-builder again, especially one who had his own secret Instagram account where half of his following was highly active in promoting pornography.

"*Don't worry. I left something in his protein shake mix to make his dick shrivel. They call us inchworms, you know. By now he probably resembles me when he's horny.*"

The hair on the back of my neck stood on end. Grubs wasn't the only one accompanying me. There was another spirit that Grubs couldn't keep away—the demon who had been watching me.

Heat branched through my fingers, curling the pages of the book I held. There was definitely a spirit of some kind shifting behind the shelves. A male spirit, I was sure. Female spirits didn't have aromas of earth, asphalt, and minty citrus like his.

I reached out, feeling for his source. All I seemed to find was a coalescing mass of aura. I shouldn't feel this way, my magic flaring and heat rolling in my belly. Not after it had only been a month since Jason and I broke up. I shouldn't feel attracted to this coalescing creep who had no business haunting my library.

I am losing my fucking mind. Am I really getting turned on by a bunch of shadows?

I continued shifting books to and from my cart, removing those I found that Grubs had snacked on. "Let's see. A witch, a familiar, and a demon all hang out together at the local library. I wonder what kind of books we'll find today?"

The shadows coalesced around me, forcing the hairs on the back of my neck to stand. "It depends on if you are discussing the book you're hiding from me." His voice was cool and silky, taking on a darker tone that I so wanted to get lost in. He was either a demon, or a poltergeist. I knew this, because he had yet to show me his eyes.

My shoulders stiffened at his reply.

Was he accusing me of hiding a book?

"Can you at least give me a hint on the subject matter of this so-called book I'm hiding from you?" I asked.

A grunt followed my question, the sound making the books on the shelf topple over. "Something you don't believe in."

I scoffed. He was talking about magic, again. "Something can still exist even if someone doesn't believe in it."

The shadows shifted closer to where I stood. "Hand the book over. Demons don't have time to play games."

My stomach twisted. *Demon*. At least he'd admitted what he was.

"Wait just a minute," I said, sliding up next to the pile of books I'd straightened, which were preparing to topple over again. "I am a librarian. Helping people—even spirits—find reading materials is what I specialize in, regardless of my beliefs. And I am sure as heck not hiding a book from you regarding magic."

The demon hovered over me, his dark features concealed by a tendrilling black shadow. "My dear Lucy, I will find what I am looking for, no matter how much you want to keep it from me. I highly doubt that you can find use for a book about magic that you don't believe in."

My phone chimed. I grabbed it from my pocket. My oldest sister had texted me.

Lucy, come on. It's Halloween Eve! Get your butt home now!

The demon dispersed, leaving me facing the bookshelves. Something pink oozed out of one of the books, which I grabbed. Try as I might, I wasn't able to pry the pages open.

My skin heated as the pink substance stretched. My hair frizzled. The bones in my fingers vibrated as my magic flared.

Bubblegum? Are you fucking kidding me?

I slammed the book closed. If I found one more nasty piece of invasive material in the stacks, I was going to lose it. This Halloween wasn't going to be like any other I'd allowed to pass in my twenty-seven years of existence.

I was going to exorcize this demon from the public library come Halloween.

2
Amon

Seething black waves pulsed through my aura as Lucy Crow stormed out of the library. There wasn't much a demon could do once a witch—especially a book loving one—made up her mind. I'd been harassing her for over a month now, but today, I accused her of hiding a magical text, which made perfect sense to me. Witches were very protective of the magic they practiced, especially old magic that hadn't been dabbled in for well over a century.

I'd followed the grimoire's magical aura to her library, where the vortex of shadows were currently so powerful, I could barely manifest into my physical form. I was so close to discovering the location of the grimoire, I could taste it. My bones rattled any time I thought about holding the magical manuscript and flipping through the gritty pages once again, especially now that the Bone Threader had threatened me.

In addition to tracking down the grimoire, there were other reasons I had been attracted to the library, and in particular, Lucy. You see, shadow magic did a remarkable thing to witches. It made her blood trill and burn and strike musical notes that enchanted a demon's soul. She became an instrument of seduction and power that pulled a demon's shadows closer to her, tethering him to her in a way that he became in danger of losing himself in her magic.

Maybe doodling images and sticking gum into one of the books in the children's section of the public library wasn't the best idea. Although my behavior was definitely not as destructive as what her grouchy familiar was getting away with. With the library closed, and my prized librarian gone, I was left hovering over the bookshelf, pondering my next steps on trying to track down the grimoire.

Even though I hadn't discovered the book, I had observed something very strange about the librarian witch's magical practice.

Any normal witch would have used her magic to remove the invasive wad of gum from the books she tended to. But Lucy Crow did not use a spell, or charm, or hex to address the gum. Instead, she had unfolded the pages, gathered the nasty ball of gum I'd spent the day grinding between my teeth, rolled it into a piece of paper, and disposed of it.

After a month of testing her magical boundaries, I'd concluded one very startling and unusual thing.

Lucy Crow was suppressing her magic.

Why, I didn't know. But magical suppression, if practiced for a long length of time, could become quite dangerous. Suppressing one's magic made a witch a target for other witches who would gladly take advantage of her magical focus.

I coalesced, solidifying myself as I was the only soul left in the library. The annoying munching sound was still coming from the stacks. A lumpy green bug was feasting on the doodles I had left in one of the children's books.

"*Your art tastes like garbage*," the inchworm said to me, his grumbly little voice echoing in my mind.

"Inchworm, I'm not here to—"

"*—Bookworm*," it corrected. "*I have a name other than It.*"

I sighed. The last thing I needed was another fucking familiar trying to convince me to pull my hair out.

"*Nice try with attempting to accuse my witch of stealing one of your stupid grimoires.*"

"Do you know where it is?"

"*If I did, I wouldn't be telling you, now would I*?"

I scoffed. "You won't scare me off that easily."

"*Try me. I have horrible breath after I've eaten lunch.*"

I backed away as the nasty little creature manifested on the bookshelf. It let a noxious plume of green gas out of its mouth. "I forgot just how protective of witches you familiars are."

"Hey, that's what us familiars do. We protect our witches from exes, assholes, and nasty demons like you," he barked. *"Now, go back to the crypt you came from before I take a bite out of your nose!"*

"Shouldn't you be preparing to, I don't know, turn into a moth or something?"

"Shouldn't you be haunting a graveyard instead of doodling in a bunch of children's books?" he huffed. "I'm going to be spending the rest of the afternoon munching through the doodles you've made and returning the books to their original form."

I pinched my brow. While Lucy hadn't discovered my other drawings, her familiar had. Since when had familiars become such obnoxious librarian companions?

I dipped back into nothingness, stepping into the edge of the Summoning. The parallel existence us demons drifted through next to the physical world was like walking through a door where the inside air and outdoors mixed, only time didn't follow. As much as I wished I could stop time, my thoughts could not linger here. The Summoning was a place for lost spirits and abandoned magic.

I needed to meet with my brothers and come up with a Plan B on how to track down the grimoire.

With my exhale, I exited the Summoning and stepped once again into the physical world. I was met by the obnoxious blare of an electric guitar. The afternoon crowd at Shadow Daddy's local bar was always hit-or-miss. But on Halloween Eve, all of the spooks in town were preparing for a little adult entertainment.

A live band played in the corner. It wasn't even five, and the bar was nearly full. Both pool tables had a dozen people crowded around them.

I spied the sunburned head of my younger brother over by the bar. Zed had the least amount of hair of us three brothers, being completely bald. Between his band and his schedule working a bunch of odd jobs, he was probably the busiest of us.

Zed liked to drink when Krim, my other brother and bar owner, wasn't here. He flirted with the waitresses and got free booze Krim would otherwise charge him three times the amount for.

"Skelly Zelly," I said, sliding up beside my brother. His fingers curled over an ashtray, a dying cigarette drooping from them. The embers burned his fingernails, but he didn't seem to notice. He was talking to a chick next to him who was busy flirting over his tattoo. I'd given him the tattoo only a few weeks ago when he'd gone through a nasty breakup. Zed had the heart of a lion trapped in the body of a wolf who had forgotten how to shift properly. "Why isn't it you up there and not these creeps?" I asked as I eyed the band, knowing how musical my younger brother was. He could hit circles on the drums better than Led Zeppelin.

Zed had a soft spot for animals, and the girl ogling his new ink had a cat tattoo on her forearm.

"No idea," Zed barked, not turning to acknowledge me.

"Where is Krim?" I asked, and the girl with the cat tattoo batted her eyes at my brother, then slinked off with her beer toward her girlfriends playing pool.

"Teaching," Zed said, his eyes following her across the bar before he swung his head toward me. My younger brother was very flamboyant and animated in ways that might make him seem gay. But he wasn't. He devoured women like chocolate ice cream on a hot summer day.

"I thought he had Friday's off," I protested, stealing the girl's seat. "Hey, you know you'll get your ass handed to you if Krim finds out you lit up in his bar," I said, knowing well that Shadow Daddy's had a very strict rule about no smoking of any kind.

Zed tapped out his cigarette in the ashtray and slammed his beer bottle onto the bar. "Krim can shove one of his nasty pastries down his throat. I need you to do me a favor. See this?" He rolled up the fabric on his shirt and showed me his forearm.

"What did you do, dunk it inside of a deep fryer?" I asked. His flesh was a crispy black and blue.

"No," he growled, his head trembling. "My gig at the graveyard is pulling double shifts, and a demon can't pass up the opportunity to make some quick cash. I dug too far into the neighboring grave, and accidentally scraped my arm against a rusty casket."

Digging in the dirt and mud, Zed saw lots of familiar kin. Many of his odd jobs brought him closer to the earth and decomposition. Krim and I called him Skelly (skeleton) Zelly. The guy was basically a bag of bones walking down the street. Despite his bony appearance, he was the strongest of us brothers. Even though he'd forgotten how to shift into the ravenous wolf that he was, he still had a powerful set of paws. I'd seen the guy win arm wrestling matches at this very bar with only his pinky finger.

While all of us demons had shifter talents, those who possessed forms that resembled creatures were preferred to serve on the demon council. Something animalistic peeked through Zed every once in a while. Watching him go through puberty was fun, his inner demons fighting over which form to take on. He would have been perfect for a position within the demon council serving alongside Dad, had he not forgotten how to shift into his creature form.

"I told you to keep it clean for a fucking week," I bit out.

"I think the rust makes it look kinda pretty, don't you think?" he replied, taking another swig of beer. Condensation beaded on the bottle, dripping as he slammed it down. "Anne said it's gorgeous, but it lacks red."

"Well, Anne can go back to ogling her sun-faded cat. Orange isn't the best pigment for skin anyway."

"I'll be ogling more than her pussy tattoo later," Zed said, his eyes meeting mine. They were bright green, electrically so. He set his arm on the bar, swinging one of his steel-toed boots away from the other. He cocked his head sideways. "You know what? You're too uptight about this grimoire business. You need to get laid."

"I don't have time for a relationship."

A wolfish grin spread across his face. "Who said you need to be in a relationship to fuck?"

I sighed. I didn't need my brother to tell me just how uninteresting my sex life had become.

Zed slapped me on the shoulder with his giant hand. "Come on, Amon. Look around you? There are plenty of women here who would love nothing more than for a nice thick demon cock to go sliding between their legs, no strings attached. You've been searching for this book for how long now? Why don't you indulge in your wild side a bit?"

"I've been searching for as long as I've been missing one of my shadows," I replied, thinking back to the wendigo's hollow eyes from only a few months ago. His hot, rattling breath still permeated my skull. "*Your fate is bound to the grimoire, Hidden One. You know what happens to a demon when he's missing one of his shadows.*"

"You know that us demons can make both witches and non-witches alike feel like a queen. We have a special talent for awakening their inner goddess," Zed boasted. "You've got a hard-on just thinking about this Lucy chick at the library. Have you considered giving her a *real* tattoo, if you know what I mean?"

I knew that Zed took the whole *marking* thing to another level. His animalistic side often emerged when it came to hunting down a true mate.

I shook my head no.

"I've got to know. Does Lucy have those big sexy librarian glasses that she's constantly straightening on her nose?"

"Nope, she does not," I replied, thinking back to the gorgeous color of Lucy's bright eyes. I liked the fact that she didn't have some thick, clunky glasses separating her gaze from mine. I liked looking into those blue eyes of hers and fantasize about all of the wild things I wanted to do to her.

"*You mean the things that we want to do with her.*"

I shuddered, slapping my arm.

"Amon, you all right?" Zed asked as he took another swig of his beer. "Or did you get caught up fantasizing about those glasses?"

"I'm just a bit tired is all," I grumbled. My shadows often had fantasies far darker than my own when it came to bedding a witch.

"What's stopping you from laying her out?"

"A familiar," I grunted.

Zed's eyes went crossed. "What kind?"

"A fucking bookworm."

Zed hiked his head back as he laughed, spittle flying out of his mouth. "Wow, Amon. You really know how to pick a witch!"

His laughter faded. I was grateful, because right now, I felt like a piece of shit. Familiars, especially the ones that were bugs, were incredibly protective of their witches. There was a reason so many Halloween stories involve the lesser-loved creatures. The earth magic that protected a witch was owned by familiars.

"I confronted her today about the energy I've felt around the library. I know the grimoire is nearby."

"What did you say?"

"I accused her of hiding the grimoire. She promptly blew me off, and her familiar basically cussed me out."

The bartender set another beer down in front of Zed, which he slid toward me. "Halloween is tomorrow. You'll be fine. You've got this Lucy librarian chick in the bag. Keep pestering her. Leave her familiar to me."

The beer stopped in front of me. I could see my own terrified expression reflecting in the dark glass. "You want to help me?"

"Of course I do. I want to help my oldest brother rebuild the confidence he used to have with witches, if you know what I mean."

I chuckled darkly. *Confidence*. What a lie that word was.

Zed threaded his fingers together and cracked them. "That's why a demon needs brothers. You've got two who've got your back in this." He tilted his tattooed arm toward me. "Before you work your shadow magic on little Miss Librarian, I need this fixed."

"Can you swing by tomorrow? I'll make time for a touch-up."

Zed grinned, his wide, wolfish mouth displaying a set of perfect white teeth. "I'll be by bright and early. Halloween is the perfect time for fresh ink."

3
Lucy

"I highly doubt that you can find use for a book about magic that you don't believe in."

Highly doubt my ass.

The demon's condescending statement boiled in my brain like a poisonous potion would in a witch's cauldron as I trudged down the street for home. There were plenty of books about magic that I believed in. I just chose not to get involved with them. Since my father passed, I had little to no interest in casting spells or hexes.

The grungy building on the corner of Sawhatch and Main Street came into view as I rounded the street. A local bar nobody seemed to remember existed appeared. Nobody in town knew who founded it, or how long the bar had been there. According to both of my sisters, Shadow Daddy's was brimming with the shadow magic practiced by demons. Yet in all of the years I'd walked to work, I had yet to see one of the shadowy figures sharing company with other humans.

My phone chimed. Alyssa was blowing me up with texts.

Girl, do you want to chat about Crystal the witch or not?

I pocketed my phone and left for the local coffee nook around the corner. A chilly breeze picked up, gripping my jacket as I swung the front door open. College students flooded the space, jostling against each other as they ordered caffeinated beverages.

Alyssa was set up at the bar with her laptop, her dark pixie-cut hair highlighted purple for Halloween. As I approached, she tilted her head my way, sliding her massive blue glasses up her nose.

I felt so bland next to her with her iridescent nails matching her favorite genre of fantasy. I was no match for her flair. She looked like something out of a fantasy novel. It was no wonder she had thousands of bookstagram followers.

She clapped her hands together. "So? How is the witchy read coming along?"

"Same as last week," I said, sliding into the stool next to her. "I still haven't found an illustrator."

Alyssa's fingers flew over her keyboard as she answered a DM. "We will find you one. It just takes time. You're self-publishing this thing, right?"

"Yes. I don't want some agent or editor telling me what illustrations to use for my first book," I replied. The world of traditional publishing just didn't sound like my thing. Crystal might be my fictional character, but like me, Crystal the witch could also see spirits. She could see them by looking through the crystals she collected.

Alyssa continued to type. "You know how shadow daddys always get me hot and bothered. They are my favorite male characters right now. I really wish there were more books with them for me to devour."

"Haven't you been to that bar before?"

"What bar?"

I shrugged, acting like I'd misspoken. Alyssa wasn't a witch like me. Only the Crow sisters and our mother seemed to know about the mysterious bar's existence in town named after her favorite fictional male characters.

Alyssa took a sip of her coffee and set the cup back on the counter. "So, back to Crystal the Witch."

"You're going to have to keep our discussion G-Rated. Are you okay with that?" I asked, knowing just how steamy some of her book promotional material could get.

She fanned her face. "I promise. I told myself that I would branch out and help some indie authors who want to self-publish middle grade and children's material." She closed her laptop, then slid her huge glasses up her nose again as her gaze settled onto me. "I know this story like the back of my hand. Some kid is going to love reading it! I can promote your book all day, but it doesn't matter how popular it becomes. If the author doesn't believe in the characters, it won't sell, end of story."

"I do believe in it. But first, I want to *see* it. Once I find an artist who can capture the storyline, I think I'll be better off. I should have just written a smutty romance novel instead."

Alyssa giggled, shaking her head. "Look, we all know smut sells, but that doesn't mean you have to write it. You have to start somewhere. We just need to get you out there so people know who you are and that you love what you write."

I propped my elbows onto the bar. Nobody said the self-publishing route for children's literature was easy, but I was always up for a challenge. It wasn't like I was trying to become a best-selling author. I would be happy if only a few kids read it. "Do you think anyone will even like this book? Be honest with me."

Alyssa grinned mischievously. "Look, the fact that you are writing a magical book to help kids cope with dyslexia? Come on. That speaks for itself!"

"I just hope that it's not too preachy, you know?"

"Go for substance over popularity. Children's books are all about pictures! That's the selling point. If the illustrations suck, so will the story, especially if we are going for a picture book." She flipped her laptop back open. "Tell me when you want me to start promoting. I can't wait to feature you with these pics!"

I couldn't believe it. She already started a Pinterest board created for Crystal's adventures. I was so lucky to have Alyssa as a book marketing buddy. I might work at a library, but I had absolutely no idea what I was doing when it came to promoting my own story.

I squinted at one of the mockups she made. "What does that say? *Witchly Wicked Crystals*?

"Oh, good thing you saw that. It's a typo!" Alyssa's fingers flew over her keyboard as she fixed her simple mistake. "How did you see that?"

I shook my head. "Dyslexia, remember? A lot of what I see is imperfect."

Alyssa winked. "Good thing you are my one and only reading witch. An editor would kill for that kind of talent."

I shrugged, wishing I didn't second-guess myself with everything I read.

As the afternoon inched by, so did my focus. Tomorrow was Halloween, and the last thing I wanted to do was get wrapped up in my magical talents. My toes curled in my boots as I thought about the interaction I'd had with the looming black spirit at the library.

I might second-guess myself when it came to reading, but the one thing I didn't doubt was when my magic flared.

Someone was following me who had a place between the worlds of the dead, and the living.

The dirt on the sidewalk shifted as a dark figure descended from the sky.

I stopped in my tracks, eager to set some proper boundaries between me and this shadow-wielding demon. I folded my arms across my chest, blinking at the strange colors forming around the black cloud that seemed to suck color out of the twilight.

His skin was dark in color, a mix between tan and honey. Wide cheekbones framed his face. Deep-set eyes sat beneath a strong black brow. His eyes were as crisp as an autumn night heavy with frost. His hair wasn't all black. Hints of red shone near his ears, catching the dim neon glow from the lights outside of the bar.

Black clothing covered his arms and legs. I couldn't tell if the fabric was leather or something else. It was shiny in places and dull in others, offsetting him against the brick wall.

I caught a whiff of firewood and leather and minty asphalt.

Something else lingered in his silhouette, an aura? The hovering mass of shadows clung to his sides like night did the darkening horizon. He didn't have horns, but holy shit, he was fucking *hot*. Before I let my fantasies run away with me, I needed to set some boundaries with this demon who thought he could vandalize my books and convict me of stealing.

I squinted at his darkening mass. What was he wearing, anyway? His pants were far too tight to be comfortable around any guy's crotch.

Stop looking at the bulge at his crotch. . .

My knees buckled as his hands withdrew from the shadows. His hands were absolutely beautiful. Why a man's hands were my kink, I had no idea. But judging by the ridges of his tendons above his wrist and deep bow of his thumb, I'd say he worked quite elegantly with them.

"Why are you following me?" I asked.

"I'm not following you," he corrected, just as coolly as he did at the library.

"Stalking is a huge red flag," I snapped, squaring my hips to face him. Nope. I was not going to take this kind of harassment. Better set this shadow creep straight right now.

"I'm not stalking you. I'm making sure they don't find the book before I do," he said.

"Who are *they*?"

Amusement glinted in his eyes as a crooked grin tugged at his mouth. "Tell me, Lucy Crow. How much do you really know about us demons?"

My mind was lost to the dirty romance novels had crowding her bookshelf. Every night she came home from the vet clinic as hungry as she was horny, she volunteered me to read aloud some of the ghastly sex scenes in her books as she prepared dinner for us.

I dug my heels into the pavement. "Well, after today, I know demons are fond of stalking *and* arguing pointlessly about books I have no possession of."

His nostrils flared.

Was he *smelling* me?

I padded toward him, stopping a few feet before his tendrilling shadows as they crept toward me. "I want to know more about this mystery book you are convinced I'm hiding."

His smile morphed into a smirk. "It's a book of shadows owned by demons."

My breath caught. "It's a grimoire?"

His gaze hardened. "Not just any grimoire off the street. The text is something that houses information on the three magics."

The wind stirred between us, sending dandelion stems curling. The air was heavy with something crisp and ancient, maybe even forbidden.

The demon's shadows thickened as they tendriled toward me. "But I'm assuming that since you aren't practicing magic, you don't really care about this book," he said, his voice quivering with what might be rage. "I suggest that you hand it over to me now to avoid future threats."

Heat branched up my spine at his words. I wasn't going to allow my magical practice to make me feel vulnerable. "And whom might these threats come from?"

"There are far more dangerous demons than I, Lucy Crow. I would hate for a witch who is not practicing magic to come into contact with one. I highly doubt you would have any defense against their shadows."

My body was trembling now, and I was unable to hide it. I clenched my fists, taking a step toward him. "I *do* know about the three magics. In fact, my family is very well-versed in them."

"Then you must know that ever since the last Earth Uprising movement, there has been a great disturbance between them."

I locked eyes with his ebony ones, flecks of color drifting in them. His gaze was too intense to be beautiful, yet I felt myself becoming lost in him.

I was the first to blink.

His shadows continued to thicken, a few of which were now touching me. They weren't cold like I imagined them to be, but oddly warm as they explored my ankles. "The grimoire documents how the three magics were created." His tone was sharp, lacking any shred of patience.

"I know what the Earth Uprising is. I know that familiars created the magical events for thousands of years, dating back to Mesopotamia. The ancient Egyptians wrote about the plagues familiars created so they could protect their witches from demons. My Dad used to journal all the time. He had a lot of hypotheses on the forgotten earth magics owned by familiars."

One of his brows drew up. Was he impressed with my knowledge? Or did he think that I was some stupid witch working in a library?

"Earth magic is owned by familiars, but it was not created by them," he corrected me again. "The grimoire specifically holds information on the *creation* of the three magics."

I held up my hand. "Stop talking. I don't even know your name."

"It's better that way," he whispered, shadows folding around him.

As quickly as I blinked, he was gone. Tendrils of condensation drifted past me, setting a chill into my bones.

Arrogant ass. Human male or demon, the last thing I needed was another self-centered asshole ruining my life.

I'd be safe as soon as I got home. Victoria had enough magic brimming around her property to keep even the creepiest of creeps out.

A cast iron fence lined the sidewalk for my remaining walk home. The entire length of the fence was decked out in glittery purple bows with skeletons hanging from them. Their skulls weren't human. They were either felines or birds—both creatures my vet sister was fond of.

As I walked, my older sister's residence came into view. Set behind groves of junipers and oak trees, the giant purple Victorian house emerged, fitting the spooky vibe of this time of year. I'd memorized the cracks in the sidewalk walking to and from this house to the library. Grubs often emerged from one of them in the morning, hitching a ride with me to work. I paused, waiting for Grubs to shift in my bag. So much for my familiar protecting me from a demon stalker.

I continued walking down the path, taking in the spooky atmosphere. So much of my family history revolved around this block. Mom moved out a few years back as the house was too big for her. Victoria inherited the property. I moved in with her not long after my breakup with Jason.

The one good thing about moving in with my eldest sister was the commute to work. Victoria's home was definitely haunted, not by ghosts, but by familiar spirits. I was just a child when we moved from the country into this house. Familiars from the fields and rolling hills between Kansas and Colorado followed us from the farm, inhabiting every nook and cranny they could turn into a home.

I had a childhood memory of being in the car moving to town, Grace wriggling next to me in her car seat. She had curly blond hair, and a mushroom pacifier sticking out of her mouth. Her pudgy little legs and arms were covered in jumping spiders.

Michael Jackson's *Thriller* blared through the open window. The second I climbed the five steps onto Victoria's front porch, a skeleton swung down from the archway, yelling "Show me yer bitties, or I'll cast a spell on yer titties!"

Swinging my hand, I knocked the skeleton aside. Every Halloween, Victoria came up with some other vulgar excuse to scare away the children from her front porch. And every year, I tried to convince her why having a foul mouthed skeleton that threatens to "*break the boners of the elderly*" was a bad idea.

"Lucy!"

My younger tomboy sister, Grace, was headed toward me. Her light brown hair swung down her shoulders as she skipped up the path. She wore a forest green dress with mushrooms sprouting near her knees. Black lace leggings covered her long, limber legs. Her feet were bare. She must have already kicked off her flip flops along the path up here.

She climbed the five stairs to the porch, holding two terracotta pots in her arms. One was lime green—her favorite color—the other was black with purple polka dots.

"I see you have some presents from the greenhouse?" I pried.

"Oh, Victoria's gonna get a kick out of what I have to show her," Grace replied, stopping with a big mischievous smile in front of me. A couple years ago, she purchased an abandoned warehouse with her inheritance from our father, tore it down, then used her magic to rebuild it into a greenhouse.

"Please tell me that you didn't bring Grubs?" she asked, her expression full of scrutiny.

I shook my bag. Nothing wriggled. "Nope. He's probably tunneled through half of the books in the children's section by now. He's preparing for his autumn chrysalis."

Grace's shoulders fell in relief. She knew just as well as I did about his ferocious appetite this time of year. She forbade me from taking him anywhere close to her greenhouse.

I sighed. At least her familiars made things pretty. Mine just devoured books and pooped on everything. Her greenhouse was often *hopping*, *popping*, and *screeching* with a zoo of a witches's companions—and that was only what lived in her potted plant collection.

The cackling cry of my eldest sister sounded from behind the door. She pressed half of her face to the glass in an attempt to scare us, smudging her mascara. The door cracked open, and Victoria's wild and wacky witch wig swung in front of her face.

"Who do I have here? Oh, it's the Crow sisters!" she cried, hiking her head back in a fit of cackling laughter. The door swung ajar, revealing her lacy purple and black dress. Of course Victoria was wearing something scandalous. She was a large, curvy woman in her mid-thirties with a personality that matched her body. Her black hair streamed over her shoulders in long wavy sheets. Half of it was colored purple, while a few of the strands are highlighted with bright goblin green. One of her breasts was lumpier than the other. Victoria was a breast cancer survivor. She had her right breast removed, thus she frequently stuffed her bra with items that made her cleavage appear uneven.

"This is heavy, can we please come in?" Grace asked, shoving past me with her garden pots. A tiny *screeching* sound erupted as she walked by.

Victoria shifted sideways, her cleavage jingling. "Come inside, my lovelies. The Halloween Eve Eve festivities have just begun!"

I followed Grace into Victoria's home, which for the time being, was also mine. She was renting a room out to me free of charge.

"Wow, you really have gone all out," Grace said, setting her pot down on the kitchen table, nearly sending a pizza box flying. There was barely any room as the space was covered in piles of crystals. Victoria liked to pull out all stops when it came to setting up her Halloween crystal altars. Amethyst, rose quartz, and a ton of smokey quartz crystals were lined up next to each other. A few candles burned in a circle, their black wax dripping onto the crystals.

I blinked a few times at the centerpiece of the crystal altar. The plastic cauldron was full of something that should by no means be handed out to children. "Are those a bunch of purple dicks?" I asked, suddenly wishing I wasn't here.

Grace cackled.

Victoria snorted. "I told you I wasn't going to be PG this year."

Grace continued cackling, matching the whimsical laughter of who I knew was Bette Midler from the TV. *Hocus Pocus* was playing on the television in the room over. The cackling cry of the Sanderson Sisters added to our trio's ambiance as we gathered around the kitchen table.

"Wait until mom sees the décor in your house. She's going to think you have a side profession other than working at the vet office," Grace said with a smirk.

I stifled a laugh.

Victoria leaned forward, reaching for the cauldron. Crystals spilled out from her right breast, one of them landing in the pot Grace set on the table.

All three of us launched backward as a loud undulating *screeeeeeeeech* exploded from the pot.

"What the hell was that?" I asked, clapping my hands over my ears.

Grace removed the crystal, digging her fingers down into the soil. She withdrew a bean about the size of a black-eyed-pea. The soil trembled as she held the bean in her palm for Victoria and I to see. "I've been propagating them over the summer. We'll see if come spring, they produce any flowers."

"They aren't magic beans, are they?" Victoria entertained Grace.

Grace's eyes brightened. "Screaming death beans have been known to help a witch do all kinds of strange and magical things. I think they belong to the forbidden spice plant."

"Is that a real plant, or something you made up?" I asked.

Grace rolled her eyes at me. "Just because you read books doesn't make you an expert in botany. There are loads of magical herbs and spices. Just ask mom. She cooks with spices from my greenhouse all the time."

"Maybe you can help me figure out what to feed Grubs before he devours the entire library."

Victoria erupted into another hysterical laughing fit. "I swear, that familiar is going to continue to ruin your sex life if he keeps his destructive behavior up."

"You and me both," I replied as I opened the pizza box and helped myself to the first slice.

"I wish some guy would devour me like your familiar devours books," Victoria replied as she grabbed two pepperoni slices.

Grace passed out paper plates as Victoria and I set out the pizza. Our youngest sister, in all of her introverted awkwardness, was probably the most sexually satisfied. Victoria hadn't had any serious suitors in months, and I was still recovering from a breakup.

Heat pulsed between my thighs. I wondered if I should bring the demon up to them. His cool, silky voice was suddenly distracting me as I reflected on Victoria's *devouring* comment.

"Just as long as you aren't dating one of those green vampires," Grace said as she grabbed a pizza slice and rolled it up. She then grabbed a bottle of Ranch dressing and lathered the crust.

"Are green vampires less dangerous than the blood-sucking ones?" I asked as I took my first bite of greasy pizza. Grace always had a new term for the hip new trend girls her age use to identify the supernatural or paranormal. While vampires had been discussed in my family before, they tended to be a hushed discussion. Victoria swore she dated a vampire once, claiming he sucked away any enjoyment she had in the bedroom.

Grace shook her head. "Green vampires are worse than the ones who go after blood, because they drain your energy. Every college girl I know right now is into this vampiry stuff. It creeps me out. I don't need anyone sucking my blood, or my energy. Energy vampires are the worst."

"Speaking of blood, who wants wine?" Victoria asked as she readjusted her bra.

Both Grace and I raised our hands.

Victoria uncorked a bottle and poured generous glasses for all three of us.

"Are you trying to convince us to spend our evening shoving crystals down our cleavage?" I asked after I swallowed my first bite of pizza.

"Of course!" Victoria grabbed the cauldron and shook it. "It's Halloween tomorrow, *and* a lunar eclipse? Come on, girls! Grab yourself some titty crystals! We're going rogue this Halloween!" She shimmied, making her cleavage jingle.

I stifled a snort. Okay. Victoria and I *both* liked crystals. In fact, the witch I was writing about in my children's book loved them too. She didn't have a cauldron, but a magnifying glass with a magical lens that allowed her to see familiars.

Crystal the witch was a fictional character inspired by my father's love for rocks. He believed that familiars were born out of minerals, as their magic was earth based.

"Come on, Lucy. When was the last real adult book you read, instead of a children's book?" Victoria asked, taking a swig of her wine.

"Can't remember," I replied.

"That's a sign you need to broaden your horizons into the deeper waters of the library science field. You never know what career opportunities a smutty book might present you with."

"Thanks for the career advice," I replied snarkily. It was true, librarians barely made more than teachers on a good day. I couldn't complain. She was letting me live in her house free of rent so I could build up my savings account again.

"Is everything okay?" Grace asked as she gazed over my head. Her eyes became glassy. "You seem a little off. I can't read auras like mom can, but you've got some residual emotional energy clinging to you. Did something happen at the library?"

I bit my tongue. Grace was far better at reading auras than I was. The shit I'd been dealing with for the past month was borderline harassment. No librarian, witch, or non-magical practicing human being, should have to deal with an infuriatingly attractive demon haunting their library.

I rolled my eyes. My sisters both thought that suppressing my magic meant that I wasn't having orgasms. Okay, I will admit, it had been a hot minute since I had a back slamming, panty shredding, hair ripping out screamer. In fact, I'd never had one of those. I'd only read about that kind of romance in kinky romance novels.

"So, are you seeing anybody that isn't human?" Victoria asked, her eyes landing on me.

Grace's gaze lingered just as heavily as she turned smoky-eyed. Both of my sisters knew that I inherited Dad's unique ability to see spirits.

I took a swig of my wine. I needed to tell someone what I'd spent the past few weeks dealing with. "If demons count as dating material, then yeah. I'm seeing someone. I have one harassing me at the library."

"Seriously? A *demon*?" Victoria gasped, her mouth opening wide.

"How long has this demon harassment been going on?" Grace asked, her tone full of alarm.

"For at least a month. Today, he put gum in one of my books that even Grubs refused to snack on, and he'll devour anything he finds."

Grace's face twisted with disgust, while Victoria cackled maniacally.

"He also said something that is eating at me. He's accused me of hiding some grimoire."

Victoria's smile turned greedy. "A book of shadows? That sounds juicy!"

"Grimoires are dangerous. Did he say anything about what this grimoire contained?" Grace asked, worry ringing in her tone.

I bit my tongue. "Something regarding the creation of the three magics."

Victoria's eyes got huge.

Grace's mouth curved down into a frown. "Why does he think you are hiding it?"

"No idea," I stammered, my magic prickling the tips of my fingers. "Then he threatened me, stating that there are other demons more powerful than him who might come after me if I don't give it to him."

"He's bluffing," Victoria chided. "He's also severely underestimating something. Nobody threatens a Crow sister unless they're willing to threaten all of us."

"Yeah, what an asshole!" Grace yelled at the top of her lungs as she sloshed wine down her front.

Screeeeeeeeech!

"What the goddess was that?" Victoria yelled, staring at Grace's lime green pot.

"I think my screaming death beans agree," Grace replied. She grabbed the rim of the pot and shook it, quieting what had erupted from beneath the soil.

I folded my arms onto the table, suddenly feeling numb. "I was so close to sending a hex his way to banish him."

"Wow, you almost practiced magic?" Grace asked.

Victoria laughed. "It's about time. A witch can't expect to explode in the bedroom if she's not expressing her magical talents."

My sisters knew I hadn't practiced magic ritualistically for years. They were waiting for the day I would light up my magical veins again. They both started to think that my magical abstinence meant that I wasn't having sex.

Well, it was true. I hadn't in a while. But not even magic could have lit the sparks between Jason and I. I had chosen not to bring my talents into that relationship, fearing it would change the way it formed. I was right. It ended with him cheating on me with not one, but multiple women, all at the same time.

Magical surges equated to uncontrollable urges in my family. And right now, I didn't want to become a victim of that.

"You need to exorcize this demon immediately," Grace said.

Victoria shook her head. "No, no, no. Don't show him any sign of weakness. Besides, he's probably just flirting with you. Demons have long been known to seek out young, attractive witches they want to mingle their shadows with."

"How would you know?" Grace asked.

Victoria smiled. "Because I'm pretty sure I dated one in my dreams before."

"Dream dating? Is that some kind of paranormal fantasy of yours?" Grace asked.

"Why not? People are reading about fucking sparkly vampires and werewolves at the same time. Are you saying I can't dream about a shadow daddy of my own?" Victoria snapped as she turned her attention back to me. "Why didn't you tell us that you were being harassed by a demon?"

"Because I knew you would both respond by trying to get me to use my magic." I shifted in my seat. This demon wasn't going to get me practicing magic, not after I'd gone so long without it.

Grace folded her arms across her chest. "If there is any time to practice an exorcism, it's now. Halloween is tomorrow! Send him back to wherever demons come from. I'm guessing that it would be a place where spirits also live, right? Doesn't mom call it the Summoning?"

Victoria grabbed a napkin and wiped the grease from her hands. "Demons, magic, or not. Sometimes a witch needs to take relationship matters into her own hands. I'm not talking about summoning *human* men into our lives," Victoria said, a wicked grin turning up the corners of her mouth. "I'm talking about summoning the magic all demons possess."

"Have you seriously encountered a demon before, Victoria?" Grace asked.

"I have. And boy, I will never forget him." Her pupils dilated as her expression turned devious. Her cheeks crimsoned into a red almost as dark as her wine. "He was either an angel, or a demon. Whatever you want to call him, he appeared right after Ben and I officially separated. We had signed the divorce papers earlier that week. I had student loan payments out my ass, no money, and was working two part-time jobs at different animal shelters. I'd been on the phone with my lawyer, working out the details on how I was going to find enough money to get back on my feet and restart my life. I was right here in the kitchen, looking at the wedding photo of Ben and I. For some reason, I hadn't given up on our marriage, even though I knew ending it was the best for the both of us. Ben disappeared from the photo. All I could see was me smiling in my wedding dress, my arm looped around a shadowy figure instead."

Grace set her elbows on the table, knocking a bowl of candy corn to the side. "Well? What happened?"

Victoria closed her eyes. "I felt a cool blanket of air cocoon around me. As it circled around my core, it began to warm, until a gentle *hussshhhhh* filled my ears. The voice undulated with my own breath, until I heard it say, "*Know your worth. You are a goddess. Until you find a man who treats you as one, you must learn to embrace your inner darkness.*"

Grace's wine missed her mouth and it sloshed down her front.

"You never told us this hauntingly beautiful story," I said, offering Grace a napkin.

"Yeah, well. I haven't drank this much wine since the divorce, now have I?" Victoria took a swig from the bottle, then slammed it next to the cauldron, making the crystal dicks shudder. "That sexy memory still sticks with me. It sent shivers up my spine more powerful than any orgasm Ben ever gave me, not that he really gave me one, anyway."

Victoria reached into a bag, tugging out a silky item. "I got both of you spirit gifts. Sometimes a man isn't the one to give you what you want in life."

4
Amon

Harassing a witch who wasn't practicing magic to turn over a grimoire should not be this fucking difficult. I could feel the Bone Threader's bony fingers turning sharper against my ribs by the day. Soon, they would be claws, gripping and shredding my shadows until I had no other option than to decay.

Spooking Lucy into tipping me off where the grimoire was hiding wasn't going to work. But I would wear her down. It might take a little more time than I wanted, but she would eventually cave in. Like Zed said, I had two other brothers who had my back and were willing to help me.

I walked a few paces down the sidewalk, pausing when the cracks in the pavement expanded and contracted in my periphery.

Once. Twice. Three times, the ground flexed beneath me.

The restless energies of the earth were breathing. With each undulating breath, my shadow wilted. I could feel magical suppression miles away. A thick, strangulating energy tugged at my navel, a drain witches often blamed on vampires was really their subconscious lack of magical creativity. Something was draining Lucy's energy, therefore, drawing her focus away from me.

There was nothing more powerful—and dangerous—than a witch who was running from her own magic.

I hadn't lied when I told her there were others that would threaten her regarding the grimoire. Green vampires were notoriously just as dangerous as their blood-sucking cousins. As soon as one got wind of the grimoire's location, they'd be swarming her library. Green vampires drained their victim's energy, not blood. They'd been known to dry up a witch or a demon's magic completely.

If Lucy had intentionally suppressed her magic for this long, she would be an easy target for the green vampire who still haunted me. The archives where grimoires were located weren't like any normal library. The books all had their place. Remove one of them for too long was like robbing a grave.

Why the Bone Threader wanted this grimoire in particular, was due to the fact that he had not created it. The text was a testament to my father's passion for preserving demonkind, and my mother's exceptionally brilliant magic. The grimoire threatened the Bone Threader. The fact that it was gone meant that another witch could come into its possession. There was always a chance that my mother's magic would rub off on another witch. To ancient greedy demons like wendigos, that could spell disaster for their ravenous, cannibalistic appetites for magic and demon flesh.

The sun faded quickly on the horizon. I had some time to kill between Zed's next graveyard shift, where he literally did dig graves. I took to the night like a bat, my shadow becoming swift and membranous. Branching over the rooftops, I was nothing but a willow-the-wisp as the wind caught me and sent me adrift.

The old Victorian house where Lucy lived was only a few blocks over. The energy drain from her section of the neighborhood tugged me closer.

I coalesced, my shadow dipping down to the first of at least a dozen hazy windows. Peering inside, I spotted a rather voluptuous woman laying half-naked atop her bed. Her face twisted in ecstasy as she glided a wand between her legs. Things had really changed in the past few years regarding a woman's sexual gratification. More and more witches were using these vibrating wands on themselves instead of using them to cast spells. I'd been around for over three-hundred years, and the magic involved with sex had started to fade. I'd begun to wonder if men in general were starting to lack skills in the lovemaking ritual.

To the next window I went, drifting silently beside the house. A giant oak tree grew outside this window, forcing me to squeeze against knotted bark and gnarled branches. Lucy was inside the window, but she was not sleeping. Nor was she using the wand her sister was busy with. She sat up on her bed with the covers pulled up to her chest. She was doing what most librarians should be doing—reading.

But she wasn't holding the the grimoire. As much as I wanted to accuse her of withholding the magical manuscript written by my parents from me, I was starting to wonder if I was making everything up. Maybe I'd become so desperate in my search to find my parent's book of shadows, that I'd lost my mind. It wouldn't be the first time my shadows deceived my sense of logic.

Green bursts of magic combusted into the air. A curtain shifted down over the window, blocking me from seeing what Lucy was reading.

The tree I perched on gave a nasty shake. Branches and leaves turned to vines as a tiny green bug began inching toward me.

"*Nice try, shadow boy. Go spy on some other familiar's witch before I bite off your nose*!"

The tree morphed and twisted as his earth magic shuddered through the bark. Luckily, all I had to do was drift away from the tree, detaching myself from the earth. The less connected to the earth I was, the better defense I had against Lucy's familiar. Her bookworm was connected to the earth, and the earth had always been the force that separated demons from witches. Even though he was no bigger than my pinky, the feisty little fucker was setting some earthly boundaries with me.

"*Go suck some other witches' energy and get lost*," he griped.

"Did you just call me an energy vampire?"

"*I can think of some worse things to call you if you'd like.*"

The tree branches whipped back and forth, one slicing through me.

I formed again—tendrils of thickening smog—only to be blown open by another assault of the violent movements from the tree. If someone walked down the sidewalk and witnessed the forces of nature and the underworld battling one another, they would see nothing but a spooky tree blowing in the breeze.

Finally, the wind settled, and I was solid enough to find my footing. I landed on the ground, which was exactly where the grubby little bookworm wanted me. With my feet planted in the soil, he could solidly hold his power over a demon.

A grunt escaped me. It sucked being at the bottom of the totem pole of the three magics.

Tree roots groaned as Grubs descended the tree. How ridiculously comical this was, watching him establish his earthly boundaries with me.

"This is going to take all night," I teased, watching the familiar's body tremble in season-splitting anger as he inched one centimeter at a time. Leaves clinging to the branches folded in on themselves as he finished his descent.

His kind had moods that could summon storms and earthquakes and anything that could otherwise set boundaries between the dead and the living. The earth was a powerful grounding force that separated shadow magic from the goddess.

Finally, after what felt like an eternity, the furious wriggling movements settled. Lucy's beyond feisty familiar reared onto his multi-legged haunches, scrunching himself into an angry accordion of fury. "*Be gone, demon*!" he bellowed, puffs of green issuing from his tiny mouth.

"You're a lot fatter than what I remember at the library. Maybe you need to go on a diet."

"*And you're a lot more of a shit-head than most demons I've chased away.*"

"Grouchy little maggot."

Perpetual silence filled with lots of quivering. For such a tiny creature, he sure seemed to have a lot of pent up rage. "*You are hereby banished from the Crow residence. Now, away with you*!" he barked, and the roots from the tree threatened to trip me.

This angry little maggot wasn't stepping down without a heavy dose of negotiating.

"Wait a fat second," I barked, holding my ground, which was starting to put off an awful scent of rot.

The roots flattened as Grubs trembled ever so slightly. Mushrooms sprouted from the earth, releasing spores as soon as their fruiting bodies bloom into the night.

"*State your name, or leave,*" Grubs growled, sending more mushrooms sprouting at my feet. The energy shifted, and I swore, the little worm was trying to cast a spell on me. "*You know earth magic will always be more powerful than shadow magic. It is the earth that provides women with the energy that makes her a witch.*"

"Only in the old teachings," I countered.

"*Like demons follow the old teachings.*"

I bit my tongue. I also happened to know that this annoying little bookworm was preparing to metamorphose. Familiars followed nature's cycles just as much as the earthly magic they wielded did. When he was locked up in his cocoon, he wouldn't be there to slide in and block my shadows from coalescing around Lucy.

I'd find the grimoire before the wendigo devoured my shadows come midnight of Halloween.

5
Lucy

The giant oak tree outside my window was way too quiet. Grubs wasn't perched in his usual spot—a tiny moss-covered hole that was his earthly window for meeting the first rays of sunlight each morning. In fact, the tree looked a little frumpy. His earth magic often kept the leaves green well into autumn.

Maybe he had gone into chrysalis early. Halloween was his window of opportunity to metamorphose. He usually waited until at least a few trick-or-treaters made their rounds in the neighborhood before he embarked on his autumn retreat.

I tugged on a pair of black leggings and a purple sweater. There was a slight chill in the air. Maybe I should go for wearing a witch hat today. Victoria had tons of them to borrow for my Saturday reading program at the library.

My heart skipped a beat. What if I ran into the broody demon again? He asked me how much I knew about demons. I didn't know much, other than the fact that the one I met was simultaneously annoying and hot. I remembered his shadows reaching for my ankles when he confronted me on my way home. My skin was still blissfully warm where one of the silky ebony ribbons touched me.

What were his shadows, really? Emotions? Magic? I couldn't tell. All I knew was that I was feeling some residual energy, or was it attraction to one of these shady characters Alyssa called shadow daddies?

I grabbed my phone and shot off a quick text to Alyssa.

Hey, what exactly do these shadow daddies do? In particular, their shadows?

Girl, you are missing out big time. You need to do a read-a-thon with me and binge some of my favorite titles!

I grabbed my book tote and slipped down the stairs. Victoria was already gone. Her jeep was missing from the driveway. It wasn't uncommon for her to go into the vet office to work a few hours on Saturday. Not having a vehicle wasn't a problem. My commute to the library was a ten minute walk from my sister's house.

A box of Lucky Charms—Halloween themed ones with marshmallow skulls—became breakfast as I poured myself a bowl.

"*You need to start experimenting with magical charms, or put some bars on your window.*"

Grubs's voice prickled inside my skull as I shoved a dry spoonful of cereal into my mouth.

He inched out of the cauldron, sending crystal dicks clattering onto the table. One of them was stuck to his head. He looked like an angry little unicorn with a purple crystal phallus pointing at me.

I set down my cereal, tempted to take a photo of him. "Why?"

"*Because demon boy was creeping outside your window last night.*"

I grabbed the crystal dick off his trembling inch-long body and dropped it back into the cauldron. "You're just trying to scare me into using magic."

"*No, I'm trying to tell you that he's not taking no for an answer today. It's Halloween. This demon is not going away until he finds the grimoire.*"

I picked up my bowl of cereal and shoved another spoonful into my mouth. "Too bad for him. I still have no idea where to find this grimoire."

Grubs continued inching toward me. "*Halloween is the one day out of the year that demons can actually bypass a familiar's earth magic. Witches are their most vulnerable during this time, not having their familiars to protect them from those beings who exist between the realms of the dead and the living.*"

I shook my head. This wouldn't be the first time that Grubs had threatened me to take the leap of faith and began practicing like my sisters. "I'm not afraid of a demon."

"Just because your Dad could see spirits too doesn't mean you inherited his ability to protect yourself from demons." He stopped before me, a gleam of something thick and protective in his aura. *"That's why your Dad gave me to you."*

"He knew I needed a bookworm to bully me every Halloween into practicing magic?"

"He knew you would be as stubborn as he was, that's for sure."

I smirked. We had this conversation for, wow. Had it already been *seven* years since Dad left us?

My throat twinged, either from emotion, or a marshmallow skull that refused to go down. "Look, I appreciate the sentiment and your loyalty, but I've dealt with restless spirits before. They're usually just passing through. They don't linger for long."

His body accordioned back and forth. *"Not this one."*

I squinted at him. "You make it sound like there are *others*?"

"That's why I'm so concerned. He's got two others that are related and younger than him."

My shoulders tightened. "Demon *brothers*?"

My phone buzzed. I pulled it out, finding a text from Victoria.

TARGET, BIATCH!

Grubs wriggled in front of me. *"When chrysalis calls, I must go. There is no force in nature that can prevent my metamorphosis."*

Before I could jam my fingers into my phone and text off a reply, Grubs already disappeared into a *poof* of purple smoke.

"Traitor!" I called after him as Victoria pulled her jeep into the drive.

I grabbed my tote and headed outside.

Victoria waved at me from her jeep, pumpkin spice latte already in hand. She wore a black dress with way too much of her bosom showing. She was definitely wearing a push-up bra. By the looks of her cleavage, she had stuffed it with something much softer than her dick crystals.

She hiked her head back, cackling maniacally just to get a rise out of me. "Check out my new bling!" She pointed to a tiny broomstick sign hanging from her rearview mirror that read:

Something Witchy & Bitchin' This Way Comes

I stopped next to her door, ready to turn on my heel and walk back inside.

"Climb in! Grace and I are going to make a last minute candy run!" Victoria yelled.

Grace sat in the back seat. Like Victoria, she wore a black dress. Her eye makeup was a brilliant green, and her hair frizzled out on either side of her face.

"Aren't you supposed to be in class?" I asked.

"Saturday lecture on Halloween? Screw that!"

"I need to get to work," I replied.

"I'll drop you off after we settle our sisterly Halloween business," Victoria cut me off. "Target opens at nine. Hop in. These witch bitch sisters are going to give every other soccer mom in town a run for it."

I climbed into the front passenger seat, where Victoria quickly handed me a piping hot Starbucks latte. She put her jeep into reverse, her tires screeching out of the drive.

I glanced up at the rearview mirror, spotting Grace playing with something that was sprouting leaves in the back seat. "Are your screaming death beans flowering?"

"No, but I have some goblin green jelly beans if you want some," Grace replied, covering up the pot with a scarf. She popped a few of the green beans she mentioned into her mouth, smacking her lips as she spoke. "It won't be until spring that I know if they're going to produce or not." Grace stuffed whatever was unraveling in her hands back into her bag. "Victoria thinks she can convince you to come over and pass out candy this evening."

"Nope. I'm camping out at the library," I replied smugly as I sipped my scolding coffee.

Victoria let out an exasperated hiss, followed by a sling of curses as she turned the corner. "Lucy, what the heck is wrong with you? Don't you know how to put down the books and have some fun with some spells for once? We can terrify the shit out of some kids!"

I ignored her, relishing in the idea of having my first Halloween in years all to myself. No crazy parties. No drunk people attempting to practice magic. The idea was complete heaven.

This Halloween, I was going to camp out at the library, completely alone, except for Grubs, of course.

Victoria's red-tailed hawk, Francine, flew above, guiding us through the traffic lights. She maneuvered ahead, swooping back and forth as she navigated the cloudy skies.

"She's not the spring chicken she used to be. I think her eyesight might be going," Victoria said.

"*Red light*!" Grace screamed.

Victoria slammed on the breaks. I held onto my latte.

"*I think you need to watch the road and not my tail feathers*," Francine said, the shrill sound of her voice filling all three of our minds.

The iconic sign of a red circle with a dot in it appeared around the bend. Victoria parked her jeep, and all three of us piled out. I braced myself for the Target adventure ahead as we approached the building. Grace and Victoria paired together like a couple of lionesses on the prowl.

Both used their magic to shoplift.

"I'll hit the lingerie," Victoria said as she led the charge inside and grabbed a cart. "Grace, you hit the candles."

Grace's green eyelashes fluttered in protest. "I did candles last time. You complained about the fragrances, remember? Then you came back with a thong that was so tight it was nothing but ass floss."

"Aren't all thongs ass floss?" Victoria protested.

Grace sighed as she tossed out one of her bony hips playfully. "Not when you don't really have an ass to begin with."

I snorted.

Victoria's purple lips curled into a smile. "Glad I don't have that problem." Her eyes dipped to me. "Lucy? Who do you want to steal today?"

"Nope. I spend what little money I make the *right* way. I'm not a thief." I headed for the paperback aisle.

Grace took my side, leaving Victoria behind with her cart.

"Fine! Find me a smutty romance novel while you're at it," Victoria called after us.

"I'm getting a thong that fits this time!" Grace cried to Victoria as she made a b-line for the Halloween section.

We walked together, giggling as Victoria rounded the corner, her energy ready to spontaneously combust. Grace and I were sure to feel her aura from at least ten aisles away. Victoria's magic was known to be flammable.

I bit my lip. I only had an hour before I needed to get to work and prep for the story time this afternoon. Maybe a few Halloween decorations for my reading were not such a bad idea.

"Out of my way!" Victoria took off to the right for the dollar section.

I brushed up beside her, eyeing the cheapest-looking skulls and pumpkins spilling out of the shelving compartments. "You know, if you come back tomorrow, this will all be on clearance, right?" I said as I grabbed one of the googly-eyed skulls.

"Lucy!" Grace said from behind me.

I spotted her frizzy hair sticking out behind a shelf covered in bras and panties.

"Look at this!" Grace grabbed a handful of lime green boy shorts and a few thongs. "I swear my ass is changing shape from all of the sitting I've been doing in class. Time for me to size up."

I maneuvered behind her, eyeing some of the panties that were selling seven for thirty bucks. Jason used to say my ass was too small to wear anything with that much *fluff*.

Grace held up a pair. "What do you think?"

"If ass floss is your thing, then go with it."

Something prickly trembled in the panties, making the fabric quiver. A pointed face with two fuzzy ears and ink-drop eyes emerged from the shelf.

A hedgehog. . .

Shit. How did it get in here?

"Quick, help me catch him!" Grace screamed as she scrambled to the other end of the aisle. It definitely was not normal for a hedgehog—familiar or not—to show up in Target.

Frantic, I darted to the edge of the aisle. Harassing hedgehogs was similar to herding cats. But let me tell you, they weren't as horrible as dealing with Grace's jumping spiders. If familiars acted this strangely early on Halloween, who knew what the evening might look like.

Grace held her hands out in front of her, fingers extending. Green sparks flew from her fingernails.

The panties shifted as the hedgehog tried to escape my sister's earthy aura. She'd been known to drive rabbits out of their dens before springtime when one of her moods went south.

The moment the hedgehog spotted me, he panicked. He seemed more frightened than anything, a mass of prickly quills rolling in on itself, taking everything it could with it.

Before he could roll away, I tossed a handful of panties atop him.

"Got him!" I yelled, dropping to the ground and cupping the frantic creature in my palms.

6
Amon

The window of All Hallows Eve was wide open. Simply put, this was when a demon's shadow got to show its true colors. Even the most practiced demon needed to warm up, especially if he was as rusty as I was. My blood needed time to flow—my blood was the ink that my shadow magic was composed of.

My boots hit damp pavement as I coalesced near the back of a grungy brick building. The sun was already climbing. I sent a tendril of vapor into the lock, convincing the door to open. The scent of metal and ink entered my nose. I rented out a space with other tattoo artists. Both were gone for the weekend, and I'd canceled all of my appointments for Halloween. Over the past week, I'd doodled so many flaming skulls, witches, and other hideous ideas that I needed to give myself a break.

"Where the hell have you been?" a voice snapped from the dark.

I jumped. Zed's gravely sound was so similar to my father's.

I flipped on the light. He stood by the counter where I kept all of my tattoo pens and ink supplies. "I wasn't expecting you until later."

"My plans with Anne's pussy didn't work out." He tugged up the sleeve of his leather jacket. "What's the damage?"

The tattoo looked more like a war wound. "You don't have to pay me for this."

"Yeah I do. This touch-up job is going to cost you some serious blood."

My boot caught the uneven lip of one of the checkerboard tiles as I walked toward my inks. My hand bumped the container, making the ink bottles quiver.

"You look awful," Zed said.

"I had another run in with that stupid familiar."

"The bookworm? Seriously?"

"He called me an energy vampire."

Zed ground his teeth as he flopped down into the chair. "Those stupid little bugs are the vampires. They think they rule everything above ground."

"Tell me about it."

"Still, it's better that you ran into him instead of Dad," Zed said, his tone darkening. "Good thing our old man is overseas right now."

Dad hadn't spoken to me in a few weeks, and I was fine with that. I had completely turned off my phone, hoping to get the point across that I, too, was ignoring his calls and text messages.

"We need to set the little bugs straight. You, Krim, and I need to come together and whip this town back into shape. I can smell earth magic like a fart on the wind, and I'm fucking tired of it."

"I've been looking for Dad's grimoire ever since the last Earth Uprising, and that was three hundred years ago."

"Wasn't it that witch you let into the archives the one who went and lost it?"

"No. Dad sealed her spirit away in the grimoire after she died, remember?"

Zed shrugged. "It happened so long ago, I don't remember much. All I remember is how she was harassing you."

I bit my tongue. After Melrose died, Dad sealed her spirit inside the grimoire. It wasn't long after that that I had gone and lost it. "It's been gone for so long, I don't know if I will have any luck at recovering it."

My nostrils flared as the scent of ancient shadow magic mixed with a certain sassy librarian. I couldn't seem to get Lucy's scent out of my nose. Her magic, while suppressed, was still powerful enough to conceal the location of the book.

The aroma was something comforting and distant. It was electricity burning through oxygen as the first bolts of lightning jolted across the prairie during an afternoon thunderstorm. I saw this wide open place whenever I inhaled Lucy's aroma. Her magic was concealing something more than my parents' grimoire.

The shadow archives housed grimoires full of knowledge about shadow magic. Everything from learning how to coalesce, to move through walls, to shapeshift, was inscribed in the ancient texts.

I sat down in the rolling chair next to my brother, eyeing the inks at my disposal. "What color are we going with?"

"Something that will last better than the red you gave me."

I grabbed a handful of tattoo pens and a few jars of ink. The magic I wielded would handle the coloring.

Looking at his arm, I knew it would be a project. I honestly couldn't tell if I could patch it up. Zed's job was by far the dirtiest of all three of us brothers. It was also the most physical. He also played in a heavy metal band, and volunteered at the local animal shelter on his days off.

Three hundred years ago, Zed was haunting cathedrals, which he helped to build the stone foundations for. He'd worked the graveyard shift for as long as I could remember, doing everything from filling potholes to working construction, or literally digging graves.

Zed leaned back into the chair, his joints cracking. "I've dealt with so many dead bodies over the years, it's time I jump into a different profession."

"Krim is also trying to change his professions. He's mentioned that teaching is getting boring, and he doesn't want to manage the bar any longer."

"Maybe both of you could work at the tattoo parlor," Zed suggested.

I shook my head. Krim didn't like tattoos. In fact, he hated them. Zed was the only demon other than my father who let me experiment with my ink on him.

"We had a gig the other night that I'm still recovering from," Zed said as his electric green eyes found me.

"Does your band have a name yet?" I asked, knowing that Zed was the only demon who played in that metalhead band of his. He was a drummer at heart and always had a thing for music. All of the other musicians were human men, and they all knew Zed was the demon powerhouse drummer who killed it almost every weekend.

"Nope. We're called *The Nameless* until further notice," Zed replied thickly.

"Better than the *Raging Boners*."

Zed laughed. "Who the hell said that?"

"That was Dad's suggestion."

Zed shook his head. "I'm not going to let our old man ruin my musical reputation because he isn't getting any."

"This skin is super angry. Are you sure you want me to touch it up?" I asked, taking note of how irritated his forearm looked.

"Why don't you just turn it into one of those ugly prickly things that's running rampant around the neighborhood? What are they called? Hoghedges?"

"Hedgehogs. . ."

"Well, they're super fucking annoying. I'm wondering why they're acting so aggressively toward me at the graveyard."

I grabbed a tattoo pen and took off the cap. I closed my eyes, focusing on the vein pulsing on the back of my hand. My blood bubbled and frothed beneath my skin.

My shadows coagulated into a substance thicker than blood—shadow ink began to form. "All right, an angry hedgehog it is," I said as I pressed the pen to my brother's arm. The design was there, hiding beneath his skin. All I had to do was tap into my shadow magic, and the image my brother wanted would manifest itself.

His skin morphed as the ink-drop eyes and spiky body of a hedgehog formed. I chuckled as a bookworm torn in half appeared next to it. My shadows sure had a dark sense of humor.

I grabbed a towel. "Clean it. I'm not giving you a bath."

Zed swiped the towel, spat on it, then rubbed it against his forearm. "Now the real question is, when are you going to give one of your tattoos to little miss Lucy?"

"That's out of the question. All I want is for her to tell me where the grimoire is. I'm not interested in marking her."

The electric green color of my brother's eyes darkened. "Amon. Stop hiding what you want from me. Us demons have marked our witches with our shadows since the beginning of time. Krim and I both know you've always had a thing for the ones who like books."

Zed's words made my shadows claw at my chest. Okay, I *did* have a kink for book-loving women. Hell, why did her bare patch of skin on Lucy's lower back make her so visually intoxicating?

Zed propped both of his elbows onto the table. "You're afraid, aren't you? Afraid you might do to Lucy what you did to the witch dad locked in the grimoire?"

"I don't want to talk about this anymore," I bit out, turning my attention back to Zed's half-finished arm. "What other color do you want?"

Zed reached into his jacket pocket, tugging out a leather pouch. "How about this color?"

I took the pouch from him. "What is this?"

"Go on, open it."

I untied the leather chord, and flipped it over. The scent of damp earth filled the room. My periphery went dark. All I could see was the garden.

I blinked a few times, escaping the residual vision provided by magic. Sitting on the table were a few pink items that settled in a burst of shimmering yellow powder. "Rose petals? Where did you find these?"

"I dug them up in the graveyard. I'm fairly certain they are bewitched with something. What do you think?"

I grabbed one of the petals. The texture was oddly papery. The petal evaporated, sending plumes of dust into the air. "Definitely bewitched. Do you have any ideas behind the origin of magic?"

"No idea. Who knows, maybe the petals could help you find the grimoire."

"How would a bunch of bewitched rose petals help me?"

"Your biggest problem is the stupid grubby worm, right? He keeps scaring you away from Lucy?"

"Yeah. For such a tiny little dick, he sure has some powerful earth magic."

"The petals will at least help keep that grubby little bookworm of hers distracted."

"How do you know?"

"The hedgehogs were going crazy for them. I found a dozen of the prickly little creatures curled up in a ball after they'd eaten a bunch. You know what dad said about familiars—the ones who are fond of soil are always digging up trouble. It's time for you to give that nasty little maggot a tummy ache."

I grabbed the pouch and tucked it into my pocket. I hoped Zed's plan would work. I was desperate at this point to find the grimoire. Giving that nasty little bookworm a pain in the gut seemed like a great way to get closer to his witch.

7
Lucy

I ended up shop-lifting, but unintentionally. It was the only way I could escape Target without getting a trillion quills lodged inside of my palm. When a hedgehog appeared in the lingerie aisle of Target, what was a witch supposed to do? Apparently, you ran the fuck out of there, cackling like a crazy person hyped up on goblin green jellybeans with bags bulging full of orange and purple thongs.

I had about twenty pairs of panties that didn't fit me, so I'd have to run by Grace's place later. She managed to snag the rogue hedgehog and wanted me to see the hidey hut in her greenhouse she had planned for it. The only thing that might help me later was the purple witch hat I'd swiped.

Without faltering, I arrived at the library two minutes before we opened. Eve's car was parked on the street. Thank goodness she was here to open. I just had to get through the Halloween reading program I'd volunteered for this morning. Only Grubs would be there with me. I'd planned on feeding him some of Grace's jellybeans to put his grumbly little tummy into a coma.

Speaking of Grubs, where was he?

I walked up to the dragon tree perched atop the bookshelf. It looked a little frumpy. A stale aroma filled the children's area. A trail of something brown and damp surrounded the tree.

Was it dirt? Mud? Great. Whatever escaped Grace's tree, I really hope that it wouldn't be a problem later on. Familiars were known to wreak havoc, especially on Halloween.

I grabbed a few books with spooky themes and organized the beanbags, chairs, and cushions around the chair I'd later sit on.

"Hey, Lucy Goosey," Eve said, poking her head in. Her nose ring with a skull dangling from the center wiggled. "I like your hat, but have you checked your email?"

"No, why?" I replied, straightening my hat so that it didn't tilt sideways.

Her black lipstick twisted as she frowned. "You might want to."

I set my books down, tugging out my phone. My inbox had the message icon lit up in the corner.

As soon as I clicked on the link, the message title from my boss appeared.

The YMCA Saturday Spook Camp closed due to plumbing issues, meaning you will have fifty children coming your way at 11 AM.

I nearly dropped my Target bag of Halloween décor. And here I was thinking that I would have five, maybe ten kids with parents tops in my story time program.

Shit. . .*fifty* of them?

"Can I help you set up anything?" Eve asked.

"Scratch all of this. I'm going to need to open up the bookshelves for this crowd."

Eve grabbed one shelf, and I grabbed another. Together, we shifted them sideways. I didn't even have my books picked out.

I jerked my hand as tendrils of smoke began to uncoil from the skull decoration I tried not to knock over. Beneath the bookshelf was a liquid black stain. The inky color reminded me of oil. Where was this mess coming from?

This was an absolute horror to walk into. What would happen if I couldn't clean it up in time?

Not only was there a stain, a giant person-sized hole was staring up at me. I blinked a few times. This couldn't really be a hole, was it? Grubs did mention that he was going to set up some precautions to keep the demon away. I was used to finding his trails tunneled through book spines.

But *this*?

I was going to *kill* my bookworm. He dug a hole to fucking China. Not only that, but a horrible smell was rising out of it.

Black smoke crept across the bottom of the bookshelves, issuing up in small white puffs. As the smoke cleared, a book came into view.

What the heck was a dirty, nasty-looking book doing here?

The moment I touched the spine, my hair stood on end. This book was definitely not part of our collection.

Flashes of yellow electricity spiraled from my fingers. Okay. A magical book was randomly here in the library? Did Grubs dig it up?

What if it was the grimoire the demon had been hunting for?

I explored the spine, searching for some kind of identification. Lumpy pieces of foreign items stuck out of the binding that reminded me of stones.

Or were they *bones*?

The pages were thick and uneven. Gritty textures pulsed beneath my fingers, brimming with magic.

Tendrils of smoke coalesced around the bookshelf. The demon was here, again. My witch hat was nearly knocked off my head as he manifested before me.

At first glance, I didn't recognize him. His face was far too beautiful and masculine. From his wide cheekbones to his angular jaw. His features reminded me of a marble sculpture with the hard, sharp lines next to the darkness of his shadows.

"Don't move. Whatever you do, don't open it," he breathed, his villainous shadows reaching for me.

I backed away from him, clutching the book to my chest. A great weight settled into my heart as my magic pulsed, sending out a violent flood of energy. The tendrils of his shadows retreated as a magical barrier between us fell into place.

While I held the book, he couldn't touch me.

"Set the book down," he snapped in a sharp tone.

Part of me wanted to listen. Another part wanted to rebel. I dug my fingers into the leather binding, which felt more like damp earth. "Why should I listen to you?"

"This grimoire is not something a witch who abstains from practicing magic should be playing with."

My fingers ignited. *Abstain*? His choice of words was strange.

Was he mocking my magical talents?

I clutched the book to my chest, feeling a wave of rebellious energy pulse through me. "Why don't I just read something from it then?"

His eyes answered before his lips did, a sneer crinkling them. "Then be prepared to live with the consequences."

Heat branched up my spine as the pages thickened beneath my fingers. Something in this book was calling to me, *begging* me to unleash whatever it was. But the force was not only inside the book—it was brimming inside of *me*. An ancient rhythm pulsed through my hands as fluid as the changing seasons.

The demon evaporated, leaving me staring at Eve. "Showtime. I'm letting them in."

The book pulsed beneath my fingers. Was the spine actually quivering? Lumpy textures bulged and retracted as I struggled to keep my grip. Whatever was inside of it, I was willing to take a chance with the consequences if it meant wiping that smirk off the demon's devilishly handsome face.

Families began to pile into the story time area. So much for giving myself enough time to round up some reading material. The book trembled beneath my fingers. Why not see what stories were locked inside of it instead?

I emerged from the stacks, walking into the circle of my eager onlookers. Many of the kids were dressed up in Halloween costumes, ready for their spooky evening of trick-or-treating. Groups of witches, ghosts, some Ninja Turtles, and a few devils stared up at me. Smiles dimpled the few faces I could see.

"Is everyone ready for a spooky tale today?" I asked, and I swore the book groaned.

The kids erupted into a fit of screaming.

I smirked. *Fuck* that demon. I'd show him what it meant to abstain from my magical practice. I had one special circumstance that I allowed myself to indulge in magic—reading.

I closed my eyes, feeling for any flares of heat from the grimoire. The moment my eyelids snapped shut, an image flashed behind them. A tree branched through my vision. The bark was as black as night. The only reason I could see its outline was from the lightning illuminating the purple sky.

Screaming erupted, breaking the vision.

My eyes flew open. All of the children were pointing and screaming at me.

"It's a monster!" one of the children screamed.

The bookshelves began to quake.

Kids jumped up, screaming as black smoke filled the room. The book escaped from my hands, landing on the ground. The cover flew open, and windswept pages flipped over one another. The pages stopped as the shadows thickened around me.

A single sentence bled across the parchment.

Amon, I'm coming for you.

8

Amon

As soon as the book opened, a terrible force gripped me around the throat. I was hurled out of the library, flung over the rooftop, and landed somewhere in the road. Hitting the pavement, my shadows were nearly ripped to shreds as the spirit of the witch who had been locked inside of the pages emerged.

Lucy's magic shattered the hex my father placed on the grimoire.

Anger surged through me, making my shadow thicker and darker than it should be. The bookworm must have dug the grimoire up. He'd known from the beginning where it was, and he was intentionally trying to give it to Lucy.

Now that another witch had broken the enchantment, Melrose would soon be searching for me.

"*Amon…*"

I shivered as my feet scraped the pavement. Her voice was already echoing in my head.

"I'm coming for you, my Hidden One," she whispered, sending my shadows retreating.

Dandelion stems curled in the cracks on the sidewalk as Melrose's sinuous vines began to unravel toward me. They buckled the concrete as they reached for my shadows.

"*How about we play a game of hide-and-seek*?" she teased, her voice high and childish.

I shifted sideways as one of the vines lashed out, curling toward my ankle.

"*Oh, come on. You didn't used to be so shy around me. I remember how insatiable your desires used to be.*" Vines became fingers, gripping for my leg, where she caught me. "*Gotcha*!"

I pulled away, shuddering as her fingers elongated toward my crotch.

"You can't hide from me forever, my Hidden One. Your daddy's spell has been broken. Now I'm going to take back from the shadow archives what I want."

Lurching away from her sharp fingers left my skin burning. *Shit.* My tattoo had a nasty finger-shaped gash sliced into it. She'd marked me so that she could track me down. Melrose would be able to smell my bleeding shadows from miles away.

The only way to cover this wound was to rub some serious dirt in it. The more earth magic mixed with the dirt, the better. Gathering what I could of my shadows, I coalesced and headed for Lucy's house.

"*You won't get far, Amon darling. You know how good my sense of smell is,*" Melrose said, her voice fading in my head as I distanced myself from her.

By the time I reached Lucy's home, the earth magic was so thick in the air, I could barely catch my breath. It was suffocating me. As difficult as it was to get a lungful of air, this was exactly the kind of magic my wound needed. The sooner I stopped myself from bleeding, the quicker I could hide myself.

I settled at the base of the giant oak tree outside of Lucy's window. Grabbing a handful of dirt, grass, and fallen leaves, I smudged the detritus into my wound. My tattoo burned, but the skin reformed.

"*Hey, what are you doing to my dirt*?" A familiar voice echoed in my head. "*Can't a bookworm chrysalis in peace*?"

My sense of relief was quickly sabotaged by the bookworm who put me in this situation to begin with.

I rounded on him, my shadows brimming to lash out from my fingertips. "Why would you give Lucy the grimoire, you little maggot?"

Grubs accordioned his body tight before me. "I did no such thing."

"Liar. I know that you've been digging for something. And that *something* just broke free from the grimoire."

He inched backward, his tiny body aquiver. "What are you accusing me of, demon?"

"I don't know, maybe the fact that bookworms are called bookworms for a reason? I know why you've been tunneling through the shelves."

"Tell me about this book you've accused me of giving to my witch," he grumbled.

"Come on, I'm not stupid. Why did you give it to Lucy? Why didn't you give it back to one of us demons?"

What little bit of brain that he had was struggling to comprehend my accusation.

"Let me get this straight. You think that I, a familiar, would spend my time digging up a crotchety old shadow book and give it to the witch I am bound to?"

"Yes, I do."

The tree trembled at my apparent lack of understanding.

"Do you have any idea what the Earth Uprising was for? It was to prevent you demons from sticking your dicks into the witches we work our asses off for!"

"*Oh. . .Amon?*"

I plastered myself against the tree as Melrose drifted above. Perched atop her broom, neck craning, red hair curling, green eyes flaring, she searched for me. She scented the wind, her nostrils flaring as she hovered only feet above the tree.

Grubs shimmied his body, sending out a plume of dust and what appeared to be pollen.

"Ewwwww!" Melrose cried, fanning her hands in front of her face. "This town is infested with maggots!"

I sighed, sloughing forward as Melrose flew over the rooftops, her pointy hat disappearing from sight.

My heart jumped into my throat, pounding as adrenaline flooded my blood. I was safe, for now. Who knew how long it would take for her to find me.

"*That was no normal witch. They never compare me to the likeness of a maggot,*" Grubs scoffed, inching toward me.

"Melrose isn't just any witch—she's a green vampire."

"*Hmmmmm. Not my problem,*" he huffed, promptly returning to his munching.

I slammed my back against the tree, making the branches shudder above me. *Shit.* This was *really* bad. I couldn't just stay here next to this grouchy bookworm and expect the earth magic to conceal me forever.

My boot was nudged sideways as something scurried out of the bushes.

"*Get back you little devil, this is my tree*!" Grubs snapped as a hedgehog darted away from me.

Hedgehogs—the wild ones Zed had complained about snacking on something in the graveyard. I'd forgotten all about the rose petals—bewitched rose petals that were full of earth magic. Maybe they could help me.

I tossed one of the petals into the air. It fluttered to the ground in front of Grubs. He took a bite out of it, and the little maggot froze.

His body trembled as a puff of yellow pollen erupted into the air. My chest swelled as Lucy's nasty little bookworm shriveled at my feet.

9

Lucy

It was mid-afternoon by the time I regained a partial amount of my sanity. Luckily, the library was closed on Sunday, so I had some time to sort things out. Like what the heck was I supposed to do with the book? And what did *Amon* mean?

Was Amon some kind of spell? Or a name? And *who* or *what* was coming?

Heck, I hadn't seen a lot of grimoires in my life, just Victoria's shady romance novel collection I was pretty sure had some kinky stuff that would make Satan blush. I'd seen something when I tapped into my magic, a tree branching behind my eyelids. The tree was ancient and gnarled, lit up with purple lightning that branched across the sky. The smell of electricity still burned my nose.

Something about the vision made my chest ache. The tree wasn't healthy. It was sickly, its roots and branches whipping in the wind as a violent storm grew around it.

I wedged my fingers into the binding. The grimoire refused to open. I glanced over my shoulder, expecting that any moment now for the demon to show.

Why did he leave so abruptly?

I put the grimoire into my tote and left the library. It was three in the afternoon, yet the sun was already starting to dip on the horizon. The air felt oddly still, like a breath drawing in before a storm. It wasn't until I was half-way home that I realized how light my tote felt. I was missing a certain someone.

Right on time, Grubs had ghosted me like he always did this time of year. Honestly, not having him chew holes through everything I touched was a breath of fresh air. This book, even if he wanted to, didn't seem like it was one his greedy little mouth parts could penetrate through. The pages were as tough as tree bark. The binding was thicker than leather.

Trick-or-treaters were starting to appear on the streets. My phone buzzed. Victoria was calling me.

I pressed my phone to my ear. "Hey I'm on my way home."

"That's grrreeattt! Come overrr and help paaaassss out candy."

I cringed. *Great.* Her Rs were slurring, and her As were twice as long. I knew for a fact that Victoria had been drinking.

"Fine, but only if I can look at your spell book collection," I replied.

"What arrrreeee you looking fooor?"

"Anything you have on demons."

Upon arriving home, I squinted at the candy bowl on the front porch. The hedgehogs were nowhere. It seemed a little odd for a bunch of nocturnal creatures I imagined would like to forage on Halloween candy to retire early into their dens for the night.

I ascended the stairs and walked inside, finding shot glasses everywhere. Victoria had definitely been slamming the hard stuff.

"Victoria?"

No answer. But I heard her voice over the shrieking laughter of the Sanderson Sisters blaring from the TV. I peeked into the living room, finding her bookshelf. The perfect opportunity had presented itself. I could do my research without her seeing what I was looking for. Victoria had books I wish I would have inherited from Dad—books that were far darker in details about magic than anything I would ever find in the library.

I thumbed through the titles, wishing I could find something that stood out. Goddess upon goddess upon moon ritual texts lined the shelves.

Victoria appeared in the kitchen, her hair frizzing on end. Her bloodshot eyes found me. "Well, well, well, what do we have here? A librarian peeping through my spell books?"

"Candy?" I replied, holding up the bag I'd bought at Target that morning.

"Set it here," she said, swaggering toward the kitchen table. "I need to sober up."

I walked to the table, relieved her cauldron was no longer full of crystal dicks, but actual Halloween candy.

"Who were you talking to?" I asked, swiping a Hershey's candy bar and sitting down.

"Grace. She's heading home from the party she got invited to. I asked her to come over, but she made her excuse to tend to her screaming death beans." Victoria sat down next to me, grabbing an Almond Joy. "That girl needs one of two things, to decide on her major already, or find a steady partner. Apparently the last girl she dated ended up being a total swinger."

I unwrapped a candy bar and shoved it into my mouth, mostly to stop myself from saying anything. I was so jealous of my youngest sister's love life.

Victoria ate her Almond Joy and flipped on her mini skull radio.

"*What was seen as a Halloween prank at the public library is now a sensation among locals. Librarian Lucy Crow is sure to go down in the history books. During her Halloween story time, the kids reported a terrifying cackling monster erupting from the book.*"

Victoria's eyes went wide. "Lucy, is this real? Are you finally practicing your magic again?"

I wanted to sink down into my chair and forget I was here.

"What a hit! My sister is gonna be bitchin' famous at the library!" She clapped her hands together. "I need to see the book this cackling monster erupted from!"

I reached into my tote and tugged out the book. I swore the air in the kitchen thickened as I set it on the table.

Victoria's purple lipstick quivered. "Hot Hades, this is wicked!" She grabbed it, trying to tug the cover open.

Ding dong!

"I'll get it." I excused myself from the table with the cauldron of candy. I opened the front door, finding three kids dressed as Ninja Turtles thrusting pillowcases toward me.

"Trick-or-treat!" they shouted in unison.

Grubs perched atop Leonardo's mask, his tiny body trembling. "*We need to talk about what escaped that grimoire.*"

I loaded up the kids' pillowcases as Grubs launched himself into the cauldron, where he inched down between the candy bars.

I closed the door and walked back inside.

"*I knew that demon was up to no good. . .*" His pudgy little cheeks bulged.

A stream of projectile vomit sprayed over my shoulder.

"Ewwww, gross!" I stammered, the candy spilling out of the cauldron as Grubs released the floodgates.

"Why does it smell like a rose bath bomb went off in here?" Victoria asked.

Luckily, whatever sparkly vomit sprayed out of Grubs evaporated into a shimmering mist, leaving the entryway smelling like a bouquet of fresh flowers.

"It's not even the evening. How much candy have you eaten?" I scolded him.

"*It wasn't candy that Amon fed me. That demon tried to poison me with bewitched rose petals.*"

"Amon? That's the demon's name?"

Victoria emerged next to me. "All right, who is Amon and what is he feeding your bookworm to make him puke flowers?"

"*He's the demon who's been haunting the library looking for that grimoire,*" Grubs barked.

Victoria's eyes swiveled between me and my bookworm, who had inched his way out of the cauldron and was now perched atop my shoulder. "Well then, what are we waiting for? Let's have a look at this grimoire!" She grabbed the candy cauldron from my hands, opened the front door, and set it outside for the kids to help themselves. She returned into the kitchen, a wicked grin creeping up her face.

I followed her. She grabbed a spatula from one of her drawers and tilted it toward the pages. With a flick of her wrist, she attempted to pry it open.

"*That won't work,*" Grubs said as I watched in amusement at my sister's bizarre drunken behavior.

"My *ass* it won't," Victoria chided, clapping her hands together, then holding them out wide. "By the power of the goddess beneath our feet, I demand that you reveal the secrets you keep!"

Purple sparks erupted from her fingers, zapping the grimoire's spine. Electricity ricocheted off it, bolting over our heads and zapping out a few lights.

"Watch it!" I yelled, ducking as Grubs sprung off my shoulder.

"*It's bewitched with shadow magic,*" Grubs said, inching his way up the chandelier dangling above the kitchen table.

"Then why don't you take a bite out of it? You eat books for breakfast," Victoria scolded Grubs, fanning out her hands as her magic fizzled and popped.

"*I wouldn't take a bite out of that old thing if the goddess promised me my own kingdom.*"

I stopped next to my sister, who finally admitted defeat. Her hair frizzled on the ends, adding to the wild and crazy witch that she was.

"*It opened when the spirit of a witch went flying out of it,*" Grubs said as he weaved a small thread of silk to the light, then descended down to the table, where he landed with a tiny *thwop*!

I stared at the book that was immune to my sister's magic. I'd seen her use that simple opening spell on cans of tuna for her cats, and the most stubborn jar of pickles in the Midwest. Was Grubs really telling the truth? He'd lied to me before. His eyesight wasn't the best, but his sense of smell was very strong. He could smell magical disturbances miles away and deep beneath the ground.

Was a witch's spirit trapped inside? Why? How? Where did she go when she escaped? Would she also be looking for the book? What kind of relationship did she have with Amon?

Victoria shook her head. "I wish I could remember some of the more powerful spells mom used to cook up a magical storm with. That witch could dig me out of my bedroom after I'd barricaded myself in."

"I never understood why you locked yourself inside your room in the middle of summer," I protested.

Victoria shrugged. "I absolutely hated summer camp." She turned to the cupboard and began sifting through spices, bags of tea, and what appeared to be an assortment of jars stuffed with moldy peach pits. She pulled away, snapping her fingers. "I remember now! It has something to do with beans!"

"Beans? You've got to be kidding me," I stammered.

Victoria laughed. "Grace has *loads* of bean plants she's preparing to winter in her greenhouse. What I would do is head over there first thing tomorrow. They'll be freshly charged with magic after Halloween. She's sure to have something that can help you open the grimoire."

"Why do you think I want to open it?"

"We both know Grubs doesn't always see things correctly. But this is a magical book, one that houses shadow magic, specifically. It will be sure to tell us just who or what this spirit was that he witnessed escaping, and possibly what she wants."

"*What if this spirit comes searching for the book*?" Grubs asked, trembling.

"Pfffft, are you kidding? Have you felt the magic in my house? Mom and Dad made sure their daughters were well protected from anything supernatural. As long as the grimoire is here, it's safe with us."

"*Amon...*"

I blinked as the name filled my skull. The image of the tree appeared again, its silhouette whipping in a violent motion as lightning branched across the night sky. Something was there between the branches, long sinuous fingers gripping for me. Rattling breath shook the air as a pair of white eyes gazed out of the tree.

"Lucy, are you all right?" Victoria asked, her hand coming to my shoulder.

"Yeah," I lied. The haunting image of that black tree vanished from my mind. But the white, soulless eyes of whatever had been there were still staring at me.

Who was that spirit? What did it want with me?

10
Amon

I'd abandoned Lucy's feisty little maggot earlier that evening, hoping that the hedgehogs would help dispose of him. I wished to my very core that they would gobble him up as quickly as a child devoured Halloween candy. Hedgehogs ate bugs, right?

I found myself wandering the streets, dodging funnels of spiderwebs, their familiar creators all singing. "*Halloween! Halloween! Tis the time when our earthly magic is ringing*!"

The celebratory chorus of the earth's magical creatures could put humans to sleep. For a demon, however, the sound could make his ears bleed. Halloween was a word created by humans only after they had heard the familiar's song about *Hallowing*—the term used to describe the process in which a demon's shadows retreat.

The one place I would be safe from both Melrose and the chorus of familiars was at Shadow Daddy's bar.

A blink and a funnel of spiderwebs later, Krim's bar manifested before me. The door was locked, but the purple neon sign of a martini glass with a toothpick stuck through a large bulging eggplant was still blinking.

I stepped forward, shifting through the glass, entering the bar. The stench of bleach and something grungy burned my nose. The room was murky dark, saturated with the musk of cheap alcohol, perfume, and body odor.

Krim was nowhere. He was doing one of two things. He was either cleaning, or elbow-deep in his tiramisu recipe. My second youngest brother worked two jobs. He worked as a chemistry professor at the local university, and was also the owner of Shadow Daddy's bar and nightclub. He used the hours from three AM to dawn for decompressing with his favorite pastime.

"Amon."

I turned to face Krim's gravelly voice that was quieter than normal. He'd probably spent his evening yelling at customers, as his bar could get pretty rowdy.

Krim was the beefiest of us brothers, and also the most introverted grim reaper of a demon, preferring to himself most of the time. And he was probably the smartest of us, too. He might look like a thug, with his big bulging biceps and thick neck. But Krim had a love for alchemy for as long as humans had shown interest in conjuring up ways of manipulating the elements.

I spotted him hunched over something I couldn't see at the bar. Green neon signs framed the backlit wall of alcohol behind him. His head was turned down, wisps of his long brown hair hanging over his face. I got the feeling he was contemplating one of two things. Either a way to quit the bar scene for good, or convert the space into a shop for his secret side passion—baking.

"Every year, I hate this holiday a little more," Krim grumbled, his expression hard in the dim green light of the bar. Empty beer bottles crowded the space a few seats away, and I was pretty sure that liquid puddle in the corner was fresh vomit. "Well? How did the gig at the library go?"

I took a seat at the bar in front of him. "Not as well as your current baking experiment."

"What does that entail?"

I set my forearms on the bar and leaned forward, crossing my good arm over my wounded one. I caught a whiff of some cloves and cinnamon and some other spice that should not be combined.

Krim reached under the bar and set out a shot glass.

I shoved it aside, throwing out my hand. "Just give me the bottle."

"You pick. But I'd stay away from the Krackin." His eyes dipped to the bottle of rum sitting on the bar next to me. "I'm pretty sure a lady was giving the bottle a blow job before I closed."

I second-guessed the liquor collection.

Krim's gaze dropped to my wounded arm, where my tattoo looked like it had gone to hell. He set a glass next to my arm, where my shadow poured like liquid black silk out from my forearm. "Perfect timing. Blood orange is all the rage right now."

"Are you really going to flavor one of your baking goodies with my blood?"

"I don't see why not. As long as it doesn't have mushrooms in it, it's edible."

"How is teaching?" I asked, desperately wanting to change this awkward conversation away from demon blood flavored pastries.

"It's always the same. I'm surrounded by a bunch of horny twenty year-olds who change their majors as much as what they sexually identify with." Krim shoved a pastry that looked like a half donut, half cookie toward me. "Taste this and tell me it's not the best thing you've shoved into your mouth all day."

I took the pastry, unimpressed with the lack of form. It was like a smashed piece of burnt toast decided to flirt with a pound cake. Taking a fork, I stabbed it into the side of the soggy dough. It jiggled uncontrollably. "Gross. It's the consistency of barf."

"Perfect. That's the exact reaction I wanted."

I shoved Krim's nasty dessert concoction away. "Why are you baking all of these goods?"

"I have an event coming up, and I wanted to get a head start. Rumor has it that Zed's band is going to start rehearsing here after hours some evenings."

"I talked with him earlier. They still haven't decided on a band name."

"Didn't they call themselves the Nipple Splinters at one time?"

Krim's phone buzzed.

"Grab it," he ordered.

"Why?"

He wiggled his sticky fingers. "My hands are covered with cupcake batter."

I grabbed his phone. "Who is Marsha?"

"A biology professor who wants a one night stand every night."

"Why are you baking cupcakes and not with her?"

"She's not my type."

I shrugged. Krim was very picky about his women, witch and non-witch alike. While he was busy turning down women left and right, I couldn't seem to figure out how to get Lucy out of my mind.

Krim's attention returned to my arm. "What's caused all of this bleeding mess?"

"I found the grimoire all right, but Melrose's spirit has escaped it."

Krim's eyes got huge. He slammed his fist down on a spoon, sending a marshmallow flying. It stuck to the glass behind him, oozing down in a sticky white and charred mass, where it lit one of the bottles of alcohol on fire. "That's serious."

"No shit."

Krim took a spatula and swatted the flaming marshmallow until the flames died. "Dad sealed her spirit into that book how long ago?"

"Apparently not long enough," I bit out. Melrose had died over three hundred years ago, however, her spirit refused to move on. She had wanted to get into the shadow archives when she was alive, died, then promptly forgot what she had been looking for. Trapped in her own confusion, she haunted me for decades, begging me to let her back into the archive.

That's when my Irish demon father, Eugene Ravenblood, got involved. Dad bound her angry soul into the book that she had stolen from the shadow archives. But even the talons from Dad's two ravens weren't strong enough to keep her soul contained—not when a book-loving witch like Lucy got involved.

I clenched my fist. "The Bone Threader recently learned that the grimoire was missing from the shadow archives. He sought me out and asked me to recover it."

"You're talking with the Bone Threader?" Krim asked, alarm ringing in his voice. "Why didn't you say anything about getting involved with that nasty demon?"

"Because I knew you would react this way."

Krim grabbed a knife and stabbed it into the bar. "No shit. That wendigo will devour any kind of magic."

I shivered. The cannibalistic demon who took over the shadow archives after mom passed was Dad's nemesis.

"Well? Who was able to open the book and release Melrose's spirit?" Krim asked.

"Lucy. She's a librarian witch who currently has the grimoire."

"And you haven't gone after her, why?"

"There is this nasty little familiar of hers that keeps getting in the way. I did feed him something Zed gave me, some bewitched rose petals that put him to sleep. But knowing him, he won't be sleeping for long."

Krim continued to rearrange his cupcakes. He placed two jumbo marshmallows on the top. Both had been shaped and decorated with candy eyes and teeth to mimic skulls. "Maybe you should stop chasing the shadows of the past, and look at what's in front of you. Dad and the Bone Threader will always have bad blood, but that doesn't mean you can't have a little fun with this witch librarian." He grabbed a sieve, cocoa powder, and began shaking it over the top of his dessert, darkening both of the marshmallow skulls. "I should have gone to culinary school."

"At least you are a professor. Chicks dig that."

"They've got to dig a tattoo artist too."

"Not the chick I want to dig my needle into," I bit out, thinking of the sexy skin on Lucy's lower back every time she bent over to shelve a book. I grabbed the shot glass, a bottle of whiskey, and poured myself a drink.

"What kind of familiar does Lucy have that keeps scaring you off?" Krim asked as he arranged his dessert.

"A bookworm."

Krim chortled.

"Melrose had them too. I'm convinced they live in the same place where she was experimenting with shadow magic."

Krim shook his head. "Look, I know she got herself killed, but she was also playing with magic only demons are meant to manipulate."

I tilted the glass to my lips and downed the shot. How I wished the alcohol would burn away the memories of Melrose as much as it did my insides. I didn't want to revisit that night when I saw Melrose in the garden, roses coiling in her vibrant strawberry blond hair. I remembered how stunning the curves of her wrist and cheekbones were as she twirled her hands high in the air. The words escaped from her mouth—an incantation that was meant to make her garden grow better. Instead, she'd summoned me out of the earth, right when my shadow was trying to manifest itself.

Krim set the sieve and cocoa powder down. "Why not bring Lucy here?"

"What would that accomplish?"

"My desserts have hexes inside of them that a witch can't resist. How do you think dad trapped Melrose's spirit in the grimoire in the first place?"

"By feeding her sweets?"

Krim's wiry mouth twisted. "Leave the hexed desserts to me. Dad won't know she ever got out. We'll trap her and send her back to the grimoire."

I shook my head. "Lucy won't give the grimoire up that easily. She's a librarian, and fiercely protective of her books."

Krim turned around his now blackened cocoa-powder dessert experiment toward me. He doused it with a splash of vodka, struck a match, then tipped at the base of the plate. "Maybe this librarian needs something sweet to munch on other than Halloween candy. I highly doubt she'll turn down an event that involves both books and sweets." He flashed his teeth as a ring of fire encircled his creation. "I call it flaming skull balls."

"Do skulls have balls?"

"I don't know, ask Zed. He seems to know things about skeletons neither of us have any real knowledge of."

The flame caught one of the marshmallows on fire, causing it to droop sideways. It caught the edge of a paper pamphlet on fire.

Krim batted out the flames with his hand, sending smoke into the air. He tapped his hand on a pamphlet next to my shot glass that read:

Shadow Daddy's Books & Baking Event!

11
Lucy

I barely slept a wink Halloween night. As soon as the sun rose, I propped myself up on my elbows in bed, too tired to get up and withdraw my curtains. I clutched my pillow as my time asleep cycled through me. My dreams were nightmares full of wickedness that I couldn't escape from. I remembered standing at the edge of a field, watching the thunderclouds build as a storm blew in. The scent of lightning burned in the air as my magic brimmed in my fingertips.

In my nightmare, I flew over Midhaven, my feet dangling below me as I took to the night sky. It took me a moment to realize why I had fled. I had just discovered the truth behind my relationship with Jason. I was running from finding his hidden emails, and his text messages to other women.

As always, I found refuge in my library. When I entered the building, a cool blanket of mist tendrilled through the bookshelves. I followed the cooling sensation as it soothed the burning anger I felt from Jason's betrayal. Shadows coalesced near the far bookshelf. A demon stood at the end, his hand outstretched.

Hunger swam in Amon's eyes like I'd never known in a man. The desire was not something I'd felt before. He wanted something beyond my body—he demanded my soul.

Then, I saw Dad out on the farm. He was climbing out of the well we used to go hunting for familiars nearby. Grubs sat on Dad's shoulder—a villainous black shadow poured out of his body and coiled after me.

Sunday morning, I left Victoria's house as soon as the sun was half-way up the sky. The grimoire was safely tucked into my tote, which I hadn't attempted to open. Part of me still felt like discovering it was a dream. Or maybe that's how I was feeling about Jason and had only now come to terms with it.

Thankfully, Victoria had gotten called into the vet clinic for an emergency, allowing me to escape a day of her questioning. Quite frankly, I didn't want to have my eldest sister probing me about this demon who was haunting the library. All I knew was that I had a book that he wanted, and having it in my possession was quickly becoming a problem.

Should I toss it back into the hole beneath the bookshelf and act like I'd never discovered it?

Quite frankly, I was surprised Amon hadn't come to stalk me. Sooner or later, I was pretty sure that he would be searching for it. The name Amon, if that was his name, of course. The sound of it sent shivers up my spine. There was something so secretive about its sound, the way it tried to hide itself away in my brain. If only my annoying familiar would do the same.

I glanced up from the sidewalk, startled at the tree I could see from the next block over. Apparently, I'd made quick work of the sidewalk, already making it to Grace's tiny house.

One of the shrubs lining the path trembled as a tiny green bug accordioned its way up a twig. "*There's my witch!*"

The twig bowed, catapulting my familiar into the air. He landed with a soft *thwop* upon my book tote. "*Why are you carrying this nasty thing around*?"

"Well, it can't go back to the library." I replied, reaching in and tugging him away from the grimoire.

He shimmied around my palm. "*Should I take a bite out of it*?"

"Absolutely not!" It took all of my strength not to flick my finger into his wriggling body.

He inched his way up my arm and perched atop my shoulder. A low rumbling sound emitted in my ear.

"You're just hitching a ride because you want to pig out at the greenhouse," I scolded him.

"I had a feeling you were headed to see your sister. No more nasty Halloween candy. I'm eating a real lunch today!"

Grace's residence came into view as I passed the grove of giant cottonwoods. This past summer, her home was nearly swallowed by the vines that exploded out of her greenhouse. Her property put off a bayou vibe, while simultaneously screaming 'I'm a witchy hippie.'

Magical energy tingled up my arms and back. Grace's property, like Victoria's, was brimming with earth magic. I skipped up the stone steps, stopping at Grace's tiny house. It definitely put off cottagecore vibes being painted green, with a roof she had painted red with white polka dots. Her mobile mushroom home was propped on a set of wheels, which had all started to rust. I remembered only two years ago, Grace had experienced what she called a *mid-witch-crisis* where she took the house out into the desert in Arizona, leaving Victoria and I wondering if she might ever return home.

I shifted aside the Virginia creeper and knocked on the lime green door. No answer. I shouldn't be so surprised. Grace was rarely inside, unless she was doing homework.

Grubs inched closer to my ear as I swiveled on my heel and headed for the earthly abode tucked behind the tiny home. I could feel his aura tingling with anticipation as I approached his snacking opportunity.

The greenhouse was a community garden project that Grace spent her freshman and sophomore years of college reviving. With some magical TLC, and her portion of Dad's inheritance, she quite literally brought a hunk of old plastic and metal beams back to life. The walls were made of foggy tempered plastic that could resist gale-force winds, and even hail storms. This past summer, a tornado touched down only a few blocks away. Somehow, Grace's greenhouse didn't suffer any damage at all. It was probably due to the fact that her greenhouse was haunted by familiars.

The door was ajar. The crispness in the air dissipated the moment I walked inside. I was bombarded with the aroma Grace would argue was the source of all familiar magic—the breath of decomposing earth—detritus.

The temperature immediately warmed as I approached the raised plant beds, some with pots lining them. While most normal flowers put off scents, Grace's haunted greenhouse was full of plants that created sounds. Disembodied voices echoed through the humid air. It was always a hassle just trying to figure out how I should navigate the constantly changing greenery.

There were her boo bushes that went *boo*! for no reason at all. There were also piles of popping leaves and walls covered in whispering vines. This past summer was a particularly bad season for what she called the *symphony of sprillywigs*, which involved the often flamboyant vocalized assault from her most precious spices.

Grace was a green witch, something I'd never be interested in pursuing. There were too many things that could bite or poison you. I'd rather find those stories in the books I was reading. Apart from having an incredibly magical green thumb, Grace also had a thing for *soil speaking*—a form of divination that involved retrieving information from the nature spirits who formed earth magic.

My tote ruffled. The temptation of everything in the greenhouse was too much for my hungry bookworm. As soon as he spotted one of her plants, he launched himself from my shoulder, diving into the leaves where he started to munch.

I spotted Grace's bed bundle in the corner by the thyme. Something was wrong. She only slept in the greenhouse when she was unsettled about something.

Grace stood near a cactus that was half-alive, half-hollow. Something was likely living inside of the holes that lined the not as spiky side. The puffiness around the corners of her eyes meant one of two things. She was hung over, or had been crying.

"Hi Grace." I walked up to her. The only thing separating us was the cactus, which started to wobble in its pot.

Her body language was just as prickly toward me. Grace was shy and reserved, even for a college student. Sometimes I wondered if she might be better suited as a librarian. But she was too devoted to the sensation of having damp soil embedded under her fingernails. Ever since high school, her mantra had always been *soil, earth, and clay keeps the creeps away.*

I spotted the flowers I thought only a few days ago were heading for the dumpster. Grace had a magical green thumb I was jealous of. I could barely keep a succulent alive, and here she was, making a half-dead cactus grow.

Her rumpled Target bag sat next to the pots. Only Grace would use her shoplifting magic to steal a bunch of potting soil. Plants bobbed next to her as she doused them with a healthy spray from a watering can.

"Weren't you supposed to be partying with your college friends?" I asked.

Grace didn't look up. She set down the watering can and stuck her hand into a pot. She turned over handfuls of soil instead, patiently, deliberately with every flick of her fingers and thumb, digging for hidden treasure through the moss.

"I got tied up doing homework," she said, which I knew was a lie. Tending to her plants was her way of easing unspoken tension. One of the pumpkins next to her flashed from orange to a startling lime green. "I shouldn't have changed my major again."

"What's this, your third time?"

"Fifth."

"Do you ever want to graduate?"

"Hey, it's not my fault that my allergies always seem to implode during the worst times possible. I'm pretty sure I'm going to flunk chemistry for the third time."

I knew the time Grace was referring to. A couple of years ago, she spent a lengthy time at home for remote learning due to a flare-up with her allergies, which gave all of us a scare. She'd come so close to death, that Mom had to forbid her from going to class for an entire semester.

Grace sighed exasperatedly. "Don't get me wrong, I love plants, even the ones I'm allergic to. But sometimes, I think they have their own thoughts and dreams that don't require me."

The pumpkins jostled as a hedgehog poked his prickly face out from them, seeming to be just as startled at the squash's change in color. I realized Grace used the pumpkins as both a snack for the hedgehog, and a den. "That's not true. If you didn't water them, I'm pretty sure this entire greenhouse would die. Also, you really spoil the familiars you befriend, even the ones who are supposed to be wild."

She laughed. "No wild familiar who enters my greenhouse ever wants to be wild again. And as for my plants, I'm pretty sure your bookworm alone would kill them."

Nostalgia flooded through me as I remember the bedtime stories Dad used to read to me. They often involved tales about how a witch found their familiar companions. "I wish Dad was still here. His stories always made me wonder how I could send Grubs back to whatever plane of existence he came from."

"Dad would have been super proud seeing that you were actually writing a book inspired by his love for nature."

Emotion swelled in my chest. Sharing my book with Dad was one thing I'd never be able to experience. Unless he came around the library, haunting me like Amon.

One of the plants shifted next to Grace. She set her hand out, catching a tiny arachnid as it slowly inched up her wrist.

"They still live in your old bedroom," I said.

"Jumping spiders are the shit. They'll even wear a raindrop hat for you if they're feeling sassy." She cradled her jumping spider companion in her hands. "Skittles, what did you do with the witch had I made you?"

Skittles hopped in her palm, bouncing between her fingers as he apparently had no answer to come up with.

I shook my head. I still didn't understand how my sister convinced her jumping spiders to wear the paper mache hats she created for them. "So what did you do for Halloween then if you were doing, you know, *homework*?" I asked, keeping a watchful eye on the spider in case it did decide to launch itself toward me.

Grace focused on the rapid leg movement of her newfound spider friend. "I don't want to talk about it."

"Come on. It can't be as bad as finding out your ex was seeing, six, no—" I flushed. Jason had been cheating on me with so many women, it hurt to count them.

"*Twelve other women*," Grubs said, rubbing dirt into my wound.

I pinched the bridge of my nose. "Either we talk, or my grouchy bookworm will cut in."

Grace's head whipped around as she searched for him. "Great, you let the most invasive species of bookworm into my greenhouse? Do you know how long it took me to recover from the last time he munched through my death daisies?"

I shrugged. No use trying to hide him now.

"Months, Lucy!" Her honey-brown curls flew out from her shoulders as she threw both of her hands out to her sides. "Out!"

Grubs dove out of sight. "*Wait, I have gossip*!"

Grace turned back to me, her eyebrow arching up. "What kind of gossip?"

"*Lucy's library is being haunted by a demon*," Grubs said. It took all of my effort not to launch my tote at the plants he's hiding in.

"Is this the same demon you mentioned to Victoria and I earlier?" Grace asked, both of her eyebrows disappearing into her mossy bangs.

"*His name is Amon, and he's bad juju beans. He also smells like dirty underwear.*"

"He was searching for this," I reached into my tote, tugging out the book. I swear, the textures changed. It was now damp, putting off the scent of mildew, and the spine was almost slimy in spots.

Grace's mouth popped open. "Wow. A grimoire?"

I nodded. "Grubs swears he saw some spirit fly out of the book when I opened it at the library."

"Why would a spirit be trapped in the book?"

"Victoria thought you might have some kind of magical plant that could help identify the name of the spirit who escaped the grimoire. She mentioned something about one of Mom's old magical recipes, and ended up with beans? She was slightly drunk when she advised me."

The plants around me drooped. Maybe it was a sign that the earth magic in the soil agreed with me.

Grace rolled her eyes. "Victoria doesn't know *what* she's talking about. She's crazy. And the fact that she hasn't even thought about how to keep you protected from this demon is what's irking me." A crazed look overcame my sister. The jumping spider in her palm skittered up her arm and launched into her plants. "I have *just* the thing that might be able to help you."

She walked over to a pot not far from me and turned it over. Out popped a dark green seedpod that resembled a rotten pineapple. "My lucky seedpod, just where I left it!" Grace cried, holding up her prize.

"You've been watching too much Hocus Pocus," I teased.

"Hey, Victoria plays that movie on rerun the entire month of August. She's obsessed with Summerween. I'm pretty sure I have the entire movie memorized." Her eyes dipped to the grimoire. "Bring that book over here. Things are about to get dirty."

I did as told, stopping at Grace's side. A wooden sign stuck out of the compost that read:

Here Lies The Home Of The Screaming Death Beans

"Set the book in the compost," she instructed as she gathered the seed pod.

I hesitated. "Are you serious?"

"Just do it!"

I cringed. Had it been any normal library book, I would have screamed. But this thing, it looked like it crawled out of a grave. Maybe that's where it needed to return.

I set the book on the pile of rotting vegetables, eggshells, and detritus, half expecting a gnarled hand to come clawing its way out.

Grace opened the seedpod, which exuded a musk so foul, I thought Grubs had released one of his noxious fart clouds. She set three of the screaming death beans, which were oddly square in shape, around the book, then resumed her place next to me. She thrusted her arm toward me. "Grab my hand, and ask with me. The beans will whisper first before they scream."

I grabbed Grace's free hand.

She tossed the remaining beans in the empty pot sitting above the book, their husks clattering against terra-cotta like runes. Raising her hand, she took mine into the air and chants out a spell, "Spirits of the earth, I summon thee. Reveal the name of the spirit tied to Amon who is now free."

An explosive *pop,* followed by a simmering *fwwisssshhhhh* filled the greenhouse. The plants released more than oxygen. They had voices, and they were singing. The voices left my ears ringing.

I closed my eyes and stared into the back of my eyelids, waiting for something to happen.

A rancid smell filled the greenhouse, leaving Grace and I fanning our faces.

Kiiiissssshhhhhhh...

Grace clapped her hands together as the rancid beans expelled a plume of noxious purple gas into the air. "It's simple. You have to kiss him."

"What did you say?"

"The only way to reveal the name of the spirit tied to this book is to kiss Amon."

"Why would I kiss this demon, when he's been nothing but a pain in the ass to me?"

"You want to get rid of him, right?"

"That's why I have two sisters who practice magic to help me."

Grace wiped the excess soil from her hands back into the pot. "Nope. This is on your turf, not mine. *You* need to set some boundaries with him, not I. Besides, I can imagine kissing him would be a lot better than kissing your ex."

I cringed. The last thing I wanted to do was think about the horrible aftertaste Jason left in my life.

12
Amon

Darkness fell over my eyes, dancing like a great horrible storm. Magic pulsed through me as I was ripped out of Krim's bar. A witch was beckoning me, caressing my spirit with her fingers that gripped for my throat.

Shit.

Melrose found me.

I knew the impatient nature of her long, thorn-like fingers too well. I was helpless. As soon as she gripped for me, the tattoo on my forearm changed into the shape of a rose.

As I plunged into the Summoning, my shadows thrashed, flickering like a dying candle as the physical world fell away. A great void of emptiness huddled around me as Melrose's fingernails dug into my arm. Damp, soggy earth enveloped my senses as my shadows fought to free themselves. But no matter how much they tried, they were all powerless to a witch scorned on Halloween. Until the sun rose, I would be at the mercy of the witch Lucy set free.

The further I went, the drier the earth became. Cracked, parched soil filled my nose. Relaxing my arms, I forced my shadows to calm. While they wanted to lash out and protect themselves, I was the one in charge. I settled into Melrose's decomposing garden, a place where familiars drew their earthly magic from. When a witch died, she immediately gained access to this layer of the Summoning.

Staggering, I fell back, gathering myself onto my feet. I clutched my throat, wheezing. "If the grimoire is what you are looking for, I don't have it."

"Why would I be looking for the cage your father trapped me in after I've been freed?" she asked, her voice high with rage.

I dug my heels into the ground. She hadn't shown herself yet. All I could see was a mass of roots, decomposing leaves, and thorn-covered vines.

One of the vines snapped in front of me, striking my bottom lip. The taste of iron filled my mouth. Not only was Melrose a witch, but she was a green vampire. Her taste for a demon's shadows was the equivalent for a vampire's desire for blood.

Her lips came to mine. She let out a moan, trailing her fingers down my chest as she forced her tongue into my mouth.

My traitorous cock bulged painfully in my pants at her advances. She wanted to unleash my shadows and make them do the wild, unforgivable things most women only experienced in their dreams.

I pulled back, ripping my lip away from her teeth.

Her face appeared, manifesting behind a shimmering green mist. "Withdrawing from me now, are we?" she asked, gripping the bulge in my pants with her fingers. "I know how aggressive your true nature can be."

I cringed at the memory. A few centuries ago, I had been uncontrollably horny with her, and now I was paying for it. "I'm not being aggressive with you. I just want you to either move on, or stay the fuck away from my family."

Her fingers traced my crotch, one of her thorn-like nails piercing the fabric. "How could I move on after what you did to me?"

My hands twitched as vines coiled around my wrists.

Melrose bound my arms with her wicked, thorn-covered vines. "How could I move on after I died at the hands of a demon who doesn't know how to properly control his own shadows? How could I not want to know that power for myself?"

"You were playing with magic that even demons can't always control," I bit out. "Any normal witch should know the risks they are taking when playing with death."

"I'm not a normal witch, now am I?" she breathed, her voice rasping against my ear. "Death does not scare me, nor does the demon who killed me."

My stomach knotted. She was still blaming *me* for her death. "What do you want?"

A high-pitched giggle followed. "I remember how you desired me, you dark, wicked thing." Her voice caressed my chest with an earthy balm. "Who said your shadows won't have the same wicked feelings for sweet, innocent Lucy?"

My throat constricted at her threat. Melrose had seen what my shadows were capable of. "Leave Lucy out of this. She didn't mean to release you from the grimoire. She had no idea you were inside."

Melrose withdrew from me, a coiling mass of vines and thorns offsetting her from the earthy Summoning chamber she'd trapped me in. Her naked body, a tangled mess of porcelain skin, emerged. Her lips were a rich burgundy in color. Thorns jutted from her breasts and her loins. Her blood formed as shiny red drops of dew that collected on the tips of the thorns. "I want to thank that witch for giving me a new opportunity to destroy what you love."

A cackling cry erupted from her.

"Stay away from Lucy!" I yelled. "She doesn't know what she's done!"

Melrose's lips curved into a smile. "I've had a long time to contemplate on how I would get back at you, Amon. I know how like me, a part of you refuses to forget what you've lost. There are far more powerful demons who can haunt this town other than the Ravenbloods." Her fingers danced along my jaw. "Us witches who practice shadow magic have long been fascinated with demons like wendigos."

The knot in my stomach tightened. "What do you want with the Bone Threader?"

Her fingers lodged into my neck, this time not playfully. She traced her pinky along my jaw, slicing through my skin. "Amon, you are going to be the one to find what the Bone Threader has been hiding from me, even if he devours you in the process."

I shivered. "Impossible."

"Nothing is impossible when love is involved. Rose petals don't fall far from the flower, my dear." Her fingers drape past my cheek. "It's time that you remember what your shadows did to me three hundred years ago."

13
Lucy

There were many reasons to take Grace's advice to heart, even if I didn't want to. For one, she practiced green magic—which was probably as pure as any goddess could get when attempting to get to the root of a magical situation, no pun intended. My youngest sister, like me, was also single. It was common knowledge among our sisterly coven that a woman not having sex was a witch whose dormant powers were to be reckoned with.

As soon as I left Grace's greenhouse with the grimoire tucked back into my tote, my mind fogged with more questions than answers. It was as though the soil and plants and Grubs's feisty attitude had somehow thickened my thoughts, forcing me to ground myself. Not to mention that my blood sugar was dangerously low. I couldn't remember the last real food I ate other than pizza, explaining why I was having a sugar crash.

And the grimoire, despite being doused in the magical soils from Grace's greenhouse, still refused to open.

I agreed with Grace in that I needed to establish some boundaries with Amon, But *kiss* him? It was highly unlikely that I would follow through with such a strange idea. I got the feeling that Grace's screaming death beans often told people to do all kinds of crazy things.

How would this kiss feel? Embarrassment twanged in my gut. Was I that hard up that I'd forgotten what it was like to get wrapped into such an intimate moment that was supposed to be reserved for lovers?

An unhealthy amount of pent up emotion curled inside of me just from thinking about pressing my lips to another man, let alone a demon. Maybe I was taking it too seriously. Maybe I should trust what both of my sisters were asking of me.

If a simple kiss could make Amon go back to wherever he came from, then I'd be happy.

My stomach gave a grouchy rumble. It was time to head home and eat some lunch. Once I arrived at the house, Grubs launched himself from my shoulder and busied himself with burrowing into Victoria's gaudy Halloween decorations. Knowing her, she would keep them up until Thanksgiving. I grabbed what I needed from the pantry, a few slices of bread, peanut butter, and jam from the fridge. I took the sandwich into the living room and plopped onto the sofa. The fabric had tears in it, and probably dirt deep down in its crevasses from back on the farm.

My heart ached when I saw the tear on the arm rest, which Mom tried to patch up. The button on my overalls caught the fabric and tore it wide open the evening after Dad and I returned from my first familiar hunt.

I remember perching next to him on the chair, feeling so big next to him as he sat in the middle and gathered us all around, just to share what had come crawling out of the well. That moment was preserved like a painting in the back of my mind.

Mom's beef stew was cooking in the kitchen. Grace's toys were scattered on the floor. Victoria's homework assignment was strewn across the coffee table. Everyone had big important things going on in their lives, and yet, they all saw me as the most important.

Dad had a way of making all of us women in his family feel like we were the only one.

I shook Dad from my thoughts as the stale scent of dust settled over me. He was here with me in spirit, but still, having him gone for what, *seven* years now? That felt like an eternity. Cancer had taken him sooner than any of us were ready for.

I stuffed the sandwich into my mouth. Ever since he passed, I saw spirits like shadows. They drifted back and forth, some passing through, others wishing they had more time to linger with their loved ones. Dad said spirits were nothing to be afraid of. I worked the remaining bits of my sandwich into my mouth, trying to process what happened over the past few days. Amon had been haunting my library for at least a month now, and up until I discovered the book, I had acted like his appearance was recent. I became used to his shadowy presences, merely coexisting with it.

The aroma of roses broke my focus.

"Grubs, stop hiding. I can smell you. Get down here, or up here, wherever you are, *now*."

"*What's in it for me?*"

I set my plate down on the coffee table. "How about me not tossing you out the window to fend for yourself with the cold snap coming in?"

The floorboard next to my chair trembled. "*You wouldn't do that.*"

"I would. I need to discuss some things with you about the book, and this demon named Amon. When was the last time that you saw him?"

He manifested next to the patch on the armrest, bursting into appearance in a plume of green smoke. "*I told you. Shadow boy was peeping inside your window. I called him out and said some nasty things in hopes of scaring him away.*"

I shivered. Where would a demon go? And if I found him, how would I actually go about this kiss Grace wanted me to go through with?

I squeezed my legs together, suppressing the gentle throb growing there. My mind traveled to Victoria's present, which I had hiding upstairs. All I could see was Amon's cold desire-filled eyes lusting after me.

No—he wants the book.

It isn't me he wants, right?

My phone chimed, which I grabbed from my pocket. Victoria texted me.

What did Grace have to say about the grimoire?

I danced my thumbs over the screen, wishing I had a better reply.

She said it's probably just a fluke and to try and find a home for it.

No way was I telling her about the kissing advice Grace gave me.

My phone buzzed as she called instead, probably knowing that there was more to the situation. "Tell Grace that her screaming death beans aren't doing their job."

"What do you want?"

"Tonight they're having some local author event at Shadow Daddy's bar! Would you be my date?"

I cringed. I'd walked by that grungy place loads of times, but I hadn't actually been inside. I always imagined it to be more of a biker stop than an event venue. But if Amon was anywhere, he'd likely be hiding out in some place named after the magic demons practiced, right?

"It starts at seven," Victoria chimed in. "Look, Halloween was a bust. This is our chance to have some real fun. I'll be home from the vet clinic in an hour and we can get all jazzed up! Who knows, maybe you and I will snag ourselves a demon."

I glanced at my calendar hanging on the wall. Why did I feel like I was forgetting something?

"Tutoring!" I cried, jumping up and grabbing my tote. "I have a new kid coming into the library this morning!"

Ten minutes later, I arrived at the library. I was such an idiot having spaced my reading tutoring appointment. A young boy sat outside the library entrance, propped on the curb. His shoulders were hunched forward as he'd drawing something with the chalk we kept outside for the kids to play with. By the time I approached the sidewalk, I could see what he had drawn. A giant gnarled tree, one that oddly resembled the tree I'd been having visions of.

Next to the pail of chalk were a few paper crafts strewn on the sidewalk—origami?

I stopped next to the boy, huffing. "I'm so sorry, how long have you been waiting?"

"It's all right," he said, standing. He handed me the folded piece of origami—a rose. "Are you Lucy?"

I took the paper rose, which was oddly heavy. "I am. I'm the children's librarian who was supposed to be here thirty minutes ago."

His face brightened in a way I couldn't tell if he was upset, or pleased. His expression was difficult to read. The boy had hair as thick and wiry as Amon's. His eyes were far apart, oddly so. Their color was brownish-green. He had lanky arms with big hands and feet. He hadn't yet grown into his body. Definitely a tween. "Hi, Lucy. My name is Jeremy."

"Did your parents just drop you off?" I asked, confused.

Jeremy shook his head. "No. I walked. I live outside of town near a farm."

That was odd. Even I knew the closest farm town from here was at least an hour away if you drove. He would have had to start walking before the sun rose to get here by this time.

"Well, Jeremy, I'm glad you are here. I apologize for being late. I hope you will let me make it up to you."

Jeremy's smile returned. "Gladly."

I unlocked the door. "The children's area is right around the corner. Why don't you grab a few books that you like, and I'll be in to set up, okay?"

He nodded, not looking me in the eye. I swore I saw a spider scurry away from his foot as he walked by.

Jeremy moved quickly through the entryway, disappearing into the children's section before I turned on the lights.

A musky odor filled the library as I followed him. Maybe he hadn't taken a bath in a few days. As I set up a reading station by pushing a few tables and chairs together, he walked through the stacks, collecting books and returning to me.

"Do you have any snacks?" he asked as he set the books down on the table.

I grabbed the cauldron from a nearby desk. "I have some leftover Halloween candy."

"I don't know if candy is good enough for my appetite. I'm rather hungry." When he replied, he flashed his teeth, which were incredibly white. They were almost too big for his mouth. "I wish you could read a story from that book you had on Halloween."

"Were you at the story time yesterday?"

His grin widened. "I was."

"I don't remember seeing you."

He shrugged. "I was wearing a costume. I don't think you would recognize me." He grabbed a few crayons and started sketching on the blank paper I'd laid out for him. "Well? Do you have that book?"

"I left it at home."

"Where did you find it?"

"It's a secret."

Something shifted behind his eyes. "That's too bad. I feel like I really would have devoured that story."

My magic pulsed in my fingers, the sensation oddly cold instead of warm. Something was off about this boy. His appetite didn't seem normal. But I wasn't supposed to judge. We got a lot of kids from low income families at the library who just needed more in their lives other than reading guidance.

He grabbed a book from his pile and scooted it toward me. "I thought this one might be good to read from."

My fingers burned. The book had a tree on it that reminded me of the one I'd been seeing. The white eyes hiding in the tree's hollow flashed before me as Jeremy opened the book.

14
Amon

"*It's time you remember what your shadows did to me over three hundred years ago.*"

Those sinister words had come straight out of Melrose's twisted mouth moments before she released me. She wanted me to find something the Bone Threader had taken from her, even if it meant me getting devoured in the process.

I fell forward, staggering until I caught myself before I went headfirst into damp pavement. The Summoning vanished. I was back in the physical world.

The first rays of sunlight branched over the sky. I felt naked as golden strands of daylight touched my face and arms, which illuminated the damage Melrose's vines had done.

The tattoos on my arms looked like they'd been through a blender. My shadows were so angry with how I'd treated them that they'd gone and withdrawn beneath my skin. They hated it when I restricted their aggression, even in the face of a witch who wanted me dead.

"*Well, well, well, look who crawled out of the sewer,*" a grouchy voice sounded from the sidewalk. Lucy's familiar was making quick work of the patch of weeds curling in the morning sun. A couple of hedgehogs scurried away from the weeds as I turned my attention toward the bookworm.

Who knew where Melrose had gone, or when she would attack me again. When I confronted her about Lucy, she mentioned that she wanted to thank her. Not a good sign. She still blamed me for her death and had yet to forgive me.

I had two options. Trap her back in the grimoire, or find the Bone Threader before she did. Would Krim's plan to help me trap her vengeful spirit actually work before the Bone Threader found out she was free? His idea with bewitched pastries was starting to look more promising.

My fingers craved soil, anything to rub the dry, gritty textures of Melrose's sharp fingernails away from my skin. I itched all over. For all I knew, those vines were really poison ivy.

Something fell out of my pocket. I grabbed my cell phone, which I hadn't turned on in over a month. I pressed the power button and waited for it to turn on. Dad avoided the message I sent him, which was probably a good thing. I hoped that Dad didn't come storming into town acting like a witch hunter like he did with most mortal settlements, scaring the living with a few choice poltergeist maneuvers to get heads turning. I was sure he'd be angry if he saw the new wounds Melrose gave me.

I could hear his dry voice ripping into me had he seen the state of my shadows. "*What did you do, Amon? Go fuck yourself up on a thorn again?*"

I shook my head. Dad had scars all over his arms and back and other places mom loved about him. I gathered what I could of my shredded tattoos and headed for my apartment.

Moments later, I settled into my living quarters above the tattoo parlor. My flat wasn't much. It was always messy and smelled like stale Chinese food from the last time I had my brothers over.

The bachelor life was a lonely life. I hadn't had a girl over in ages. Exploring a real relationship had never been an option for me, given the angry and unpredictable nature of my shadows.

I walked into the bathroom and turned on the tap in the shower. I tore off what was left of my shirt and pants and stepped beneath the steaming water. As the water worked over the tension in my neck and shoulders, my tattoos began to change. I knew for a fact that many of them wish they could wash down the drain.

One of the tattoos on my arm morphed until a hand appeared. The middle finger elongated toward my elbow as it flipped me the bird. My shadows were pissed, rightfully so. They were as lonely as I was, tethered to a world without much love for demon kind. Demons were revered for our magic, and feared for what could result from it. My meeting with Melrose had only reinforced how badly I wanted to be desired by a witch, not feared by her. I honestly couldn't remember the last time I had been touched with affection, let alone flirted with.

I couldn't get Lucy's smell out of my nose. Her magic was electricity setting fire to the air, and it somehow permeated a deeper part of my soul. How much I wanted her to want me with the same vengeful ferocity displayed by Melrose.

My cock hardened as I imagined what it must feel like to slam her against a bookshelf. How badly I wanted to make that sweet round ass bounce as I plunged into her.

I pumped my hand over my cock, finishing myself in seconds. I couldn't be this hot and bothered when I faced Lucy next. I had a feeling my shadows might get the best of me before Melrose did.

I turned off the tap and toweled myself off.

My phone buzzed. I retrieved it from my pants pocket. Zed had sent me a text.

> **Come to the graveyard. Something real strange has been digging the graves I'm pretty certain isn't the hedgehogs.**

The graveyard wasn't far. Of all of the odd earth-shifting jobs that Zed worked, this was probably his least favorite, as he always had a heck of a time getting past the familiars who find their homes in the first few feet of earth.

The first thing I saw was a massive pile of dirt with a few gravestones jutting up beside it. Zed had a shovel resting on his shoulder. His tattoo was exposed, muscles in his forearm glinting with sweat and morning sun. I knew I'd be touching it up for a second time before the week was over.

"Didn't I tell you not to let it get dirty?" I scolded, stopping beside him.

"Yeah, well. There are more people dying to get in here than there are folks willing to dig graves," he gripped as he set the shovel down and turned to me. "Whoa? What happened to you?"

"Melrose."

Zed's eyes went wide. "How? Didn't Dad seal her spirit away in one of his grimoires?"

"Yeah, well, that grimoire ended up at the library. Lucy found it before I did and opened it."

"Meaning Melrose's spirit is out?"

I nodded.

Zed glanced over his shoulder. "Fuck. Does Krim know?"

"He does. Tonight, he's agreed to help me try and trap Melrose back in the book with one of his baking experiments."

"Who has the book?"

"Lucy."

"Lucy is a witch, right?"

"Partially. She's not practicing her magic."

Worry crowded my youngest brother's electric green eyes. "Shit, where is Melrose now?"

"No idea. But she said a couple of things that concerned me. She said I would be the one to find what the Bone Threader hid from her. Then she said she wanted to thank Lucy for setting her free."

Zed's eyes dropped to the dirt pit. "No shit. I think I know whose claws are responsible for digging in the dirt."

The earth was disturbed all right. Gouges lined the dirt where Zed had been digging. Massive three-pronged grooves criss-crossed each other. Whatever had been digging here had some seriously large claws.

Silence fell between us.

"What could the Bone Threader be digging for?" I asked.

"The tree of shadows was cut down after Melrose died. I'm convinced it's regrowing somewhere here in town."

"*Regrowing*?"

Zed nodded. "I've been finding a lot of roots that I've never encountered when digging graves before."

"Could the roots regrow under the library?" I asked.

Zed rolled his neck, cracking his vertebrate. "Considering the fact that you found the grimoire there? I assume you might be right."

My gut twisted. I was not liking this picture at all. Not only was Melrose on the loose, but we had a wendigo digging closer to where Lucy spent most of her time working.

I needed to get to the library.

Voices sounded from the stacks as I manifested in the library. I recognized Lucy's voice. The other belonged to a child, a young boy. Yet his sound sent my tattoos scrambling up my forearms.

I hid behind the bookshelves and peered through the opening. Lucy was sitting next to a young boy who had a pencil in his hand. "Miss Lucy, I can't do it."

"Give it another try. You can spell the word tree. Sound it out with me," Lucy replied

The boy held his pencil over the paper in concentration, then wrote the letter T.

"Perfect. And the next letter?"

He wrote the letter R, then set his pencil down. "I can't remember the other letters."

"You are so close, don't give up! I'll help you this time." Lucy held her hand over the paper. Purplish-blue light fizzles out of her fingers. The last letters, two Es, manifested on the paper. The letters glowed a vibrant electric blue before they faded to black.

"You lied to me," I said, emerging from the stacks.

Lucy jumped as I approached.

The boy didn't look up, but Lucy did. Her expression was fire and daggers.

"How long have you been there?" she demanded. The freckles on her nose burned red. That sexy, angry look of hers was going to strike me dead.

The boy stood up. "I think that's enough tutoring for today."

"Same time next week?" Lucy asked.

"Yes. I'll be here on time." The boy didn't acknowledge me as he left for the exit.

"And what did I lie about?" Lucy snapped at me.

"You *do* practice magic."

She closed the book, her fingers leaving a trail of brilliant blue energy as the pages sealed shut. "I only use my magic under one circumstance—if it has to deal with reading."

"Is this your own magical service?"

"If you are asking if I get paid to do it? No." She glared at me. "I just volunteer on Sunday mornings when the library is closed. My boss lets me open the reading room just for tutoring purposes."

"I saw that kid's face light up. What does your magic do?"

"Reading is all about confidence. Building it, and keeping it, so they keep coming back to read more. I had dyslexia as a child. Growing up, magic helped me to cope with it."

"Isn't dyslexia a reading disorder?"

"Dyslexia is more than not being able to read. It's how our brains process symbols and make sense of our world, both visually, and audibly," she corrected me in a matter-of-fact tone. "It's estimated that one in five children have dyslexia, and one in ten adults do. It's something many people live in silence with, instead of learning how to cope."

Her words resonated with me somehow. When she admitted that her reading had not always been whole, I thought about my shadows. How that inner void has always rustled against my ribs, emptiness filling me with questions I had yet to answer.

Lucy's gaze found me. "Why did you jet out of here like a bat out of hell after I discovered the grimoire?"

"There have been some new developments regarding the spirit that you freed." I reached down, grabbing the drawing the boy made.

Our fingers touched.

The moment her magic touched mine, I saw the tree of shadows. Its long black branches whipped in the wind as lightning burned across the sky. I was transported there momentarily by Lucy's magic.

Her hand pulled away from me. "What just happened?"

I looked away from her as the intoxicating smell of electricity setting fire to the air burned through me. "Your magic, that's what. It's awakening something that's long been dormant."

"You're mistaken. I don't openly practice."

"Magic is not something that we can predict when it will emerge, or what it will do once it's started to flow. Can you encourage with your magic like you were doing with reading? Yes. But, control, no."

Lucy blinked. Her eyes dropped to my lips, her gaze thickening as she found my eyes again. "You saw it too, didn't you? The tree?"

"I've seen it since the grimoire went missing from the shadow archives."

Lucy's brow furrowed. "Shadow archives?"

"Come to Shadow Daddy's bar tonight. My brother Krim owns the bar. He is hosting a books and baking event. I'll share more with you about the book's history."

"Why do you want me to come?"

"Krim wants to help us trap the dangerous spirit that escaped the grimoire."

My bicep burned as one of my tattoos inched down my forearm. "*You know you don't want to leave this witch. You still haven't had your fun. You want to pin her against the bookshelf and—* "

I slapped my arm.

Lucy jumped.

"Sorry, I thought I saw a spider," I stammered, rolling my sleeves down. The last thing I needed was for my shadows to start expressing their desires for her.

Lucy was still assessing me, her lips curling into a smile. "I'm in. When does it start? What do I bring?"

"Seven this evening. Make sure you bring the grimoire."

15
Lucy

Amon's voice still lingered in my ears like a cool, velvety fog. "*Make sure you bring the grimoire.*"

As evening inched closer, I checked my phone for what felt like the thousandth time. Grace had ghosted me. But Victoria was blowing me up with text messages about how scandalous she should be with her wardrobe.

My mind drifted back to my tutoring session at the library when Amon had shown up. Why the fuck did he have to look and smell so delicious? My fingers still burned with magic after his hand brushed over mine. I wondered if his touch had been an accident, or if he was just as curious about magical chemistry as I was.

No, you don't. I wanted him gone, not drifting into a fantasy of being in the shower with him. *Fuck*. I wasn't supposed to feel this way. Not after Jason. Not ever again with another man or a demon, if I could help it. How was I going to actually go about this kissing maneuver that would make Amon disappear?

I just wanted him to leave my books alone. Any time I saw his shadow, memories of Dad seemed to creep up from my subconscious.

My stomach pitted as Victoria's purple jeep pulled up outside. The front door slammed shut as she found her way into the house. "Lucy!"

"I'm upstairs!"

Thundering footsteps followed.

Victoria quickly found me in the bathroom. She bustled past me, grabbing a pair of fake eyelashes. "I still need to doll up. We're both going to land ourselves a hot date tonight."

I jammed my thumbs to my phone, typing out a message to Grace.

Hey. I'm going for the kiss tonight. What kind of kiss do you think your screaming death beans were suggesting?

I don't know—get creative. They're a bunch of fucking beans for goddess sake.

I pocketed my phone. This was going to be one wild night. I lathered on some mascara. *No. This isn't right.* Was I really trying to doll up for the possibility of kissing some demon?

Amon's handsome face appeared in my memory. Damn, he was so fine with his thick wiry hair and deep-set eyes. First thing first. When I arrived at the bar, I was going to need some serious alcohol in my system if I was to go through with this kiss.

We arrived a little after seven, barely finding parking. Apparently this books and bakes event was bigger than I expected. I lugged my tote with the grimoire tucked inside, ready to get this kissing exchange with Amon over.

As soon as Victoria and I walked into the bar, gravity seemed to tug against my book tote. I wasn't Grubs shifting around in there. Something else was at play—magic I assumed belonged to demons.

Victoria clapped her hands together. "What a lovely magical atmosphere! I don't know why us sisters don't hang out here more." She made a b-line for the bar, where an incredibly bulky looking guy was busy preparing drinks and *pastries*? The sight was almost comical. He looked like he could give a biker a run for their money with his pinky finger.

His eyes drifted up, locking onto me. The look was almost identical to Amon when he was busy harassing me.

"Wow, he's super yummy," Victoria said as she practically skipped to the bar where the bar owner was staring at me.

I followed her, finding a place in front of him. This must be Amon's brother, Krim.

Krim looked nothing like Amon. For one, he was far beefier, and his hair wasn't black. It was reddish-brown, almost sandy. And his eyes were the kind of blue that made you think of far off exotic places.

Like me, he was wearing a cardigan, which made me feel a bit better. We could have been twinsie librarians. Only he had flour smudges on the sleeves that were rolled up to the thick leather elbow patches. Something about this bartender made me think academic.

Victoria's boob practically fell out of her dress as she flopped both of her forearms onto the bar. "Hello. What do we call you, infamous bartender?"

"I'm Krim Ravenblood, bar owner and Amon's younger brother."

I squinted. *Younger* brother? He was much larger than Amon in size, and had a voice twice as deep.

"Charmed," Victoria said, throwing out her hand. "I'm Victoria Crow. This is Lucy, my younger sister."

Krim's eyes dipped to me. "Yes, I know. Amon told me to be expecting you right around seven."

I bit my lip. The last thing I wanted was for Victoria to think Grace set me up on a date with this demon. "Where is he?"

"Amon's running a bit behind, but I promise, he will show." His eyes dipped further, landing on my tote. "Do you have a book that you would like to put on display with the others?"

I nodded, swallowing the lump in my throat. Krim obviously knew I'd brought the grimoire. According to Amon, he was supposed to help capture a dangerous spirit who escaped it.

The corners of his wide mouth turned down. A hint of something uneasy flashed across his blue eyes. "Go on and have a look around at the tables. There are a few you can choose from to set up."

Victoria glanced between me and Krim, and I knew she was going to spend the entire evening batting her fake eyelashes at him. "What do you suggest two witch sisters have to drink if they want to get lucky?"

The corners of Krim's wide mouth turned up. "I guess that depends on what kind of luck you're looking for."

I cringed. *Fuck*. This was going to be a devastatingly long evening.

"I'm going to have a look around at the tables," I said, quickly finding a reason to excuse myself. I busied myself passing some of the bookish booths, trying to figure out which one will be best. A creepy, hollow sort of feeling branched over me, like something prickly was reaching up my legs.

Another woman approached the bar, making the same doe eyes at Krim. Victoria had some stiff competition. But my sister was large, and her hips had more sass loaded in them than an elephant matriarch. She wouldn't let the skinny, sickly-looking woman wearing spider web leggings and a mini skirt sneak in flirt with Krim while she dominated the bar.

I couldn't see the newcomer's face, but what I could make out was that she was skin and bones. And why the heck did it smell like a rose bath bomb exploded?

"Lucy."

I jumped as Amon's voice sounded behind me. His tone was lower, harsher than normal. There was no silky after-sound that followed.

"You didn't bring the grimoire, did you?" he asked.

"Didn't you ask me to?"

"Change of plans." His eyes drift to the bar, where the skeletally thin woman had Krim looking sick.

Jealousy wrecked my sister's profile as the incredibly handsy woman moved all over him. She stroked the side of his face, his neck, until she tickled his earlobe with a long pinky fingernail.

"That's Melrose," Amon said, stepping forward and blocking me from seeing what's going on at the bar.

I squinted, barely believing my eyes. "So *that's* the spirit who escaped the grimoire?"

Amon's hand came to mine. His touch was callused and unbelievably warm. We'd touched in the library, but this touch had possessiveness written all over it.

In one swift movement, he tugged me aside. He released my hand and pointed to a stack of beer kegs. "Hide here."

"Why?"

"There is another spirit in town that is more dangerous than Melrose. And he might be closer than I thought." Amon set his arm on the wooden shelf behind me. He leaned, dangerously so, pinning me against the kegs he wanted me to duck behind.

Here was my moment. His lips were dangerously close to mine. I could taste the mint on his breath—feel the protective flame in his eyes.

This was as private as any place I could get in a bar with people swarming around me. *Okay. Here goes.*

I grabbed his face with my hands and leaned toward him.

I closed my eyes as my lips crashed into his.

A grunt escaped Amon as I worked my lips over his mouth.

His taste was a mixture of smoke and something citrus.

His hands dropped to my hips forcefully. The sheer gravity behind his touch was enough to make my knees buckle.

Oh, fucking goddess, he tastes and feels glorious.

He pulled his lips away from mine. "Stop," he grunted. "What are you doing?"

I was breathing like I'd run a mile. His body pressed against mine, forcing me back against the wall. But my back didn't slam into anything solid.

The bar fell away, and I was literally hanging midair, tendrils of smoke, vapor, and ash coiling around me. I was swallowed into a void of earth, vines, and darkness.

16
Amon

Before I could gather myself, the Summoning ripped Lucy and I away from the bar, vines lashing and crashing around us like an angry monster. This couldn't be happening. Lucy wasn't supposed to *kiss* me. Whatever she did, she unleashed something vengefully dangerous from the grimoire, and now both of us were at her mercy.

Lucy was subconscious, her body hunched over in front of me. I was barely able to keep my grip on her without my shadow coalescing.

Fuck.

I needed Lucy like lungs needed oxygen. As I traced my hand down her hips, my cock hardened. The Summoning was where my shadows took on many separate minds of their own. I really didn't want Lucy to meet them.

"*But she's so vulnerable.*"

No. I would not fall under the spell of her magic, especially with his dangerous voice filling my head. I needed to break her out of here and send her back to the world of the living, or else.

I couldn't let her get sucked into the Summoning. Not even the most experienced witches could survive the dangerous nature of shadows like my own, unless, of course, you were a vengeful spirit of one named Melrose.

I reached under Lucy's legs, lifting her up. She felt so weightless here.

"*She is ours,*" another voice echoed that didn't belong to my shadows. It was far deeper, pounding against my skull as it thickened in the air. "*You know you want to taste her.*"

I spun as the echoing laughter filled the Summoning like thunder. My shadows retreated as a much more sinister demon manifested around me. "Show yourself!"

Something grabbed me around the collar, tugging me back. Lucy's body ripped out of my grip. The Summoning fell away as gravity grounded me back in the mortal world. Kegs toppled to the ground as I fell forward.

"You fucking asshole," Krim's dry voice ground into my head.

I suddenly realized who had a hold of me. Judging by the clock, *hours* had passed. It was nearly midnight. The bar was completely empty.

"What. The. Fuck. Was that?" Krim growled, his voice gravely and dry. His grip felt like a vice upon my neck.

"Where is Melrose?" I choked out.

"I spent the past hour dealing with her while you disappeared into the Summoning."

"I wasn't expecting Lucy to *kiss* me," I barked.

"Well, while you were fooling around, Melrose just made off with the grimoire."

My stomach hollowed.

No...

"Where is Lucy?" I asked. Her lifeless body had only moments before been in my grasp.

Krim tightened his grip on me. "You didn't tell me that Lucy wasn't practicing magic."

I grabbed Krim's beefy hand, forcing my fingers through his. "Tell me where she is, or I'll fucking deck you."

Krim put me into a headlock. "I asked you to invite Lucy so I could help you trap Melrose again. I didn't ask for you to fuck around with her."

"How was I supposed to know that she would kiss me?" I protested.

Krim's fingers blackened. His fingernails turned red, a sign that his beastly reaper form was beginning to manifest.

Krim's aura thrashed as a hood descended over his face.

Green sparks flashed in my periphery as another demon manifested.

Zed entered the bar and sat on one of the stools next to me. "I had the shittiest of the shittiest shifts ever. I need a drink!"

Krim's reaper fingernails elongated, turning into scythes as they inched for my jugular.

"What did I miss? And why are there tiny crystal dicks all over your bar?" Zed asked, swinging his head toward me.

"Zeeeeeedddd," I gagged, barely able to choke out a cry with Krim's palm crushing my neck.

Zed grabbed Krim's jacket, lugging him off me.

I fell to the ground, wheezing.

"Okay. What did I miss?" Zed asked as Krim shoved him away.

"Amon here has lost the grimoire, meaning the Bone Threader is going to be coming after our hides any minute."

Zed's eye sank into the back of his bony head like the skeleton he was. "Fuck, Amon. Is that true?"

Krim withdrew into his hood, his eyes glowing red. He extended one of his arms, pointing toward the exit. "Get out."

I staggered to my feet. "Come on, guys. I need help getting the grimoire back."

Before I could center myself, Krim was barreling toward me, his hood descending over his face again. His arm extended as he sent a blast of his reaper shadows toward me. "I said get out!"

17
Lucy

I sat up in bed, dazed beyond reason. Whatever happened at the bar had to be a nightmare. No way had a simple kiss done what it did to me.

I also had another vision of that haunting tree. . .

In the vision, a little girl stood by gnarled roots that arched unnaturally. She had red hair and a pretty green dress. The smell of roses permeated the air as she tried to ascend the tree.

She called out someone's name, which escaped me.

Water appeared out of nowhere, flooding the ground in an instant.

The next thing I knew, I was falling. . .

Everything pierced right through me like a thorn from a rose bush. The vines were everywhere. Dad was there, walking away from me.

I leaned over my bed, my stomach trying to turn in on itself. What did the nightmare mean? The moments all juxtaposed with one another, echoing and bashing against my skull. I vaguely remembered leaving the bar last night with Victoria.

I remembered Krim stepping in, then some woman began screaming. Why did her voice sound like the little red-haired girl in my dream? Her voice is high and shrill, like glass shattering. In the midst of vines exploding out of her body, someone said her name.

Melrose.

Her name sent shivers up my spine.

As soon as I heard it, Amon forced me back into some dark tunnel I couldn't escape from. Amon's taste from our gloriously dark kiss still lingered on the back of my tongue. His shadow clung to me like a satin curtain that refused to let me go.

My phone chimed.

Fuck.

It was Monday. I was pretty sure I needed to open, as Eve was on vacation. Jumping out of bed, I tugged on a pair of leggings, a cami and cardigan. Somehow, I felt naked.

My gaze dropped to my tote resting on the ground. It was empty.

The book, where is it?

I grabbed my tote, flipping it over. Like magic, it vanished.

Shit.

Had Amon tricked me? Did he take it?

I scrambled downstairs. A note from my sister was pinned on the refrigerator.

Had an emergency surgery on a parakeet. Will be home for lunch if you want to discuss what happened at the bar. Text me.

Texting Victoria was the last thing I wanted to do right now. Grace's greenhouse was in the opposite direction of the library, but I really wanted to talk with her. Did kissing a demon make magical items they desired go *poof* into thin air? Something told me I shouldn't have listened to one of her magical plants, because now my ears wouldn't stop ringing. I could hear their little voices, almost laughing at me.

The last thing I needed to see right now was a shadow tendrilling across the ground.

Amon manifested, his black boots hitting the damp pavement on the sidewalk. He crossed his arms in front of his chest as his gaze leveled with me. His dark eyes were swimming with questions and fury. "Why did you kiss me?"

His voice was like a cold wave of salt water breaking over my body. I staggered backward, overcome by the force that wanted to wash me away, or envelope me.

"I thought kissing you would get rid of you," I replied, suddenly wishing I hadn't pressed my lips to his. I could still taste him. What kind of spell was I under? Why did I ever take advice from a bunch of screaming death beans?

I wanted him to kiss me again and *again*. I wanted him to pin me against the bookshelf and—

"Lucy," he said, breaking my fantasy. "Where did you get the advice that kissing a demon would get rid of him?"

"How about a bunch of screaming death beans?"

He pinched his furrowing brow. "And I thought your grouchy bookworm was a pest. Well, now we're both screwed. The demon I mentioned that's more powerful than me? The Bone Threader is a wendigo, and he'll devour more than the bodies of his victims. He devours the magic of both witches and demons."

I froze, suddenly paralyzed at his words. Devouring magic? Why would a demon want to do that?

I stomped my foot. "Wait just a minute. You told me to bring the book to the bar. How was I supposed to know some crazy ass witch would come and steal it and piss off some wendigo?"

Amon's gaze hardened.

I dug my heels into the ground. "Do you know where the grimoire is?"

"Melrose stole it after you kissed me. If we don't retrieve the grimoire from her, the Bone Threader will do to your library what he's already started to do to the shadow archives."

"Wait, what would he want with *my* library?" I yelled, anger rising in my chest. "The books I deal with don't have magic locked inside of them. Why would the Bone Threader want to devour them?"

Amon's eyes darkened. "It doesn't matter if your books house magic or not. You are a witch, and you've been handling non-magical texts for some time. Your magic is all over your library, not to mention you have the help of your gluttonous little sidekick to help spread your magic all over the books."

"I don't understand."

Amon reached into his pocket, tugging out a small leather bag. He tipped it over, spilling rose petals. "I tried to poison your little maggot with rose petals Melrose bewitched, hoping to keep him away from the grimoire. Instead, he led Melrose right to it." He stuffed the bag back into his pocket. "Now *you* need to fix this."

"Wait just a fat second. How do *I* need to fix something that *you* went and made worse? Hasn't anyone told you not to feed a bookworm anything magical?"

"He's your familiar. Speaking of the maggot, where is that little dick?"

I folded my arms across my chest. "No idea. And good luck trying to find him when he's gone into chrysalis. It could be weeks before he turns up. The last time he metamorphosed, I didn't see him for over a month."

Amon's teeth bared. A vein in his neck throbbed as some of his thick dark hair fell in front of his eyes. He looked exactly how I felt.

I threw my hands out to my sides, balling them into fists. "Look, I still have no idea why I should care about this grimoire, or why I should even try to help you get it back. Who wrote it and why do you care so much about it?"

Amon blinked. "My parents wrote it together. Their magic was bound within its pages. I owe it to them to return it to the archive where it belongs." He dropped his arms to his sides, mimicking my posture. "I need to know. What was it that you saw in your vision of the tree?"

"A pair of spooky white eyes, why?"

"Look past them," he demanded, and I was sucked into his gaze. The shadows drifting in his eyes held a force too powerful for me to look away. "What else did you see?"

I shivered. It wasn't what I *saw*. It was what I *felt* that still haunted me.

Dad was walking away.

I remembered the day Mom got the call from the hospital. The day I thought my lungs had caved in.

The day I learned dad was gone.

My eyes burned as I turned away from him. "I'm not going to help you retrieve the grimoire. I don't care anymore."

Amon took a step toward me. "You *do* care. Why do you think your magic is reacting?"

I glance down at my fingers, which had gone numb with cold. My fingernails put off a dull purple glow. "You can't make me."

"I'm not asking you, I'm *telling* you," he pressed. "The magic we are dealing with is too powerful for a witch who isn't practicing magic to—"

"—I stopped practicing when he. . ." my breath caught. "I saw my dad walking away from me. I stopped practicing magic when he died." My lungs made the same quivering movement I felt seven years ago. "It was a vision of death, a memory of him dying."

Amon's eyes softened. "Now I understand. The tree of shadows guards death. It is death that connects the three magics."

When he turned, my hand flew out to touch him. "Please, I don't want to be alone right now," I requested. Why I requested this of him, I didn't know. My body wanted to curl up and desperately be alone.

He stopped short enough for my fingers to brush by the tattoo on his forearm. It was damp with the cold feeling I'd spent the past seven years running from. "You're bleeding."

Amon flexed his arm. "This cut is nothing compared to what a wendigo can do to you. Melrose has thorns. The Bone Threader has teeth that will rip right through you."

Even though his words were supposed to scare me, I felt numb. "Where are you going?" I asked, pulling my fingers away from his arm.

"I'm going to talk with that boy you were tutoring. His appetite is going to become a problem if I don't confront him now." Amon's shadows enveloped him, leaving me alone once again.

My stomach knotted. The boy had been hungry when I'd tutored him. Was he really this Bone Threader who was threatening to devour my library?

18
Amon

Neither Krim nor Zed were going to help me track down Melrose and steal back the grimoire. Tuesday drifted by, leaving my shadows and I restless. It wasn't until the end of the week that I wondered if I was ever going to recover it.

The boy Lucy had been tutoring said he would return to the library at the same time in a week. I thought for sure I would be able to track him down before Sunday came around. But wendigos were smart, frighteningly so. I got the feeling he knew that I was looking for him. I just hoped that he wouldn't find Melrose.

The time that passed gave me time to think about Lucy. Her stupid familiar had gotten us into this mess, and of course, he was making the excuse to go off and metamorphose. Seemed like some ridiculous form of vengeance.

Then, there was that kiss. . .

I retraced my steps, trying to distract myself from the emotions I was starting to feel. Lucy was to blame for all of this. I couldn't allow myself to fall for her, not when I was at risk of having the Bone Threader devour my missing shadow.

Walking along the sidewalk, I retraced my steps over and over, taking careful note of where I'd been since Krim kicked me out. I couldn't pick up a single trace of magic from the grimoire. The book's aura was nothing but a dying ember now.

My boot caught a groove in the pavement. Three long angular grooves connected with each other. I swallowed. The Bone Threader left his mark, and he wanted me to follow.

I padded to the street corner where the grooves tapered off, reconnecting in a straight line. I passed a few convenience stores before the smell of grease and

salt permeated the air. A giant purple and pink neon sign flashed before me read:
Greasy's Diner

My heart raced as I entered the restaurant. What was I going to say to him? What might he say to me? Who knew how he would appear, or how long he would keep me waiting. Wendigos were predators, and they had a habit of playing with their prey.

I found a seat in the back of the diner. I slipped into the booth facing the entrance, wanting to keep eyes on my father's nemesis.

A waitress sauntered over to me with a notepad and a pen in hand. "What are you having today, hon?"

I scanned the menu. All of the greasy food items made my already upset stomach queasy. "Root beer?"

She flashed a flirty grin and winked. "You got it, sweetie."

My forearms burned as my tattoos darted across my skin. My shadows were the first to know when another demon was approaching.

A young boy walked into the diner. No adults accompanied him. I recognized him instantly as the boy Lucy had been tutoring.

When he turned his head my way, my tattoos retreated beneath my skin. From far away, his eyes appeared sunken. They flashed red as he spotted me.

I chewed the inside of my cheek as he walked up to my table, plopping down in the booth across from me. "*Amon, Eugene's son. How long did it take you to figure out my identity*?" he asked, his voice echoing inside of my head. His voice was unnaturally deep. Hearing it come from this baby-faced child made it sound even more eerie.

"*Should I move my mouth*?" he asked, red flickers of light dancing in his hollow eyes.

"*Probably. Otherwise, it will look like I'm a pedophile having a very bizarre staring contest with a child.*"

"I'll act like you're helping me with my homework, then," he said, his voice slightly higher out in the open. "Word has it that Lucy has a great way of helping others with her reading talents."

A few heads turned our way as he didn't know the power of his own voice.

My fists clenched. His words were vindictive. "Why have you taken a sudden interest in Lucy? A few weeks ago, you had only been interested in me and my missing shadow."

The Bone Threader scratched his head and glanced at the menu on the wall. "My stomach has not been feeling well. Order me a chocolate milk, and we'll talk. It's time we discuss the grimoire."

"I can't understand why you chose to disguise yourself as a kid, of all things."

"Playing innocent is the only way I don't scare the pants off people when I'm out in public. Besides, I always take on the identity of the souls others have lost." He set his small hands onto the table. His fingers flexed, and I caught a glimpse of the claws beneath the bones. "My appetite is a peculiar thing. I've created grimoires for so long out of the bodies of demons, I sometimes forget what the magic of witches tastes like."

I shivered. Those claws had seen *many* shadows. They were responsible for weaving together demon flesh, bone, and sinew into grimoires.

"Why aren't you at your brother's bar?" he asked, rubbing his hands over his stomach.

"He doesn't want me anywhere near his place, in case *you* decided to show up."

An earthy chuckle escaped him. "That's unfortunate. It seems as though your family affairs with the shadow archives have begun to crumble."

The waitress returned and set my root beer in front of me along with a papered straw.

"He will have chocolate milk," I said.

"Sorry, we're all out," the waitress replied.

The Bone Threader reached for my drink and the straw. "This will do just fine."

The waitress busied herself with another table as the Bone Threader ripped the paper off the straw. He did so methodically, as though he was peeling flesh off a bone. "I gave you a timeline to recover the grimoire, and you failed to deliver. My appetite can only be suppressed for so long, before my inner demon takes over."

My shadows cowered, gathering around my ribcage. They were protecting my lungs and heart in case the Bone Threader decided to lash out and rip a chunk out of my flesh.

He set the strands of paper onto the table and plucked the straw into the plastic lid. "I know you want to preserve your parents' work in the shadow archives. Your mother had a talent you inherited," he licked his lips. "You see, I have long hungered for these talents that I refuse to bind away into a grimoire. I want to keep your mother's magical talents for myself."

Bile burned in my throat. "My mother's magic is mine to carry on. It's not for you to devour."

He gnashed his teeth. "Devour? No. I plan to keep your mother's magical talents for myself. I cannot wait to remove the Ravenblood name from the shadow archives forever."

I clenched my fists. "How will you do this? There's no way you can keep my mother's magic alive if you kill me for it."

"Melrose has already agreed to help me take it from you. You know how I stole something from her in her youth, something she has never been able to recover?"

My stomach knotted. "How she died?"

The corners of his mouth turned down. "Amon, I know you are not stupid. You know that when an individual dies quickly, they often forget how they depart this world. This is unfortunately what happened with Melrose." A waitress walked by with a tray full of cheeseburgers. The Bone Threader's nostrils flared as he scented the greasy food. "As I age, my appetite has formed around one thing that does not satisfy my hunger, no matter how much I crave it."

His words jostled me. I always understood a wendigo's insatiable hunger to revolve around bewitchment. "What do you crave, other than magic?"

"Think about the souls you have been interacting with. There is something all of you have in common, including yourself. You lost your mother. Melrose lost a brother. Lucy lost her father."

I grabbed a napkin on the table and twisted it. "Is it, *death*?"

The Bone Threader's lips puckered as he inserted the straw into his mouth. His throat bulged as he sucked my soft drink in one gulp. A belch followed.

He wiped the back of his hand over his mouth. "Death is the thing I crave, but it is also the one thing I cannot have. Us demons, we wield magic that embodies death. The one thing I cannot cannibalize, is myself."

I twisted my napkin so hard, it tore. This was new information to me. "And yet you continue to devour demons to turn our shadows into grimoires?"

"I must do what I can to survive. A demon's shadows are the one thing that is closest to death, therefore they are the most appetizing. But my hunger will never be fully satisfied. And I cannot kill you to get what I want. A wendigo is always hungry for what he cannot have. Death is an insatiable monster when paired with loneliness."

My insides churned. *Shit*. I had the book in my fingertips, and Lucy Crow let it slip away. I'd run out of time. "Look, Melrose has the grimoire now, she—"

A massive belch erupted from his mouth. He leaned back in his chair, clapping his hands on his stomach. "The grimoire is currently in my belly. Why did you think I had such an upset stomach?"

My body went cold. "How did you get it?"

The Bone Threader continued to pat his belly. "Melrose fed it to me shortly after she stole it from the librarian you are currently crushing on."

"Prove to me you have it," I demanded, instantly regretting my request. I also hated the way he brought up Lucy like he was trying to taunt me.

He belched, and a piece of origami came flying out of his mouth. I instantly recognized it as the roses I'd seen all over town. Rose petals Zed had been finding.

I grabbed it, unfolding the gooey paper. I recognized my parent's magical bond. "You have the book. Now, leave this town and go back to the Summoning."

He licked his lips. "I've already tasted what *you* now want. That little maggot of Lucy's didn't dig up the book. I did, and I used the magic inside to create the bewitched rose petals. I know of a certain librarian who shares your mother's passion for reading. All I had to do was get you to distract her familiar."

I slammed my fist on the table, making the shredded pieces of paper jump. "You used the rose petals to draw Lucy's familiar away from her so you could taste her magic?"

He grinned nastily. "I know how much *you* want to taste her magic as well. I know how similar you are to me. I know what a demon's shadows can do to a witch he desires more than death itself."

My shadows heard everything the Bone Threader said. He'd *tricked* me. This whole time, he was using the grimoire as a way to get closer to Lucy.

Ebony tendrils of darkness unraveled from my ribs, threading out onto my arms. I felt their cold, silky strands branching up my neck and onto my face. If I didn't defend Lucy, my shadows would. They possessed the primal urge to defend the witch they wanted to claim as theirs.

"Fuck off. If you touch her, you die. Lucy is ours," I growled, my voice rattling as multiples in my throat. My shadows gripped my neck, adding their possessiveness to the tone of my voice.

The Bone Threader grabbed the shredded pieces of paper and began to unfold them. "I knew you had feelings for her. Just remember that my skin is the backbone of your daddy's archives. Don't go shredding it like Melrose has done to your arm. My shadow isn't like yours, Hidden One. I will devour everything I can of the Ravenblood's family archive before I am done."

I blinked.

The Bone Threader was gone.

The origami rose he belched up shriveled, curling into a gooey ball.

I paid for the root beer and left the diner. My breathing was so heavy, I could barely see straight. *Shit*. What defense did Lucy have against this monster who wanted to devour my mother's magical talents she also possessed?

19
Lucy

The first week of November was a hazy mess of frustration and frost as autumn crept into town. An unsettling ache lingered in my bones. The last discussion I had with Amon was a week ago. It was Sunday afternoon, and the boy I had tutored last week had not shown up. Maybe it was a fluke that Amon suspected that he was really a wendigo.

I'd spent the past week working at the library in a haze about everything I'd experienced since Halloween. There had been discussions about a demon that was threatening to devour something Amon called the shadow archives. I was starting to think that demons were as flaky as men when it came to anything book, or magic related. So why the hell was I even thinking about the *R* word right now?

The last thing I needed to fantasize about was a relationship. . .

I busied myself in my morning ritual, preparing myself some toast for breakfast. Since Victoria had been in and out of the vet office so much, I'd been put in charge of feeding the hedgehogs.

My phone chimed. New message notifications filled my screen. My Outlook flooded with emails, stating that for the next few weeks, I had no story time bookings.

What the hell was going on?

I grabbed my tote and made my way down the street. I nearly tripped as my boots caught a deep groove in the pavement.

I staggered forward, catching myself as I rounded the corner. I didn't remember seeing so many gouges on the sidewalk yesterday.

A sign was posted on the library's front glass door.

**LIBRARY CLOSED DUE TO CONSTRUCTION.
DANGEROUS SINKHOLE DISCOVERED.**

I read the last line again. "A *sinkhole*? Seriously?"

Either Grubs had tunneled his way to China to chrysalis, or the universe just plain hated me. With him gone, and no library to return to work, I was a sitting duck. I got the feeling I wouldn't be going back to work until this grimoire business was settled, meaning one thing.

I had to interact with Amon, whether I liked it or not.

Like Grubs, Grace had gone and disappeared on one of her random camping trips she said was for a species identification exercise for her botany class. I knew it was really an excuse to capture and bring home more familiars who would enjoy her plant collections. She had tasked me with watering the plants in her greenhouse.

I had nothing better to do, anyway. I was trying to stay out of Victoria's way as much as possible. Apparently, she got so hammered at the books and bake event, she didn't remember how either of us ended up back at her house.

I reached the greenhouse just as the sun was rising. I wanted it to warm up a bit and burn off the morning fog. The earth was brimming with energy, the kind that made a witch drowsy with a false sense of security. While the soil worked its magic on my nerves, I internally planned on how I was going to tackle the load of chores Grace had given me.

I grabbed a shovel and dug it into the compost pile. The dirt was hard, like it hasn't been turned over in years. My sister didn't judge the health of her plants by how much water they needed. She monitored their growth with *aura readings.* Grace always told me that plants could tell you more about how they felt simply with colors.

Her *Vibes* chart was hanging on the far wall. A handwritten aura diagram highlighted a few words: *The Forbidden Blooms*. It looked like some moth had gotten a hold of the edges and devoured what had been written below.

Water too much, and I get extra weepy.

We are screamy.

Don't forget to prune weekly, or I get awfully smelly.

My phone buzzed in my pocket. Mom texted me.

I got a notification that the library is closed until further notice. Something about a sinkhole? Is magic involved? I guess I won't be able to rely on you bringing me my book holds. Also, Victoria tells me you have a new boyfriend?

My face flushed. I really wanted to slap Victoria upside the head now.

Another message from mom came through.

We need to talk. Do your old lady a favor and run an errand for me.

What errand?

Those things from the greenhouse Grace calls silly sprigs? Can you bring some? Make sure you grab the slightly yellow ones. I want to bake up a fresh batch of muffins.

I'm on it.

Mom's living arrangements weren't far. It had been at least a couple of weeks since I had gone to visit her. *Shame on me*. She lived in an old Victorian home similar to my sister's house a few blocks away. The trees in her neighborhood were less mature than what grew around Victoria's home, so a few years ago, mom began planting. Her house was the only house on the block with hedges that weren't junipers. Despite the Midwestern environment, she somehow convinced her own hedges of dragon trees to grow. Judging by the wilted state of her plants, I'd say she was also behind in her winterization ritual.

I walked up the flagstone pathway, passing the lilac bushes that had yet to be cut back. A circle of stone mushrooms Grace created in one of her sculpture classes sat beside the path. They spiraled around a bird bath I gave mom a few summers ago.

The sound of booming music echoed from inside the house.

I reached the green front door and knocked.

The music died.

"Oh no, it's the bookworm!" A woman cried behind the door. Mom's roommate was spunky beyond her years, and even though the doctors told the seventy-something ex-nurse to use a walker, she refused. The last time Alba was given unsolicited advice by her doctor, she rebelled and spent the afternoon chasing me around the living room on her new pair of roller skates.

Alba opened the door and let me inside.

"Alba? Where's mom?" I asked, walking into the home that smelled like a perfume bomb went off. Goddess, I hoped I wouldn't be stuck living like this when I was older. I'd rather live alone than with women who smelled like bad floral soap.

"She's already in the kitchen setting up shop," Alba replied.

I stepped sideways. No roller skates today. But Alba definitely had a new trick up her sleeve I knew she was dying to share with me.

"I got a trampoline, you know, one that's meant for cracked up old ladies like me? I've been trying to figure out how to get into the pool next door," Alba said, her face lighting up.

I laughed. "Remind me to join you when summer rolls around."

"Lucy? Is that you?" Mom's voice sounded from down the hall.

"Cindy, your daughter has arrived!" Alba returned to the living room and flipped on the TV. The music I'd heard blaring resumed, along with a workout video of greasy bronze men wearing nothing but yellow banana hammocks.

My magic flared as I walked into my mother's kitchen. Goddess magic knew when goddesses of the same kin were about. I felt the tug guiding me into the kitchen as my mother's aura pulled me toward her.

Dad used to say that she was a lightworker—a special witch who helped people find their way through their darkest of days.

Mom turned, a messy brown bun flopping atop her head. She wore a yellow apron with a giant acorn on the front. Even though she was pushing sixty, she had more hair than any of her daughters. She refused to cut it, but looped it up into a messy braid atop her head.

Her eyes met mine, and magical sparks spilled out of her like an exploding firework. Mom could read my aura better than any of my sisters. I could tell from how her magic was reacting that she was reading something very detailed on me.

She clapped her hands to her cheeks, sending white puffs of baking powder into the air. "Oh, he's a keeper!"

I shook my head. Here she was, making assumptions about my demon boyfriend before I'd even acknowledged his existence. "Where do you want the sprouts?"

"Right here is fine," Mom replied. She motioned toward her bamboo cutting board, which was already loaded with cheese and spices.

She trailed her wooden mixing spoon through the air. "There is definitely some emotional turmoil going on. I haven't seen you this upset since high school, when that guy who worked at Hot Topic didn't give you the nose piercing you wanted."

Her energy popped and sizzled over me as she practiced one of her 'aura cleansing' techniques. Meanwhile, I was having embarrassing flash-backs about the horrible idea of ever impressing a guy by getting my nostrils pierced.

Mom's gaze dropped to the sprouts I dug out of my tote. "Ah, those look healthier than the last time Grace experimented with banana peels and mush-rooms in her compost! I try to avoid her greenhouse this time of year. My last encounter with her sprillywigs involved me getting cussed at."

After I set the sprouts down on the table, I plopped down on the stool across from Mom. "Things have been interesting over the past week. Victoria is busy with work and Grace is gone. Grubs has also ghosted me."

"Leaving you to spend time with this new boyfriend of yours, I hope?" Mom asked as she grabbed the sprouts and began dicing them up with a knife. I swore some of them sizzled as they fell into the bowl full of sugar and eggs.

"Mom. . ."

"What? His aura is all over you! I can practically feel that kiss he," she gasped as she churned the ingredients. "Oh my, *where* did he kiss you?"

My belly warmed. The moment Amon's thick, shadowy musk coalesced around me will forever be crystalized in my mind. Our kiss didn't feel like any kiss I'd experienced before. I agreed with mom. It did more than linger.

"This energy feels so conflicted. Tell me about this kiss, and how it occurred," Mom interrupted my thoughts as she whisked her eggs and sugar. "I'm just glad to see that you're moving on from that Jason fellow."

I set my elbows on the table, gazing at the eggs combining with sugar as Mom's movements hypnotized me. I vaguely remembered Mom and Dad making this recipe when I was probably six. The scent of cinnamon, combined with their laughter, was pure bliss in my memory. Relationships really were like baking. All it took was for one wrong ingredient to go into the mix, and everything fell apart.

For me, it was the fact that Jason had been cheating.

Mom released the wooden spoon, but it kept spinning. A lot of her magic went into her time spent in the kitchen. She grabbed the bag of flour and measured out two cups, then poured it into the bowl. "I'm fairly certain my youngest won't settle down until she's found a partner who will bake with her. But you, on the other hand, you've found someone special. Tell me about this new boyfriend?"

"Demon," I corrected.

Mom dropped the vanilla extract onto the table. "Is this a new fantasy of yours?"

"No, Mom. He's the real thing, a shadow-shifting spirit that you and Dad used to make up stories about."

Mom's eyes flashed. "That would explain all of the residual energy around you. You didn't see it coming when he kissed you."

"That's not how it went down. *I* kissed him."

Mom's spoon went flying, sending muffin batter into the air. "Why would you kiss a guy you barely know?"

"Because I was dumb. Grace had some crazy experiment going on in her greenhouse, and I listened to her. I was desperate. He's been harassing me at the library for a month. I wanted to get rid of him."

"You listened to one of Grace's greenhouse experiments? Wow, you must have been desperate."

"I don't know what I was thinking."

Mom's expression softened. "Neither did I when I first started dating your father." Warm daylight illuminated her face. The lines of grief made her look so stoic and beautiful as she aged. "Demons and witches have been enemies long before fairy tales were written. But we've also been forbidden lovers. The magic we possess is something they have long sought to win over. Why was he harassing you?"

"He was looking for a book, one that he's been searching all over town for."

Mom's eyebrow arched. "Could this book be a book of shadows?"

I nodded. "I know that witches have long tapped into their inner goddess to find their magic in the earth. Familiars have been our companions to help us with this." I flexed my hands, thinking of Amon's cool, silky voice, and how his sound alone could make me see shadows drifting in my periphery. "I guess I've never asked about the shadow magic that demons possess. What are these shadows, exactly?"

Mom set both of her hands on the table. "A demon's shadows are an extension of his soul. They are his primal nature, his artistic expression, all wound up into one." Mom's cheeks and chest crimsoned, turning nearly the same vibrant hue as her mixing bowl. "It is with a demon's shadows that us witches can unleash the desires only known by our inner goddess."

"What do you mean, desires?"

"You know, the things us women don't usually discuss, unless you are Victoria. She's very open about her sexuality and what she wants in the bedroom."

My body heated. Suddenly, I felt like I was a tween getting the sex talk again.

Mom's eyes dipped away from me as she continued in her mixing. "Demons are sinfully beautiful beings."

"Did I hear something about forbidden lovers and desires?" Alba asked, skating by the kitchen.

"Alba, dear. My daughter and I are having a heart-to-heart. Come back later when the muffins are ready."

Alba grumbled something about *forbidden desires*, then turned the music up full blast.

Mom waved her hand, sending one of her light incantations into the air. Her magic created a sound-proof barrier of shimmering dusty glass, which muffled the music. She grabbed a new spatula from the drawer and began mixing again. "I want to hear every detail about this demon."

"His name is Amon. He's one of three brothers who live in town."

"He has brothers?"

"Yes. One of them owns Shadow Daddy's bar up the street. I've met him, but not the other."

Mom's mixing became more furious. "What I want to know is why he has such a strong interest in my daughter."

"Since when do you know so much about demons and this shadow magic they practice?"

"Your father and I have known they've lived among humans for a long time, blending in, finding opportunities to mix their shadow magic with a witch when an opportunity arises. Witch families have long mingled with their kind, producing children with magical abilities that would make Merlin look like a clown. Your father had family members I know for a fact had talents that allowed them to practice shadow magic."

I squinted at mom. "Are you saying that Dad's family has demon blood?"

Mom's mouth curved down. "I know he did, and your father was ashamed of it. Every time I wanted to share that secret with my daughters, he became argumentative with me. So I swore to him that I would never share. But almost a decade later, here I am, breaking my promise."

My shoulders stiffened. Dad wasn't shady at all. He was the most kind, loving individual that when he left, our family of women nearly fell apart.

Mom grabbed my hand. "Your father had a love for all things small and insignificant. That's why I fell in love with him."

I saw the emotion in her eyes, but her voice didn't register.

"Lucy, you are so much like your father. He would be so proud of you. Stick by Crystal the witch. I have a feeling her story is what this world needs to hear. There are too many fairy tales out there that talk about magic, but they lack the best part of the story."

"And what's that?"

"That magic isn't always the answer we're looking for. That sometimes, we have to overlook something we believe to be magic for us to find value in it one day. If there was anything I learned from your father, it was to pay attention to the smaller things in life. Learn to read the subtleties that nature provides. It's often the things we overlook that house the most magic."

Alba waved her hands in the kitchen entryway.

Mom flicked her wrist, and her soundproof barrier evaporated.

Alba pointed her hand toward the hallway. "There is a tall, dark, and handsome gentleman at the door looking for Lucy?"

20
Amon

As soon as I entered the home, I was assaulted by the intense gaze of three women. One was human. Two were witches. One of the witches was what my shadows wanted to protect more than anything.

Relief rippled through me, but it was short-lived. The Bone Threader or Melrose could show up at any moment.

"Oh, he is *so* beautiful. Victoria is going to be so jealous," the older witch said as she fanned herself with a wooden spoon dripping with yellow batter.

I took a few steps toward Lucy, stopping next to her. "Lucy, are you okay?"

"Why wouldn't I be okay?" Lucy asked, taken aback.

"Can I speak with you in private?"

"No, you cannot," the other witch answered. "What you have to say to my daughter, you can say to her mother." A bowl full of batter began to levitate off the counter. "My name is Cindy, and you must be the demon named Amon who has been harassing my daughter?"

"If harassing is protecting, then I agree with you," I replied.

Cindy's gaze intensified. I ducked as the mixing spoon went flying for my head. The old lady grabbed it and licked the batter off it.

I crossed my arms in front of my chest, addressing the witch named Cindy who was Lucy's protective mother. "Here's the thing. Lucy is in danger."

"*Danger*?" Cindy stammered.

"I'm sure you've seen the strange marks on the sidewalks. The familiars around town have also been spooked by another demon."

"What kind of demon are we talking about?" Cindy asked.

"His name is the Bone Threader, and he's a wendigo," I replied.

The old lady with the spoon gasped.

Cindy clapped her hands on either side of her mouth. "A wendigo? Oh, no. We don't mess with those. They're cannibals!"

"Well, this one has an appetite for books, specifically those that contain shadow magic."

"Then let him eat the grimoire," Lucy protested. "As long as it keeps demons away from my library, I'm happy."

I shook my head. "He's already stepped into your library, making it a possible target too."

Lucy's face twisted. "When?"

"That boy you were tutoring the other day? I confirmed that he wasn't a normal boy. Melrose fed him the grimoire shortly after we left the bar the other night. He's been planning this all along. The Bone Threader set a trap, so he could get a taste for your magic."

Lucy's face scrunched. "Ewwww! Why would he want to taste my magic?"

Cindy set her hands on her daughter's trembling shoulders. "Why is this wendigo coming after my daughter?"

I glanced from mother witch to her librarian witch daughter. "Lucy has magical talents that the Bone Threader has long been trying to devour, magic that my witch mother possessed."

"How did this wendigo even learn about Lucy's magic? I'm sure you've met her bookworm. He would never allow a demon as dangerous as a wendigo to get anywhere near her," Cindy protested.

I chuckled. "Lucy's bookworm has been feasting on bewitchments from the grimoire that have rendered his magic useless."

Cindy's mouth opened and closed a few times before she spoke. "There *must* be another witch who has experience with this magic the wendigo wants. Is your mother alive?" she asked, the fierceness of a lioness reflecting in her eyes.

"No," I replied. "If she was, we wouldn't have this problem."

"What can we do to protect my daughter from this nasty demon?"

"One thing is for certain. I'm not letting your daughter out of my sight."

"She can stay here," Cindy argued. "I have magical barriers out the wazoo all around my property. How do you think I keep the solicitors away?"

"Lucy is not safe here. The Bone Threader can smell a witch's coven from miles away. Having a member of a witch family mingle in one location will only make his appetite more dangerous. He has already created a sink-hole in town. I don't think you want him tunneling close to your house."

The house creaked at my words. A hazy figure drifted into my periphery. I swore I saw my own mother standing there, her aura extending to me.

I blinked, turning back to Cindy.

"Amon, what is your last name?" Cindy asked, her brow arching up.

"Ravenblood, why?"

"Crows and Ravenbloods?" Cindy asked, a twinkle in her green eyes. She patted Lucy's shoulders. "Go with him."

Lucy whipped her head around. "What? Mom, are you sure?"

"He's telling the truth," Cindy said. "I recognize the same look in your father's eyes when he was worried about one of us."

My shoulders relaxed. I could breathe again. "I promise to keep your daughter safe."

"Can we at least call each other?" Cindy asked.

"As long as you don't send magical sparks across the phone to each other, I don't see why not."

Lucy hugged her mother, then the older lady, who hadn't stopped gawking at me.

"I'm sure you'll have some forbidden desires to share with us when you get back!" she teased Lucy.

Lucy flushed as she left for the front door with me.

I had won her over, momentarily. But I could tell Lucy didn't yet believe me about everything. It would take some convincing I knew only a true book-loving witch would appreciate.

We exited the home and stopped on the stone path in the garden facing each other. A chilled breeze whipped through the lilacs. Before, we'd been foes. Now I had a feeling that our ideas about magic would be different before all of this was over.

I held out my hand.

"Where are we going?" she asked before she took it.

"First thing's first. I need to find a spell that's going to protect you from the Bone Threader if he does decide to attack."

"Where would we find that?"

I squeezed Lucy's hand. "I'm taking you to the shadow archives. It's time you see the library that houses shadow magic."

21
Lucy

Amon's dark shadows coalesced around me as my mother's garden disappeared. My legs went slack as the earth fell away. Wind whipped past my face, tangling my hair.

My body was weightless and free. Rooftops and trees drifted below me. This couldn't be happening.

Were we *flying*?

I squeezed what felt like Amon's arm. He became a tendrilling mass of velvety onyx mist.

"We're going higher. Hold onto me," Amon said, his voice echoing from everywhere.

I clenched what I could of his shadows as the onyx mist thickened. The town below became smaller. Clouds drifted past my body, chilling me to the bone.

"I've never been flying this high over town. Wow, this is. . ." My breath was literally stripped away. I could see the damage the Bone Threader had done to town. His marks had scoured the streets and ripped through trees. Goddess, it looked like a tornado had swept through Midhaven. Who knew that a wendigo could cause so much damage in so little time.

It wasn't until I saw the library that I understood the magnitude of his power.

"He's circling the library," I bit out, tears trailing out from the corners of my eyes.

"That's why we can't go anywhere near there," Amon replied, his ebony shadows swathing around my core.

My stomach dropped, not from the height, but from the possibility that I could lose the one place in town that made me whole. I couldn't stand to think what my life might be like if I didn't have my wonderful world of books.

"Quick question. Why is this wendigo called the Bone Threader?" I asked.

"He weaves demon bodies together as though they were threads. The result ends up in the shadow archives," he replied nonchalantly.

I swallowed. "How do we get to the shadow archives?"

Amon's grip on me tightened. "That's for me to know and for you to find out."

As we spiraled somewhere between clouds and sky, I saw him. Well, *most* of him.

Amon's upper body appeared. Shadows threaded out of him like vines and feathers. He was something out of both a nightmare, and a dream. Goddess, my mother was right. Demon's really were sinfully beautiful beings.

My ankles compressed as solid ground met my feet. We weren't in the country, or in town. So where the heck were we?

The air was thick here, much too humid for this time of year. Twilight settled around the strange, eerie place. Was it a forest? A building? I couldn't tell what the towering structure before us was, but it was beautifully creepy.

Black feathers scattered across a frosty path. Dewdrops clung to the fibers. Everything here was thick and slow, as though time had escaped long ago.

"Where are we?" I asked, clutching my sides to subdue my shivering.

An archway made of stone loomed before us. Roots crept out of each crack and crevasse, holding the archway together. This was more like the entrance to a catacomb or a tomb than to an archive.

Amon walked forward, his footsteps echoing off the stones. Light flashed in the dark tunnel the archway guarded. A disembodied voice grumbled, sending gooseflesh rippling up my arms.

He set his hand on the keystone at the center of the archway. The ground crumbled away beneath the archway as a stone staircase manifested. Wind whipped out of the tunnel, scattering the feathers.

He caught one of them in his hand and brought the edge to his lips. He licked the dew from the fibers, tossing the feather aside. "This is a secret entrance to the shadow archives my parents created together," he replied. "Welcome to the Ravenblood's personal archive."

He began his descent of the stairs, leaving me to watch him disappear into the torchlit tunnel.

I darted after him, nearly slipping on the damp stones as I followed. His stride was long and with purpose, making me feel small. I'd recently asked Mom about the shadow magic practiced by demons, but I didn't expect to have an entire archive at my fingertips so soon.

Heck, I didn't even know if this archive had books. What if the grimoires were really monsters?

"Wait up!" I called after him.

Amon didn't slow his pace. His steps quickened, so I took off in a jog to catch up.

We rounded a bend where a giant moss-covered root nearly landed me on my butt. I slammed into Amon's back, which was no longer solid.

He was transforming into something.

His body was evaporating, leaving nothing but the vertebrae and bones protruding from his ribcage. Skin and hair became fibers interwoven with another, flexing and separating.

"What's happening to you?" I asked, backing away from his frightening transformation.

The soft caress of feathers came to my wrists and arms. They draped down my neck, my sides, until the firm grip of two hands lay upon my shoulders.

Amon was no longer a physical body. He took up the entire space as though he was air. "What lives in this archive is not necessarily physical," he said as he took my hand, guiding me forward. "The shadow archives house magic that exists as spirits."

"What do you mean, *spirits*?"

Amon drifted behind me, his shadows coalescing at my sides. "The magic of both witches and demons who have lived and died lives on in this archive."

My thoughts drifted to my father. How I wished I could share this place with him. After Amon's description of shadow magic, I wondered if a piece of him lived on here.

"How is this happening?" I ask as the room seemed to rearrange itself. Walls of dirt began to shift, and roots crept between stones, releasing mist into the air.

"The shadow magic is responding to you," he replied, his heavy bony hands steering me toward a wall.

The archive was cast in low light. There were no bookshelves, but layer upon layer of roots that formed deep gaping hollows. The earthy structure created its own light, emitted by tiny glowing particles that resembled fireflies. They hovered like in the air, making Amon's sinuous black feathers shimmer with green iridescence.

The walls had symbols on them. There were mostly birds, bugs, and spiders. Some of the symbols resembled serpents, while others looked like stars.

Amon stopped me in front of the wall with the symbols carved into the stone. His hard body pressed against my back protectively.

"Why are there so many spider symbols?" I asked, taking note of the ten, and sometimes twelve-legged pictographs that dominated the wall. I could easily see how someone could interpret the symbols as monsters.

"Iktomi represents the web of the shadow archives. His web is the fabric that holds the archives together. But he is only a small part of what created it. When a demon dies, a wendigo takes the pieces of his body and recycles it into a grimoire."

My breath caught. "This archive is made from the bodies of demons?"

Amon's fingers flexed on my shoulders. "Yes. This archive has a dark history."

"How long has the shadow archive been around?"

"It's existed ever since magic was created. My parents used to tell me that the structure is the ancient den all familiars emerged from. When they appeared on the earth, they abandoned their den, which soon became a shadow archive for demons."

I scanned the space, finding that other passageways led off into different directions. "Who created the tunnels?"

"Probably a giant ancestor of your bookworm. Who knows."

The ground trembled beneath my feet, sending a chill up my spine. What if some ancestor of Grubs was *still* living here? And what if it had as many legs as the spider symbols?

"What do you want me to do?" I asked, watching as the roots fold over each other. The lumpy spines of books appeared beneath them.

"You must choose which grimoire you want to capture."

I swallowed. *Capture*? "You make it sound as though the books here are alive."

A dark chuckle rumbled past the cusp of my ear. "You would be surprised at how much life you can find in magic that involves death. Historically, the grimoires from the shadow archives have been used to seek truths only seen with magic."

"Truths?"

Amon grazed his finger across one of the book spines, making it shiver. "We can hide truths from ourselves, even in death. The grimoires have magic that helps to decipher truth often lost by spirits."

I scanned the books. "How does one even begin to read the truth?"

"Sometimes it's about letting the magic read you." Amon's hand extended beyond mine, touching the books. Magic pulsed out of them in thick waves. The energy was malleable. I could morph it with my mind, as long as I had Amon's cool body pressed against me.

Amon's hands withdrew from my shoulders. His protective weight was no longer present. He threw out his arms, the caged animal inside of him released. Like sculpted stone, symbols began to bleed through his skin. "Read me."

"What do you mean, *read me*?" I ask, my breath catching at the sheer beauty of him. Amon's crooked smile broadened as his eyes found me. Lightning flashed in them, great storms of magic and power illuminating the darker parts of him. "Stop ignoring your talents. Read me like you read one of your books."

I stared at his chest, his arms, everything his tattoos encompassed. I couldn't ignore the trail of dark hair that extended down his torso. Everything was shifting, spiraling to the point that it made me dizzy. The symbols on his arms lit up like lightning.

My throat constricted. "I can't read you."

"Yes you can. I've been watching you, Lucy Crow." His feathers grazed my cheek, their softness comforting. "Now, trust in your magic. Everything else will flow."

My memories of the symbols were buried somewhere, but I didn't know where from. I had seen them, but where? Why were they flooding through me like a thunderstorm?

I closed my eyes, focusing on the pulsing energy I had written for Crystal's secret seeing ability. I might not have a crystal in my hand, but I had Amon's shadows assisting me.

They folded over me like silk, his feathers spreading like a protective halo. His aura pulsed, a red iridescence shimmering against the emerging blue outlines of the grimoires.

I focused on the energies pulsing between him, the grimoires, and myself. Our auras blended and folded, until we were dancing together. The colors combined, forming into a shimmering orb of energy. I touched the orb before it dispersed, releasing a gust of wind that sent Amon's feathers flying.

I opened my eyes, finding him gazing at me.

Pride flickered in his eyes, a proud glimmer acknowledging what I'd accomplished.

The wall bulged as more roots emerged, and a great wind tunneled past me.

"Don't let the shadows win," Amon said as he retrieved his feathers with a flick of his hands. The ends traced my cheeks and arms, drawing my focus away from the wind. "They will test you to see if you believe in them or not."

I dug my heels into the ground. My own magic surged, the scent of something burning filling my senses. The roots were angry, lashing out from the hollow.

One struck my cheek. Dampness filled my mouth. I tasted blood.

Heat burst through my fingers as lights pulsed through me. Another element emerged not from the wall, but from below. My shoes became damp.

Water, *so* much water. It welled up like a spring from the ground. I had to make it stop, or the archive would flood!

The fire in my fingers escaped, torching the wall and igniting the roots as they thrash out at me.

A vision flashed in my mind's eye, a vision of a black tree.

I focused on the elements whipping through the branches—the wind, and rain, and lightning. I felt the earth tremble as the tree grew. This tree, whatever it was, had somehow tapped into my own magic. Its roots were drinking, draining my power before I could master it.

One of the roots gripped my wrist. A book emerged from the hollow, the spine threaded with roots and vines as it struggled to free itself.

"I got one!" I cried, falling backward.

Amon collected me back into his shadows.

The water retreated from the archive, as did any body heat I had left. I was soaking wet, and freezing. The book was lodged between us, a mass of gritty, damp earth pulsing with magic.

Amon's arms relaxed around me, and I saw his eyes for the first time in what felt like ages. They were so full of light, not dark and cavernous like the archive.

His lips curved into a lopsided grin. "Nice job."

I gripped the sodden book in my hands. "What do we do now?"

"We get the hell out of here before the archive realizes it's missing."

The hollows in the walls began to draw in air again as though they were inhaling.

I spun on my heel, preparing to dart back toward the staircase.

Amon's hand came to mine, black, bony feathers sticking out of his wrists. "We don't exit the same way we entered," he said, leveling his gaze with me. He was no longer a creature that seemed to fill up the entire archive like air. He was solid again, standing before me. His dark hair was misshapen and feathery in texture.

He plucked a few of the black feathers out of his hair and ran his hand through it to tame the rebellious mass, then took off for another tunnel.

"Why do I get the feeling that not many books get checked out from this place?" I asked as I followed, tucking my new grimoire under my arm. "Who re-shelves the materials, given the books are returned?"

"They are self-organizing."

I grabbed his hand. "You're kidding me."

"I'm not. There is no use for librarians in this archive. The shadows that live inside of the books all work to organize themselves."

Amon squeezed my hand as we entered another tunnel. I was enveloped with so many questions about the history of this archive and why it was formed.

We walked in silence, a dribble of water or a shifting stone occasionally filling the void. The quiet was oddly comforting. This archive wasn't only a home for books—it was a living, breathing place that I couldn't get enough of.

After I'd seen the rawness of Amon unfold, I started to think that maybe demons weren't what they appeared to be. They were more than just shadows. Their stories were brimming with history. I couldn't wait to see what magic this new grimoire held. Maybe it would tell me more about Amon's story.

22
Amon

As we ascended the tunnel, light illuminated the walls and the elated look on Lucy's face. Her excited expression didn't reflect the shock I was feeling. I had taken witches into my family's shadow archives before, but never had I seen one do what Lucy did.

A book of elements was what Lucy had withdrawn—what all witches derived their magic from. These elements were earth, water, fire, and air. And Lucy had somehow summoned every one of them. The elemental texts were so old, they rarely emerged as books. Their messages were often found in forests, rivers, and oceans. Their language was composed of the unpredictable nature associated with the elements. The last time I had seen one of the elemental grimoires up close, my mother had still been alive.

I stumbled in my footing as her hand grazed my face. "What are you doing?"

"You still have feathers sticking out of everywhere," she teased.

"Better feathers than bones," I said, knowing that my shadows only took on that feathery form when they were infatuated. I was lucky they decided to go with feathers today and not some of the more gruesome things they had been known to mimic.

Her touch was soft and warm and curious about the hidden parts of me. I had a problem. The scent of Lucy's magic buried itself into my skull. I needed to get my shadows under control, or they would be ripping out of me to explore her themselves.

As the tunnel narrowed and we left the shadow archives behind us, the smell of cold night air distracted me from her for a moment. As shimmering silver stars emerged in the night sky, I focused on where I must take her next.

My shadows gathered around us both. When they dispersed, we emerged in a dimly-lit room. The windows were cracked open. Drapes drifted in the wind as I settled us in for where we would stay the night.

"Where are we?" Lucy asked, as she walked into the space.

My stomach twisted. This definitely wasn't the most romantic spot, but it was safe, and that was all that mattered. "We're at my apartment."

Lucy spun, taking in my living arrangements. Thankfully, I'd done some housekeeping. There weren't any whisky bottles or cigarettes left over from my brothers. And the sink was clean.

"Demons live in apartments?" she asked, clutching the book of elements to her chest.

"Where did you expect us to live?"

"I thought you might cocoon up at night like my familiar does and just disappear when you feel like it."

I chuckled. "Neither the Bone Threader nor Melrose can find us here."

"How come?"

"Hold out your hand."

Lucy did so, and a beam of moonlight fell into her palm. There were so many colors and textures, her magical aura creating all of it. I traced my finger over the grooves, loving how soft she felt. The lines were like little rivers rushing through a forest and into the prairie.

"Has anyone told you that you hide your magical talents well?" I asked.

The skin on her chest crimsoned. "Has anyone told you that you hide your personality behind a bunch of bones and feathers?"

"That's my nature, and the meaning of my name. One who is hidden, I will always remain."

"Get out. Amon means *hidden one*?"

"It does. My mother named me Amon because she felt that she could never meet all of my hidden shadows."

I draped my hand over the magical aura hovering in her palm and sent it up toward my ceiling. The colors broke open, flashing, then disappearing.

"Let me guess, you have a magical barrier around your place?" she asked.

"Just like your Mom had at her home, only mine is much more established and resistant toward wendigos." A feather formed in the air. I snatched it and handed it to Lucy.

She took it from me and tucked it behind her ear.

Jealousy panged my gut. "You witches are lucky. Your magic is always so colorful."

Lucy stroked the feather, making the colorful iridescence shimmer in the moonlight. "Is your apartment the only place we are safe?"

"Krim's bar has a shadow barrier too. But Shadow Daddy's is getting ready to close, and I don't want to disturb my brother's late night baking experiments."

Lucy's eyes went wide as she glanced at the clock. "Oh my goddess, it's after midnight!"

"Settle in. Shower is that way." I motioned to the hall. "We can eat something if you'd like."

"Do you have any suggestions for twenty-four hour takeout?"

"Greasy's Diner?"

"No, I hate that place. My ex used to eat there all the time. I'm pretty sure he was also eating the waitresses."

My cock twitched. I might not be a wendigo, but I didn't think eating anything other than Lucy could satisfy my appetite tonight. While sex was necessary for a witch and demon to bond their magic, it wasn't the only thing that made the goddess erupt. I was desperate to see how she reacted to the touch of my shadows, who eagerly wanted to explore her.

I'd learned a little while ago why Lucy was intentionally suppressing the goddess that lived inside of her. She stopped practicing her magic after her father passed. I needed to dig deeper, or the Bone Threader would take advantage of her.

"Why don't we look at this book?" she asked, holding up the text.

I peeled another feather off my shirt. "We will. But first, you should call your mother. She will be worried sick about you."

Lucy grinned as she set the grimoire down on my coffee table. "I can't wait to share my adventure to the shadow archives. She will absolutely love it!"

"*And we can't wait to share ourselves with you.*"

I slapped my arm.

Lucy's brow furrowed. "Are you okay?"

"I'm fine," I ground out as one of the horny voices of my shadows threatened to come pouring out of me.

Lucy turned, gathering her things in the silver aura drifting through my window. Her face was a porcelain sculpture etched in moonlight. The subtlety of her features contrasting against the mess of my creative space had me transfixed.

I can't do this. I needed to get myself under control, or the Bone Threader would win. He knew how unpredictable shadows could become toward a witch when it came to the possessive nature of our inner demons.

I eyed the book of elements. "Once you're settled, we'll take a look at that book."

While Lucy grabbed her phone and dialed her mom, I went out onto the balcony of my flat. Maybe some cool night air would help silence the insistent voices in my head.

"*Come on, Amon. Stop hiding us from her. You know you want to throw that book in a ditch and take a look at her sprawled out on your bed.*"

"*No, the kitchen table!*"

"*How about we tie her to the bed and introduce her to your belt collection?*"

I shook my head. So much for fresh night air.

I walked back inside, hoping to distract myself with something other than the witch who was making me go mad. My tattoos were thick and matted on my forearms. They were way too comfortable with discussing taking Lucy to bed.

Lucy tossed her phone back into her bag. "Just like I thought. Mom was more excited than worried."

"Your mother is a very trusting woman. I was amazed that she suggested that you go with me without having met me before."

"Mom's a woman of instinct. She's taught all of her daughters to trust their guts over anything else. All of us sisters are so lucky to have her."

Something deep in my chest ached. I rubbed the spot, wishing the place that had been numb for too long wouldn't feel the way it did. How much I missed my own mother.

I sat down on my sofa and tugged the book of elements next to me. "Well?"

A strand of Lucy's hair fell into her eyes, taking the feather with it. "Well, what?"

I snatched the feather as it fell onto the book, hovering momentarily as it finally settled atop it. Lucy's intoxicating scent exploded through my nostrils. "Do you want to hear the story about how Melrose became locked in the grimoire from this book, or from me first?"

"I thought you said I had to capture the book so you could cast a spell to protect me from the wendigo." Scrutiny twisted her expression. "Am I missing something?"

My jaw clenched. Yes, she was absolutely missing something. All I wanted right now was for her to be close to me. I hated rushing magic. Casting spells and hexes could wait. Right now, she was safe. Was it selfish to want to take advantage of her closeness?

I slumped on the sofa, trying to appear less intimidating. *Fuck.* I was so out of practice. What was wrong with me?

Lucy's eyes scanned my hand, then arm, where my tattoos continued to darken. "Somehow I think hearing the story about Melrose from you would be much more intimate."

"Oh, Amon! Please, take me now!"

"If only you could hear the dirty things she's been thinking about you."

"Where do those tattoos near your cock go? I want to lick you like a popsicle."

I crossed one of my legs over the other before my shadows got any devious ideas. *Shit*. Apparently they were already listening to her thoughts.

Lucy sat next to me, mimicking my guarded posture. She also crossed a leg over the other, eagerly awaiting my story regarding the book of elements.

"Any questions before we begin with this bedtime story?"

"I do have one. You mentioned that you had brought other witches into your family's archive. Was Melrose one of them?"

"She was. Three hundred years ago, she lost someone dear to her." I shrugged. "And I wanted to help her, because I was in love with her."

Lucy's eyes drift away from me, returning quickly. "What did she lose?"

"She'd lost a younger brother. How he died, I can't recall. It was so long ago that even his name escapes me now. He had been a sickly child who moved from the city to the country to find medicine. That's when my mother met him."

"Your mother?"

"My mother was a medicine woman. She was very connected to the earth spirits, or what modern witches today call familiars. She possessed a very rare magical talent that involved all four elements, or directions. She was very close to an ancestral spirit named Changing Woman, a spirit who was known to give guidance to witches practicing spirit medicine." I spun the feather in the opposite direction. "My mother's tribe had a healing tree they would visit when they offered prayers to their ancestors. The tree of shadows, or the sacred spirit tree. They believed this tree housed all four directions, or elements."

The feather continued to spin, catching moonlight and reflecting colors between us. The cover of the book began to change as branches and roots threaded over each other.

Lucy's eyes widened. "That tree I've been seeing, it's this tree of shadows, isn't it?"

I nodded. "I think it's been showing up to you for a reason. The tree of shadows exists in the Summoning, a place where all three magics dance as one. The energy there is very powerful. Sometimes the magic that forms there is so powerful, that the spirits who get too close to the roots become trapped. When I was a boy, both my mother and father forbade my brothers and I to go anywhere near it."

"I know that your mother is deceased. Is your father still alive?"

"He is, but he's not around. He works overseas most of the year for the demon council."

"We're the opposite." She shifted uncomfortably on the sofa. "My father passed away seven years ago. Cancer took him sooner than any of us were ready for."

My shoulders rose then fell as I blew out a sigh. "I'm sorry. It's not easy losing a parent. I miss my mother all the time."

She glanced at me. "What happened to your mother?"

I flexed my hand as my fingers had suddenly gone numb. "When I was still quite young, long before I even knew Melrose, my mother became so enchanted by the earth spirits, that she became swept up by their magic." Emotion clogged my throat. "My father found her body at the base of the tree one day. The tree of shadows is where my mother died."

Lucy's hand came to mine. "I'm so sorry."

Her touch was so present, so different from what I was used to feeling. Distance and loneliness was my true being. "I still feel her spirit at times, but not like I used to. There is a part of me that I lost that day. A part of myself I don't think I'll ever recover. And quite frankly, I don't want to." I pulled my hand away from her. Lucy's comfort was too much. I didn't want to be vulnerable like this. I gazed down at my palms, watching the stains of ink blur behind my tears. I shouldn't be this weak, not with Lucy so near.

I needed to protect her from being swept up by the magic of that tree like it had my mother.

Her fingers traced over my forearm. "When I first met you, I thought these were just tattoos. Now I understand that they have histories of their own."

"Histories?"

Lucy's eyes clouded with fatigue. "You just said that there was a piece of you that you lost. What I don't understand is why you don't wish to recover it."

I grabbed a blanket from the edge of the sofa and pulled it over her. "I lost that piece of myself so long ago, sometimes I think it's best if I just forget it completely."

Lucy shifted closer to me, her soft body fitting snuggly. "How old does that make you?"

My throat became dry. "Try over three-hundred years."

Lucy looked up at me, curiosity brimming in her blue eyes. "Well, you don't *look* old. Do demon's usually live that long?"

I shrugged. "My father has always said my brothers and I got the best of both worlds with magical genetics. We got his longevity, and our mother's creative spirit. I was born in July when the moon was missing her face, so my shadows apparently took advantage of her missing identity and multiplied themselves."

Lucy traced her finger over my forearm, finding the serpent that snaked along the veins bulging toward my wrist. "So this whole multi-shadow streak of yours is due to you being born on the *new* moon?"

"I guess. I never really put that much thought into it. I've gotten by just fine without having all of my shadows," I replied. I could care less about my fragmented shadows right now. All I wanted was for her to continue caressing my skin. Her touch made me feel whole.

Lucy yawned. "Three-hundred years seems like an awfully long time to be missing a piece of yourself."

She tucked herself close to me, her body soft against my ribs and torso. I breathed in her scent, overcome with her presence. I didn't want sleep to separate us. I wanted this moment to linger on like my loneliness had for all of these years.

How weak was I that I could break so easily at the simple touch of Lucy's magic?

23
Lucy

Rain fell in thick cold sheets around me as the sky turned gray. I was sitting in the library, waiting for Jeremy to appear for tutoring. Lightning ripped across the sky and the children's room was filled with the bright electrical light, blinding me momentarily.

Something wasn't right. The library was completely empty. My breathing shallowed as I felt the sensation of someone watching me.

I walked through the stacks, picking out books I thought Jeremy would like. When I pulled the books off the shelves, they had no titles, nor images for me to read. All of the books had the image of a gnarled black tree on their covers.

With my stack of books in my arms, I returned to the table. That's when the rain came pouring down. Fear twisted in my stomach. If Jeremy had walked from the country into town, he would have gotten caught out in this rain. I needed to go find him.

I took one of the books with me. I could take it to him.

As I raced through the stacks, my foot caught in a hole. I tripped, falling into a tunnel. The scent of damp earth filled my nose. I'd lost the book with the tree on the cover. My fingers scraped against gritty dirt and other items as my hands broke my fall.

Shimmering white items lay everywhere. I touched one of the slender items no bigger than my finger. They were bones, *finger* bones. Black feathers drifted on the air, settling atop them.

I grabbed one of the feathers, and a great gust of wind carried me forward, blowing me through the tunnel. The gust was so powerful, it stirred the bones in the tunnel. Larger bones appeared. Legs and arms and rib cages poured out of the earth. No skulls emerged. These skeletons were missing their identities.

I climbed out of the death tunnel, kicking as the scent of fresh air broke my focus. The clap of thunder echoed above me as I emerged. A stone archway glistened over my head.

Roots threaded through the stones, their tangled masses growing atop the archway. They thickened and connected to the trunk of a giant black tree. Grabbing one of the roots, I hoisted myself up and climbed until I perched atop the archway.

The earth leveled out, revealing a wide open field before me. The purple storm clouds continued to flash with explosive bouts of lightning.

A figure stood in the field not far from me. Their face was turned away, blackened hair whipping out from their side as they turned to face me.

The figure was a woman. Her skin was as white as the lightning flashing above. Tears streamed from her eyes. They fell to the ground, pooling into a river that changed direction as it rushed for me.

The water from her tears surged over the ground, catching my feet. It took all of my strength not to fall backward as the water rushed forcefully.

A hand emerged from the water, reaching for the roots. I tried to reach for the hand, but the water swept it away. Who was there? Who had been swept away by the water? Was it the woman who had tears streaming from her eyes, or someone else?

Something was in the tree. A monster with multiple arms maneuvered through the branches, its arms and legs bent unnaturally.

One of the branches cracked.

A sickening *thud* followed.

I raced toward the sound. *No*. Somebody had fallen.

A hand gripped my shoulder. The woman with the white face pulled me back. I fell away from the tree, fading as the branches overpowered me.

A little girl rushed forward, crying as she dropped to the boy on the ground. She sobbed as the woman tried to comfort her. The scent of roses filled my senses as the roots from the tree of shadows took me under.

The scent of coffee jolted me. I sat up on the sofa, blinking into the dull sunlight draping through the window.

Amon stood in the kitchen, his back turned toward me. He was shirtless. Black markings covered his neck and shoulders.

A tattoo of a monster was there—its large, cavernous mouth belonged to that tree.

Amon turned, facing me, coffee mug in hand. "What did you see?"

The smell of that place—the wind, rain, and lightning. I needed to get it out of my skin and hair. The Bone Threader had been hiding in that tree.

I scrambled to my feet. "I'm going to be sick."

I tore down the hall, racing for the bathroom. Once inside, I slammed the door behind me and dropped to the floor. Whatever was causing this, magic, or illness, it had completely messed with my emotions.

"Lucy, what's wrong?" Amon's voice sounded from behind the door.

Clutching the toilet bowl, I prepared to wretch.

A hand came to my back. It took me moments to realize it belonged to Amon. How he got inside the bathroom with the door closed, I had no idea.

Amon's hands reached under my arms, helping me to stand. He closed the toilet seat, then set me atop it. I shivered uncontrollably.

Amon's eyes met mine, silver flecks of light shining in their ebony depths. "What did you see?"

"A tunnel of death. It was right under that black tree. The tree grew on top of the entrance to the shadow archives."

Amon's eyes searched mine as I tried to remember what I'd seen. The branches of that tree reflected in his dark irises. I could smell the Bone Threader's rancid breath on my neck as he descended the tree.

"Your magic must be responding to something. What else do you remember?" he asked.

"There was this woman standing in a field. When she turned to look at me, tears flooded from her eyes. They formed a rushing river that changed direction, flooding toward me."

"The water changed direction?"

I nodded, shivering.

Amon's brow knitted. A few feathers prickled from the thick black hairs, softening his expression. "You might have seen Changing Woman. She was the spirit my mother looked to for guidance with her magic. What happened next?"

"I saw someone climbing in the tree. Then I remembered the story you told me about Melrose's brother, and how you couldn't remember how he died. . ." My stomach caved in. "It happened when I was there. He was in the tree. I heard him fall, hit the hard ground." I grabbed his hand. "Amon, I heard his bones shatter."

Amon squeezed my hand. "Lucy, it's okay. It was just a vision."

A face flashed before me. A face I had seen before. The white eyes. The wide smile. They belonged to the same spirit.

I squeezed Amon's hand. "Her brother wasn't the only one climbing that tree."

"You saw another spirit in the branches?"

"I did." I pressed my face to Amon's neck, breathing in his scent to replace the stench of the wendigo's breath. He smelled like ink and rainstorms. "The shadows in that archive are hiding something the Bone Threader doesn't want us to uncover—something tied to Melrose and her brother's death."

"Both Melrose *and* her brother?"

I thought back to the tunnel with bones, but no skulls. The skeletons were missing their identity, because something had stolen them. All I could see was the tree Jeremy had drawn at the library, and the word I had helped him to write with my magic.

I pulled away from Amon's neck. "I think I know who Jeremy's true identity is. I think Jeremy is really Melrose's brother."

Amon's eyes widened. "This is huge. Lucy, if you're right, you just made a huge discovery in how we can defeat the Bone Threader."

"How?"

"You've discovered the Bone Threader's identity—the soul of the last victim he consumed. Identity is a wendigo's biggest weakness."

I began shuddering from head to toe.

Amon stood and turned on the shower tap. "Your body is in shock. We need to calm you down."

Steam filled the room as he helped me into the shower. I was wearing my clothes. And he was wearing *shadows*?

He helped me under the tap, positioning me beneath the stream of hot water. I soaked it in, thinking about Changing Woman's tears as the river flooded toward me. She was directing me to see something in the vision, a different side to the story behind the spirits from Amon's past. What the Bone Threader had tried to hide from Amon was the truth behind their death.

His hands stroked my shoulders and spine, his touch igniting me. His words from the shadow archives came back to me, hovering over the cusp of my ear. "*You would be surprised at how much life you can find in magic that deals with death.*"

"Are you doing better?" he asked, keeping his hands above my waist as he continued to stroke my back. He rubbed small circles, his touch convincing the tension in my muscles to leave.

Amon's body had done something in the steam. He wasn't feathers, or skin, or the bones I had seen. He shifted between a man, a bird, and a stream. My heart fluttered. Demons were such intricately beautiful beings.

"Why do you change form so often?" I asked, touching one of the tattoos that snaked down his forearm toward me.

"It depends on my mood," he replied, gruffness in his voice.

"What is your mood right now? I'm having a hard time reading it."

"I'm starting to think that reading isn't the only thing you are good at, that maybe, I'm," his voice was clouded by the steam. "Lucy, I want to know what makes your heart sing. I want to worship you." His eyes met mine, dangerous flames licking from their ebony depths.

His hands lit me on fire.

"Don't stop." I grabbed for him, but my fingers met hot water. "Stop hiding from me."

"I'm not trying to," he growled, frustration ringing in his voice.

Goddess, I wanted the hidden parts of Amon. *All* of him. Right now, no exceptions. But why couldn't I seem to gather him?

"Amon," I breathed. A moan escaped me. Even though I couldn't press my hands against his chest, he already found my breasts. "Don't stop what you are doing."

As his shadows thickened around my legs, the waves of Amon's body against my own began to pulse. I became trapped in an endless sea of mist, pleasure, and shadow. My clothing dissolved from my body as Amon's darkness explored me.

"Tell me what you want," he breathed, the hunger in his voice echoing.

This can't be real. This must be a fantasy.

Pinned against the wall, I had no place to run. Every time his shadows slid to a new spot, my body ignited. My hips gyrated as Amon's silky shadows explored my breasts and belly. I rocked my body closer to him, trying to find a rhythm.

His tattoos uncoiled from his arms, their cool touch burning my skin. The shadows morphed their form, shifting between serpents and hands.

I jolted as one of the serpents raised its eyeless head. A forked tongue flicked out toward me.

"Don't worry, they don't bite," Amon said, holding his hand out and allowing the serpent to coil between his fingers. "My serpents are meant for one thing only—pleasure."

He lowered his hand between my legs, joining the other hands as multiple fingers slid over my opening. My back arched as the fingers pulsed, stretching me. Tension wound in my belly as he inserted his fingers. What I assumed were the serpents teased and circled my clit, bringing me to the edge of release.

"Relax into me," Amon said as the fingers slid out of me.

I closed my eyes as the steam from the shower and his voice broke over me. His hands gripped my hips, propping me onto the tile ledge. The shadow serpents caressed my belly and thighs as they coiled around my legs.

Amon's face appeared out of the shadows, his drenched hair stuck to his forehead. He buried his face into my neck. "This is when you tell me what part of me you want next."

Oh, fuck. I have options?

"You've seen what my shadows can do. They can do more, *much* more. What more do you want?"

I wrapped my arms around his neck, tugging him close to me. "I just want you right now."

He planted a kiss onto my neck, resting his face against me. "I wish I could say that I was that simple."

I found his cheek, kissing him as his stubble rubbed against me. His lips found mine, and I savored every flick of his tongue. He pushed his tongue into me like the fingers had earlier, and I was reliving the fantasy of being filled by *so much more* of him as he stated.

The shadow serpents coiling between my legs slithered up to my chest, gliding between us. Were they jealous?

Something hard pressed against my opening that wasn't the head of a serpent.

"You feel so good," Amon grunted. "I want to burry myself inside of you. Would you like that?"

My mind blanked. I thought I was on the pill. I hadn't stopped taking it after I broke up with Jason, right?

I kissed his neck, tasting the salt on his skin. "I want to, but I can't yet."

Amon withdrew himself from my aching pussy.

I reached out, touching what had to be his cock. Amon was *huge*. My fingers grazed the head, trailing along his thick length. Where did he end? I wish I had a condom or *something* to keep going where we both wanted this to go. But Amon respected that I wasn't ready to *take all of him* as he suggested, even if my body ached for him.

Oh, it had to be a tongue—no—was it more than one?

The nipping and sucking dipped below my navel, hovering inches away from my slick. I withered against his shadows as they continued to please me.

A hand clasped around my throat as teeth scraped across my jawline. "Just wait until you feel me inside of you."

"Fuck," I said, opening my eyes.

"Exactly," he replied. "*Tell me you want me*," a voice lower than his interrupted. The steam was so thick, I wondered if it was changing the sound of his voice.

"Turn around," he demanded.

"*She's too afraid of us to do so*," another voice said. "*She must do as she is told if she is to trust in her magic.*"

Amon held me, possessively so.

"Who was that?" I asked, trembling from my own arousal.

"My shadows want you as much as I do," he breathed, the desire in his voice as scorching hot as the steam. "You are safe with me. I won't let them have you. You are *mine*, Lucy Crow."

I moaned as his fingers glided over my slick, expertly flicking and circling over me. His body evaporated, but the pleasure remained. The water pulsed down my front, creating an explosion of ecstasy.

24
Amon

I took Lucy's sodden clothes with me out of the bathroom and strung them up in the kitchen with the help of my shadows. A few of my feathers detached from the ebony sinew, spinning to create a wind tunnel. Within a few minutes, Lucy's clothing would be dry. But that didn't mean I wanted to see her cover up her beautiful body.

I dried myself as well, collecting the misshapen mass of my shadows as Lucy's spontaneous arousal burned all around me. Her orgasm was sweet and intoxicating, and now my shadows wouldn't leave her alone. That sexual release was not expected, nor was the magic that came pouring out of her like a river, in the shower, with half of my shadows fighting over her.

Fuck. My shadows had gotten way too kinky. There was no way the attraction between Lucy and I would last. It would end in one of two ways as all of my intimate relationships with non-magical women or witches did. They either ran screaming out of my flat, or straight up told me to go to hell.

Images of her in the shower played like a video behind my eyelids every time I blinked. Her panting against the wall. Her hands gripping for me. What kind of noises would she make when I plunged my cock between her legs?

Her magic burned into my nose—it had changed me. I still felt her pressed against my tongue and hands. Her breasts. Her skin. Her taste as I ate her out like a starved animal. She was just as starved for that kind of pleasure as me, only Lucy was *mine* to please.

"*You mean ours...*"

I chose to ignore my shadow's greedy comment. Lucy's magic wasn't only palpable, it was transforming quicker than I'd ever seen in a witch, especially one who had for so long, suppressed the goddess. The mess of *Inked* magazines in my corner were no longer tossed about, but stacked neatly according to their color. And my art pens—I'd never seen them look so perfectly propped into jars next to my collection of whiskey bottles. If my mother could see this, she would be laughing. She'd told me long ago that I needed to find a witch who could help me organize my creativity.

I plopped down on the sofa, bracing myself for when she emerged. She was either going to be pissed, or so turned on that she would beg me for more. It would take all of my strength not to have my shadows rip out of my body and pin her to the wall.

My bedroom door cracked open, letting the steam from the shower into the hall. Lucy emerged in the living room, her body wrapped in a damp towel. She was still woozy and glowing from her orgasm. Her chest rose and fell as she studied me.

Damn it to hell. Why am I doing this to myself?

A strand of her hair fell into her face. "That was amazing."

"Did you enjoy it?" I asked, pride swelling and deflating in my chest. I squashed the triumph I wanted to feel. Most women didn't enjoy my kind of kink when it came to sex.

Fuck. I could get high off this new expression of her magic.

Her gaze met mine, smoky with desire. "I would have enjoyed it more had you not run out on me."

Every part of me ached to grab her and return to the shower. Lucy didn't understand. I couldn't physically be there with her, or my shadows would have all had their say. All of me at once was not something I'd been able to share with a witch, *ever*. Only one of my shadows was capable of doing terrible things. The last thing I wanted to do was to end up hurting Lucy.

My crotch bulged as her smoky gaze traced a line down my front. "Sorry, sometimes the serpents get a little out of hand."

Lucy's lips curved into a smile. "Having a snake in your pants is one thing. But multiples?" She set her hand on the doorframe, slumping as her desire-filled look thickened. "I'd like to see more of them again."

"We need to make sense of what you saw in this vision," I said, hoping to change the subject away from what my shadows were begging me to do.

"*What are you waiting for? You've opened the floodgates*!"

"*Slam her against the wall, now*!"

"*Tear her wide open and give her what she's craving*."

Lucy's eyes burned with fury, and satisfaction. She still had that magical after-glow from her orgasm. "I told you what I remember. What is there to make sense of?"

I waved my hand.

Lucy jumped when she noticed her clothes suspended in the air, my feathers fanning away the last bit of moisture.

"Get dressed, and we'll look at how to move forward with this," I said. I could hear the dismissive tone in my voice. I didn't sound how I felt. I'd always hated how I could hide not only my shadows, but my feelings for those I cared about.

She grabbed her clothes. Instead of returning to the bedroom to change, she dropped the towel and exposed herself.

Her legs. Her stomach. Her breasts. . .

"*She said she liked the serpents. She is ours. . .*"

Before I could stop myself, I was across the room, gathering her in my arms and stroking her hair away from her face.

Lucy's skin began to glow.

She held her arm out to observe the colorful changes in her aura. "What is happening to me?"

"I don't know. But you seemed to have experienced a flare in your magic."

"That was no magical flare, that was an explosion. Am I reacting to the elements from inside the book? If so, which one?"

I stared at her aura as more colors came fizzling out of her like solar flares. I was so jealous of her magic. My shadows were as black as night, but Lucy had so much color to play with.

"Judging by the colors in your aura, I would say that you are experiencing every element."

"Why do I get the feeling that you want to play with them?" she teased, looking up at me.

She was right, I *did* want to play with her magical energies. Lucy's aura was like a box of crayons for some kiddy school boy to rip open and start coloring with. Only I wasn't a school boy. I had urges that could not be satiated with simple coloring. There would always be another part of me that would want to take her magic and turn it into a painting.

I forced my arms away from her, dropping them at my sides. "Will you please get dressed?"

She grabbed my hand and shoved her bra into my palm, then turned away from me. "Help me dress."

"Did anyone ever tell you that it's not a good idea to turn your back to a demon?" I asked, taking in the curves of her waist and ass as she further exposes herself. The bra was a tangled mess that would be a crime to use to cover up her breasts.

Another magical flare burst from her arms. "Make it stop."

"I can't. *You* can't."

She grabbed her bra. "Fine, then I'll figure it out myself!" As she dressed, I felt like such an idiot standing here, ignoring all of the urges that were blowing through me.

She spun on her heel and grabbed the book of elements from my coffee table.

"What are you doing?"

"I don't care what this stupid wendigo wants with my magic. I'm taking matters into my own hands."

Lucy jumped as the book sprung open. Flames erupted out of the pages, as did a whirlwind that spiraled like a liquid serpent up into the air. Lucy released the book, which levitated before us as it hissed and popped. In a fiery display of sparks and electricity, the book promptly disintegrated.

We both stood awestruck, staring up at the shimmering yellow dust that hovered above us.

"What the hell just happened?" Lucy asked, completely flabbergasted.

I tried and failed at stifling a laugh. "I think the elements just spoke for you."

"I thought that stupid book was supposed to help protect me. Why would it just disappear like that?"

One of my tattoos mimicked the shape of the liquid serpent that appeared moments before the book destroyed itself. "The shadow magic inside apparently decided that *I* am the one who is supposed to keep you safe." I grabbed her hand, tugging her close to me. "I'm not letting you out of my sight. The Bone Threader will find you, and he will hurt you."

"I don't think he will, not with your shadows protecting me," she said with a smirk.

"*Kiss her, you fool, or I will take her mouth and...*"

I shook my head, forcing my shadows' devious thoughts away. I wanted to give in and enjoy this witch, and devour every last drop of her magic.

My phone buzzed, shaking me out of my fantasy. I grabbed it, sticking the speaker to my ear.

"Amon?" Zed's voice sounded.

"What the fuck do you want?"

"Dude, we finally got a name for the band!"

"That's nice. Anything else?"

"Yeah. I've been such a dick to my big bro. I wanted to apologize for the other night. I should have stuck up for you when Krim kicked you out. Are you holding up alright?"

Lucy's hand was still intertwined in mine. My tattoos snaked down to my palm as they reached for her. "I'm fending for myself, if that's what you want to hear. Why did you call?"

"Come over to Shadow Daddy's so I can make it up to you. And bring Lucy, I want to meet her! Also, I've been digging around town, trying to track down anything I can about this wendigo."

I ground my jaw. The only reason I would consider taking her to meet my brother was because I needed to get my shadows to cool down. Being close to Zed should help prevent me from doing anything regretful, like I'd almost allowed when we were in the shower.

"We'll be there in a few." I ended the call, pocketing my phone.

Lucy grabbed a strand of my hair and tucked it behind my ear. "Where are we going, Hidden One? I can call you that, right?"

Daylight streamed in from my bedroom, illuminating the bed that should be how we spent the remainder of our morning. "My brother Zed said he wants to meet you."

Her fingers grazed my cheek. "You didn't answer the second part of my question."

I grabbed her hand. "You didn't give me time to answer." I pressed my lips to the top of her fingers, kissing each one.

"I take it that's a yes?" she whispered.

"I can't promise that you won't see the hidden parts of me before all of this is over." When I released her hand, a flash of her aura burst from her fingertips, dispersing my shadows before I could take her skyward.

Lucy smirked at me. "You don't have to whisk me off my feet at every opportunity you get. I have legs. Why don't we walk to the bar?"

I was so jealous of how her aura flared. When she looked at me, her aura didn't dull like I thought it would, being that I was all shades of onyx and ebony. When she looked at me, her aura became more vibrant.

25
Lucy

My magic was blooming out of nowhere, and I was so sick of seeing the colors that I could puke. I needed to stretch my legs and work through the new colorful sensations, but all I wanted to do was return to the velvety satin fabric of Amon's shadows. The one thing I did like about my magic was how Amon seemed to be reacting to it.

My mind kept drifting back to my hot, steamy explosion in the shower. Amon had pleased me first, something Jason never imagined doing. Now all I wanted to do was rip his pants off and finish him the way he did with his "*I want to worship you*" comment.

It was apparent that his shadows had more to do with his magic, and his sexual appetite, than I thought.

We passed a rock shop, one of Grace's favorites. The crystals inside had so many colors exploding out of them that I must have lost my mind.

I stopped to peer through the window. "Wow. I can't believe how many colors these rocks are putting off. Crystal would be so impressed."

"Who is Crystal?" Amon asked, sliding up beside me.

"She's a fictional witch character in a story I wrote."

One of Amon's brows arched as a perplexed expression took over his face. "You write?"

I turned away from the window and started walking. Why did I have to open my big, fat mouth?

Amon took two steps with his long legs and caught up with me. "I thought you just liked books. I didn't think you were working on one."

I shrugged as we padded down the street toward Shadow Daddy's. "I've always wanted to be an author and share stories that I love. I figure that not everyone will love it, but someone will, right?"

Amon shook his head, sending a few of his stray black hairs into his face. "I could never write. When Dad wanted me to go into the family grimoire business, I backed out." He cocked his head sideways. "But you, on the other hand, it sounds like you have this book thing all worked out."

I chose to focus on the new colorful energies sprouting out of every crack, tree root, and patch of earth that wasn't asphalt along the sidewalk instead of acknowledging Amon's compliment.

Amon's elbow nudged my arm. "What's this book about?"

"I told you, a witch named Crystal."

"I got that part. What inspired you to *write* it?"

My footsteps sped up. "My father's love of nature. Most of what I appreciate about magic comes from what he taught me as a child."

Amon kept pace, his feet hovering over the sidewalk as he drifted beside me. "What does Crystal the witch do?"

"She gathers crystals that have magical symbols locked inside of them. Once she has so many crystals, she can eventually put together a spell that she can read, one made of the earth magic created by familiars. The whole idea for the book was to use magical symbolism to help children cope with dyslexia."

"Sounds like a great start for a book, except for the familiar magic part."

"So what is your artistic outlet, then, other than harassing librarians?" I asked, knowing he'd lived in this town for a while.

A wicked grin crept up his face. "I can tell you that it's not baking shitty pastries like my brother does."

I laughed. "My oldest sister tells me that demons are rumored to turn destructive if they don't have an outlet for their creative magic."

"She's not incorrect."

"What makes a demon turn into a cannibalistic monster like the Bone Threader?"

"It's boredom. Wendigos are created when a demon becomes so bored with his shadows, that he begins to feed on others." He ran his hand through his hair, making it spike. "My father tried to stop the Bone Threader, but by the time he sank his teeth and claws into the archives, it was too late. Every grimoire created after he took over was created with his shadow cannibalizing ways."

I slowed my pace. "Wait, so the shadow archives haven't always been that way?"

"No. The Bone Threader took over the shadow archives after the death of my mother."

Amon's words hit me hard. Empathy wallowed in my gut.

"So, this book you're writing, is it a novel?" Amon asked, steering the conversation away from death.

"Oh, no. It's a children's picture book. After meeting you, I might need to put a few chapters in about the ferocity of demons. Piss me off, and I might turn you into the villain."

"So you think I'd make a good ferocious villain in your book?"

"Yeah, I do."

Amon grabbed my hand. He hiked his head back, chuckling darkly. "Oh, Lucy. You have yet to learn about a demon's true nature. We are not always the most straightforward of creatures. But ferocious? Nah."

I knew he was flirting, but it wasn't working. I just wanted to get my magic under control and return it to its state of dormancy. My mind raced back to the kinky serpent sex we almost had while in the shower. "Why do I get the feeling that your tattoos like to be kinky?"

His mouth quirked, and I couldn't help but notice that he wasn't disagreeing with me. "You already know them a lot better already than I do."

"What if I told you that I'd like to get to know them better?"

Amon's face crimsoned.

My belly warmed. Kinky was an understatement. Amon's tattoos had unraveled from his forearms and caressed my belly. The sensation had been both cool and warm, and slightly tingly. It felt like being stroked by a feather that knew just the spots to tickle and leave alone.

I walked faster, but Amon tugged me back, forcing me to match his lollygagging place. "We've spent enough time stressing over a grimoire. I want to know more about this children's book you've written. When's it getting published?" he asked.

"Why are you so interested?"

"Because it's something you love, right? You should see the colors in your aura right now."

I flushed. Jason *never* took an interest in my writing projects. "I've just never had someone ask so much about a story they didn't know about."

Amon's cheeks dimpled. The tall, lanky demon actually looked childish.

"I have the entire book written, but I haven't yet found an artist. I can't find anyone to illustrate the contrast I want in Crystal's quest to find all of the elements."

"What do you mean by contrast?"

I squeezed his hand, loving his callused warmth. "You know, varying shades of light and darkness."

"*Well, it's sure dark where I am right now.*"

I stubbed my toe in a crack on the sidewalk as a familiar voice crowded my head. "*Grubs?*"

"*Hi. Have you missed me?*"

"*Not really. I thought you went off to chrysalis?*" I added.

"*Well, I was. Then I sort of got stuck.*"

"*Where?*"

"*You should see the tunnels beneath town. A whole bunch of my cousins are here. We've found something. You know those rose petals Amon gave me? I think I know who bewitched them.*"

"*Melrose?*"

"*No. They came from a witch though.*"

"*Can't you just tell me who this witch is?*" I pleaded.

"*No can do. That would be violating familiar code with the earth. A witch's hair, nails, bones, and any piece of nature her magic has touched is guarded by us. What's buried remains unheard, unspoken, and unseen, until, of course, I bring it up for you to see. But that would require me getting out of this claustrophobic situation I've found myself in."*

I pinched my brow. Grubs could be such a pain sometimes. Why couldn't I have gotten a black cat as my familiar like every other stereotypical witch?

"*I heard that.*"

One of Amon's brows arched. "Is someone talking to you?"

"Grubs is. He's just being annoying."

"Tell the little fucker that I'm taking care of his witch better than he can."

My bookworm's annoying voice died away as we rounded the corner onto Main Street. The neon Shadow Daddy sign wasn't lit up.

Amon tugged me sideways, steering me toward the alleyway. I swore the bricks on the building began to vibrate.

"What kind of band does your brother play in?" I asked as the music pulsed through me.

"Heavy metal," Amon griped. "And it sounds like they're just now warming up."

"It's hotter than Hades' taint in here!" a gravely male voice echoed through the door.

Amon sighed. "I really hope that's not the new band name." He held the door open for me, and I walked inside. Whoever had yelled before wasn't wrong. The air was scalding hot. A blast of cinnamon and something floral swirled around me as Amon's shadows propped the door open.

"Zed, why is it so fucking hot in here?" Amon growled, his shadows dispersing as soon as we entered the bar.

I fanned myself from the heat, and from the sight of him. Amon was all darkness and ebony silk again. Why must his shadows turn me on?

Another shadowy mass approached me, belonging to whom I assumed was Amon's brother. But his textures weren't silky. They were like choppy water after a storm blew in. They also didn't exude Amon's delicious musky scent.

"Krim left his ovens on overnight. He's been baking like a crazy person," the shadows replied, until the choppy waves fell away. I swore I saw a skeleton standing there, a pair of drumsticks clutched in his bony hand. A man dressed in a leather biker jacket with black pants appeared. No hair was present on his shiny, bald head.

"Krim bakes when he is stressed," Amon chided, nerves ringing in his voice.

"Yeah, well. With all this new business with the wendigo, I can't blame him," Zed said, his electric green eyes glowing as they swept to me. "Ah, this must be Lucy the librarian my brother is so lucky to have in his boring life." He thrust a just as callused hand as his older brother out for me to take.

I took his hand, and his fingers cracked under my grip. For someone having such a large, bony hand, the sound was disgustingly accurate. "I didn't volunteer to help him. He pretty much told me to."

Zed pulled his hand away, flashing a set of perfect white teeth. "Amon tells me you got a wendigo threatening to devour your library?"

"Not only that, but I hear he's going to do some irreversible damage to the shadow archives."

Zed grabbed the drumsticks from his pocket and swiveled one of them between his gritty fingers. "Well, we might just be able to scare him off with this jam. Boys?"

Three other men lifted their guitars and a microphone. "We're ready!"

Zed withdrew into the bar, leaving me to fend for myself next to Amon. His shadows behaved strangely. Some coalesced, while other figures distanced themselves, seeming to have quiet discussions about what to expect from Zed.

A couple of spotlights illuminated the four band members as they took up their places in the center of the bar.

Zed flopped down on a stool behind a drum set and hiked his drumsticks over his head. "Release the Nematodes!"

An electric guitar and two bass jammed off a horrible warbling chord as Zed slammed his sticks into his drums.

"Wow, the Nematodes? That is super lame," Amon chortled, waving his hand as the heavy metal exploded. His shadows formed a buffer, preventing the music from interrupting us. I'd seen my mom perform this simple spell dozens of times, yet Amon's magic felt quietly intimate.

His hand came to mine, one after another, until my fingers were interwoven with what felt like a dozen different shadows. Their touch was cool and inviting, each exploring my wrist and fingers.

"What are you looking for?" I asked, startled with the sudden display of affection from so many of them. A bead of sweat trickled down my ribcage.

"Shadow serpents respond to vibrations," Amon growled.

My gaze dropped to his crotch. "Judging by the serpents in your pants, I'd say that you are rather turned on right now."

Amon's jaw hardened. The veins in his neck bulged. The serpents retreated into the tall shadow bodies that surrounded us.

Lighting and thunder broke the music, exposing another side of him that I hadn't seen before. His hand forced through the shadows, finding my wrist and grabbing it. He held my arm up, inspecting each of my fingers like he was reading them. "I need the light of you that compliments my shadows."

I'd never had a guy express that he *needed* me before. I was overcome with the textures of him. His constant cooling and unbelievable warmth. His gentleness.

He pressed his lips to my index finger, closing his eyes. An eyelash fluttered down from his face, brushing past my wrist as he planted the most sensual kiss on my palm. The roughness of his stubble grazed my skin, making me shiver.

"Don't stop," I whispered back to him.

"I can stop. It's *them* I don't trust to listen if you ask me to keep going."

My heart skipped. That rolling wave of pleasure from the shower filled my gut all over again.

The music finished, striking a high screeching note that broke my focus.

Amon caught me as my knees gave out. He helped me regain my footing. As the music faded, muffled clapping sounded behind us.

"Is the Neeeematooooode's all you've goooot, Zeeeeddy? Come oooon. You shoooould have stuuuuuck with my suggeeeeestion for the Raaaaging Boooon-ers."

Amon's eyes glassed over. "Dad?"

An equally glassy-eyed demon stared at us both. He sported a wicked wide grin nearly identical to the one I saw a few moments ago on Amon.

26
Amon

Dad's bloodshot eyes were as thick and murky as the two black ravens sprouting from his broad shoulders. Their feathers bowed and frilled with angst. The birds were a direct correlation to my father's quirky moods, meaning one very dangerous thing.

He had been drinking.

Lucy was still in my arms, not fully supporting her own weight. I released her, but the sweet scent of her magic burning in my nose did little to comfort my panic. Dad, even in an alcohol-induced stupor, would know his eldest son had been drinking in a witch's magic.

He stood up from his place at the bar, knocking a couple of shot glasses to the ground as he swiped his hand across the counter. He squared his hips, locking his cold gray eyes with me. It was the first time in months that I'd given my old man a stiff look. He looked like fucking hell.

His hair was disheveled, clumps of silver straying from his ponytail. What was usually a clean-shaven jaw was rough with wiry, reddish-brown hair. A purple smudge I thought might be a bruise blemished his cheek.

"Dad, why are you here?" I asked, studying his swaying movements. He had to be wasted.

"Zeeeed said he finally got a naaaame fooooor his baaaand! I had toooo come seeeeee for myseeeelf."

Lucy giggled. "He's drunk."

"No shit he's drunk. The fool can't even walk straight."

Zed held his drumsticks over his head. "What did you think? Loud enough to scare away a wendigo?"

My stomach twisted at Zed's question.

Dad's ravens erupted from his shoulders, their shadows splintering into an explosion of ebony feathers.

"Weeeeendigo? Wheeeere?" he stammered drunkenly. He spun on his heel, swinging a punch in the air.

I grabbed his shoulder, stopping him. "How much have you had to drink?"

"Noooot enoooough," he growled, staggering toward the bar to grab another bottle. Dad was much stronger than I, and I couldn't stop him from grabbing a bottle of Jack Daniels.

The brown whisky poured out, dribbling down both sides of his lopsided mouth. He tossed the bottle aside. "Come on, Amoooon. When was the last tiiiime I got to enjooooy a stiff driiiiink with my fiiiiirst boooorn? Wheeennnn youuu coooooming to Ireeeeeland with meeeee?"

"Not when you are this drunk," I mumbled. I could only imagine the kind of drinking he did in Dublin, where the demon council headquarters were located.

Dad pumped his fist into the air. "Come on, my booooys! The niiiight is stiiiilllll young!"

Zed shook his head as he approached me. "He thinks it's night. He's blasted. Krim's going to come into a real shock when he sees that Dad's downed most of his alcohol."

Dad always showed up unannounced. Ever since he started working overseas for the demon council, he barely set foot in this cozy little town.

"What do we do with him?" Zed asked, his green eyes flashing to mine.

"Sobering up a demon when he has this much booze burning in his blood could take days," I said, pinching my brow. This was the worst possible way I wanted Lucy to meet my drunken asshole of a father. "Something's happened. He's always liked his alcohol, but I've never seen him like this. He doesn't just come into town and get slammed without reason."

Zed backed away. "This is all you. Besides, we've just started practice. We need to rehearse our jams for this weekend's performance."

My stomach hollowed.

Lucy was fast approaching my intoxicated father.

"Hello, sweeeeetheart, what's your name?" Dad asked. "Are yooou a wiiit-tttch?"

Lucy's freckles darkened at his question. "I am. A librarian witch, in fact."

"What doooooes thaaaaat mean? That yoooou liiiike to reeeead speeellll books? My soooon has gooootten into trrrrouble with wiiiitches before. One ennnnded up trying to kiiiill him, so I had to looock her spiiirit into one of my griiiimoires."

"All right, that's enough," I said, sliding in between them. "Dad, what do you say I take you back to my place and get that tattoo on your arm taken care of?"

Dad's bloodshot eyes darkened. "Laaaaacy and I weeeere just getting to knooooow each other, riiiight Laaaaacy?"

Lucy laughed. "I think Amon has a great idea."

I linked my arms with my intoxicated father, but he fought me. "I caaaan get theeeere myself, booooy."

He disappeared, then manifested outside the door.

I sucked in a breath. Thank the darkness he didn't suspect that I took Lucy into the shadow archives. Must be the alcohol.

Dad turned on his heel, his stride too quick for either of us to match. When he was out of earshot, I grabbed Lucy's hand and tugged her toward the door just as Zed's band began playing again. "Come on. The sooner we get him sober, the sooner we find out why he's really in town. He's a crazy old man, but he doesn't drink like this unless something is really wrong. Just don't let him know that I took you into the shadow archives, all right?"

"Why not?"

"The last time I did, you know what happened. He had to lock the vengeful spirit of a witch into one of his grimoires."

Lucy laughed. "I'm not dead, and I'm not a vengeful spirit, am I?"

"No?"

"Well, somehow I feel like that was all just tough talk. What is involved to get him sober?"

"You'll see. One demon's creative outlet is another's sobriety."

Lucy grinned from ear-to-ear. I half-expected Dad's random appearance to end whatever we had going right now.

"You're brave sticking up to him like that," I said.

"You should have seen the crap I gave my father as a kid."

"My relationship with my old man definitely isn't the healthiest."

"What's his name?"

"Eugene. I swear, my father and I are nothing alike. He's all bark and sometimes a nasty bite."

"There isn't anything wrong with being like your parents. What I really want to know is if you have as many tattoos as him?"

I shrugged. "It depends on the day. A demon's shadows are often disguised as tattoos on his body."

Lucy squeezed my hand. "I saw one on your back in your apartment. I think it's fucking hot."

My neck burned at her statement. The monster on my back didn't always have the best appearance, and here Lucy was getting turned on by it.

27
Lucy

I followed Amon out of the bar as he attempted to chase down his drunken father. Even though things were about to get hot and heavy before Eugene appeared, I'd sensed hesitation on Amon. Darkness had been pouring out of him, unrestrained darkness that had its own hands gripping for me.

What did the darkness want with me? Was Amon able to control it?

"Shit. He's like a fucking toddler when he's drunk," Amon's voice stirred me out of my promiscuous fantasy.

Eugene was halfway down the street, chortling off curses as he maneuvered between parking meters and trees. He narrowly missed other pedestrians as he worked through the lunch crowd. Amon's father was hilarious. He reminded me of a mix of a biker guy, mafia, and a cowboy. His personality was nothing like his reserved firstborn.

A couple of ravens swooped overhead, diving toward the drunken demon. I had no idea where we were going, but it was pretty hilarious watching Amon try to reign in his father.

Amon fell back, apparently giving up, landing into stride next to me. "He knows the way to my shop. It's best just to give him space when he's this way."

"Your shop?" I asked, completely perplexed.

Amon grinned. "It's right below my apartment."

As we ventured down a couple more blocks, we stopped at the corner of the street. Eugene slammed his fist on the glass shop door. "Opppen up! I'm heeeeere to get my iiiink on!"

"Dad, I'm right here," Amon said, sliding up next to him and tugging out a key. He pressed it to the lock and opened the door.

Eugene was the first inside. I stood under the blinking green sign: **Shadow Ink's Tattoo Parlor**. I'd passed by this tattoo parlor loads of times, but I had never been inside.

Amon set his hand on my lower back and escorted me through a doorway. The scent of chemicals hit my nose as I followed Eugene into a dim-lit room. I'd only smelled the aroma when I went with Victoria into a tattoo parlor to see if an artist could do something creative with the scar over her missing breast after she had the cancer removed.

The vibe of this place was not like the tattoo parlor Victoria and I visited. An artistic organization lingered in Amon's space that made me wonder if he really worked here.

"So this is what you spend your time doing when you're not hunting down grimoires?" I asked as I slid up next to the stack of *Inked* magazines stacked on one of his tables.

Amon shifted past me, grabbing a jar of something that was much too thick to be ink. "And exorcizing spirits from my intoxicated father? Absolutely." He busied himself with a stack of sketchbooks, shoving thick pieces of paper here and there. Pencils, paintbrushes, and pans of pigments were scattered everywhere.

I absolutely loved the way his colored pencils and brushes stuck out of recycled paint cans. There were three separate drafting tables spread about the room, each overflowing with art supplies. Amon's space had completely changed my thoughts of what he did at the end of his day. The demon I had imagined spent his free time harassing witches was oddly, an artist.

Five glass jars were stuffed to the brim with varying shades of dark feathers. They made me think of the gorgeous hues of green and purple iridescence I'd seen on Amon when we were in the shadow archives. "Wow, you really have a lot of feathers."

"I collect them. I find that bird feathers have all kinds of textures that are far more interesting to paint with than a paintbrush."

My chest warmed, fuzzy at the thought. Another quirky thing I liked about him. "What species of bird are these feathers from?"

"Mostly ravens, but I'm sure there are a few crow feathers mixed in there. I hear the two mix together quite well," he replied, winking at me.

Eugene walked to the far wall away from the shop windows, where a collection of portraits hung in black wooden frames. "Wow, you guys aaare looking oooolder than I am. Pretty soooooon, you will aaaaall be wearing diiiiiiiapers."

"All right. We're draining the spirits out of you, now," Amon barked, grabbing an oddly shaped metal pen.

Eugene sat down on the stool by the table, rolled up his sleeve, set his left arm palm up on the table, then gave his son a wicked grin. "Iiiink me, booooy!"

"What color are we using?" Amon asked as he set his pen down on the table, then tugged on a couple of latex gloves.

"Whateeeeever you feeeeeel helps cooooompliment myyyyy eyes," Eugene chimed.

"Black it is," Amon replied. He rolled up his sleeves as he loaded a black ink cartridge into his tattoo pen. It was the first time I got a good solid look at his forearms.

Amon's skin was covered in black tattoos. Plants, feathers, and even some constellations were strewn in there. The message hidden behind symbols must all translate to something magical.

"Lucy, pull up a seat," Amon instructed me, eyeing the stool next to him.

I sat down between them facing the wall with the portraits, forming a triangle of me, Eugene, and Amon. I swore one of the portraits winked at me.

Amon held the tattoo pen up over his father's arm. "Ready?"

"Maaake me prooooud," Eugene replied, a hint of pride ringing in his gruff voice that just might be sobering up.

Amon pressed the pen to Eugene's forearm, which put off a faint buzzing noise. As he worked on his arm, his own tattoos began to change. A snake emerged, as did thistles and acorns. I blinked. Were those *mushrooms*? I had seen the natural symbols for a brief moment in the library when I'd first opened the grimoire. Were the symbols connected to Amon's shadows?

If so, why hadn't I seen them until now?

"*I don't share my tattoos with just anyone. Powerful shadow magic is housed inside of the symbols. And yes, those are mushrooms. . .*"

My breath caught as Amon's cool, silky voice blew through me. "*Since when can you read my mind?*"

"*Your magic has connected us somehow. My shadows have been telling me all about your detailed opinions of me.*"

I flushed so hard it felt like I might light on fire. How many details did he know when it came to my secret fantasies about him?

Amon chuckled at my panicked thoughts.

"What's so funny?" Eugene asked.

"I just know that Lucy is going to love this when I'm done."

I wanted to slap Amon upside the head. I just prayed to the goddess that Eugene wasn't listening to our dirty conversation too.

"*Don't let him know that I took you to the shadow archives, got it? If he finds out, he'll skin me alive.*" Amon's voice made my hair stand up. He continued tattooing his father's arm, keeping his eyes off me as his smirk intensified. "*If you keep fantasizing about me, my shadows will take advantage of you, even if you aren't practicing your magic.*"

Fuck. What if I *wanted* them to take advantage of me?

Eugene flexed his hand as the needle moved from his wrist toward his elbow. "Feel the burn, embrace the shadow!" he bellowed, spittle flying out of his mouth.

Amon didn't flinch as his father slammed his feet on the ground. He made circular motions with his pen until Eugene's skin turned a deep shade of red. Bands of ebony flooded out of his fingers, making me jump.

The ebony shadows dispersed, evaporating before they touched either Amon or I. Eugene unclenched his fist and he stopped slamming his feet.

"Ah, that's better, son. You sure know how to drain the devil out of a demon's blood."

Eugene was a different man after his son's artistic touch. He held up his arm, grinning madly. "What do you think, Lucy?" He flipped his arm to face me. An image of a raven with a curved beak and hauntingly beautiful eyes stared back at me.

"I can't believe how much detail there is," I said, ogling at the feathers and the shine on the raven's beak.

Amon grabbed a cloth and wiped the blood away. His inkwork was beautiful. What I wouldn't do to have him mark something like that on me.

Eugene flexed his arm. "That was what, a few minutes? You should see what he can do if he has you for an hour."

Amon's face burned red as he began to sanitize the tattoo pen.

Eugene's eyes weren't glassy any longer. They found me, mischievousness glinting in them. "Ah, Lucile, is it?"

"Lucy," I corrected.

"Great. Well, fuck. I feel like a complete idiot. How drunk was I when we first met?"

"Pretty drunk, but I've seen worse. My sister can drink like a piranha. She's a vet who spends her time taking care of familiars."

Eugene straightened his collar, where a couple of black feathers sprouted. "Familiars? Wow, she must have a big heart. They are some of the most frustrating creatures to care for. Amon should know. He had a bunch when he was a boy."

I glanced from father to son, wishing I had more insight. "I always thought demons and familiars were enemies."

Eugene rapped his fingers along the table. "Historically, we weren't always that way. The relationship between witches, demons, and familiars has significantly changed since the last Earth Uprising."

My stomach lurched. Familiars, siding with demons? Grubs would *never* approve. I tried to picture a childhood Amon with a bunch of bookworms crawling up his legs. "Is this true?" I asked Eugene's son.

"Not one of my proudest moments," Amon said as he organized his pigments.

I turned back to Eugene, admiring how his new tattoo was interacting with other tattoos I hadn't noticed until now. His bicep had three other ravens, all of which had inched down his arm to inspect the newcomer. "How did getting a tattoo sober you up?"

Eugene set both of his hands on the table, splaying his gnarled, scarred fingers, which all had tattoos on them. "Tattoos are a great way to tap into a demon's blood, as well as the true nature of his shadows."

Amon shifted a glass toward his father. "Down this now, or you'll be sick."

Eugene took the glass. "What is this?"

"One of Krim's anti-hangover concoctions I actually trust."

Eugene downed the liquid, his eyes returning to me after he slammed the glass down on the counter. The tattoos on his bicep burst into the air, manifesting as two birds. Their faces were no longer two-dimensional, but bulging with feathers. Their eyes were liquid ebony, shimmering with personality.

"Who do we have here?" I asked.

"Anger and Sadness," Eugene replied as he held out his forearm. "They're spirit familiars."

"You mean *dead* familiars?"

"You tell me if they are dead or not. Spirits often display a whole new appreciation for life."

Anger and Sadness perched on Eugene's shoulders, their feathered heads swiveling to inspect Amon's new tattoo creation. They started to chatter with one another in a language that I couldn't understand.

"Would you get them out of there?" Amon said, tossing his arm into the air.

Anger and Sadness stayed put, digging their talons into their owner's shoulders.

I stared at them, completely confused at the situation. "I didn't know that demons also had familiars. Considering how mine has always talked about demons, I thought they were only a witch's companion."

Eugene roared with laughter, his eyes bulging at my statement. "Loyal to witches in life, their souls become loyal demon companions in death."

Suddenly, I knew where Amon's "*life found in death*" beliefs had come from. Who would have thought that *spirit* familiars were involved?

The two birds had completely caught my attention with their frilling necks and intelligent chatter. "My sister Victoria would love this. She's always wondered where the spirits of familiars went when they died. Why are they named Anger and Sadness?"

Eugene shrugged. "Sadness comes and goes as he pleases. But Anger, he's here to stay. His talons are much stronger than Sadness's. I've gotten too many scars from him gripping on my shoulder when he's in one of his foul moods."

Anger's head tilted sideways as his ink-drop eyes found me, seeming to peer into my soul.

"Their names remind me of a quote from C. S. Lewis. He said that he sat with his anger long enough that she shared her true name was really grief," I said.

Eugene's eyes softened. "Sounds pretty accurate for Anger's personality."

Anger took off, flapping his transparent wings until he perched on a shelf hanging by one of the portraits.

Eugene folded his arms. "I had Amon paint every single member of our family who has worked in the shadow archives."

"You painted these?" I asked, amazed at the details in the eyes, noses, even the slivers of gray hair. For monochromatic black and whites, Amon is an incredible master of light and shadow. Amon's artwork was exactly the style I had fantasized about having illustrated in my children's book. Crystal the witch was all about experimenting with the darker places found in nature. Yet now all I could think about was the other darker, longer, *bulging* pieces of Amon that were nowhere near appropriate for a children's picture book.

As I studied the ink portraits of the demons' faces, I started to see more differences than similarities in them. Maybe their bloodline was just as convoluted as witches.

I'd also noticed something very concerning. All of the subjects were *male.* There were no *female* demons.

Eugene was already across the room, eyeing the different tools his son used to create art with. "All of my sons work normal jobs you witches seem to forget are important. It's the price we pay to get closer to you witches. The backbone of human society would snap had it not been for our presence."

I clasped my hands, twisting my fingers together. "Enliven me."

"We're the creative minds. The artistic influences—the catalysts behind change. We don't tend to go with the designated grain in any way humans deem necessary, so most of the time we blend in, undetected."

"How come?"

Eugene set his elbows on the table. "You witches think you have it hard with being persecuted? Try being a demon. We cope by raising magical barriers around our lives so that we can exist alongside witches and humans peacefully."

"How does a magical barrier work?" I asked.

"It's a simple memory trick, what most witches call a charm." Eugene's eyes drifted to the portraits. "Each of the portraits has a different spell housed in the shadow ink that helps camouflage the walls of this building on which they are hung."

I gazed out the windows, noticing a few men lighting up their cigarettes outside. "They don't know we're here, do they?"

"Nope," Amon replied. "To them, we're just an alleyway, or a field. Krim can do the same thing with Shadow Daddy's. Why do you think it's the bar in town that has a reputation for not having a lot of business?"

"Because humans temporarily forget it exists?"

"Exactly."

Eugene grabbed one of the magazines and flipped through it. "Speaking of business, I don't get why you don't have more customers, Amon. Human artists don't have the magical touch us demons do."

My body heated at Eugene's words. I'd been cravings his son's callused fingers. I studied Amon as he gathered more of his tattoo supplies, for this apparent creative tattooing ritual that was commonplace between demons.

My curiosity returned to the male portraits on the wall. "Are there any female demons? Or are you all just dudes?"

Eugene shook his head. "No female demons exist. They did historically, but they went extinct well before my time. This is why we are so attracted to witches. You are the fertile vessel that carries on our demonic bloodline."

"Why are you acting like Lucy cares about our bloodlines?" Amon cut in.

"She asked, didn't she?" Eugene flexed his arm while his dark eyes twinkled mischievously. "You witches are the reason us demons still exist. I was happily married to one for the best years of my life."

"What happened to her?" I asked.

Eugene's face thinned, his wide cheekbones appearing sunken. "That's a story far too long to understand properly. It deals with a council most witches don't like to discuss, one that performs regulations on the shadow archives."

I blinked. "Sorry, I didn't mean to pry."

Eugene folded his arms again over his chest as he dodged my question about his late wife. "I guess it's time that I tell you about the news, Amon." His voice shook. "My face won't be joining your relatives up there after I move on."

Puzzlement took over Amon's expression. "What do you mean?"

Eugen's throat bulged. "I no longer work for the demon council."

Amon's eyes dilated as he rounded on his father. "Is that why you're back in town?"

"Yes," Eugene admitted.

Confusion riddled Amon's expression. "What did you do? Quit?"

"*Quit*? Are you kidding me?" Eugene roared, his voice filling the parlor. Anger and Sadness jumped into the air, sending feathers everywhere. "You really think I would quit after everything I've done for you boys and your mother?" He sat back down, folding into his chair. "No, the elders *fired* me."

Amon's mouth opened and closed a few times before words escaped. "Fired one of their most experienced record-keepers?"

Eugene's eyes swiveled to me before they found his enraged son again. "About that, I might have fudged some magical records on the Ravenblood's behalf."

"Why would you do that?"

"Amon, you haven't lived with the backlash like I have. I've defended the magic witches practice for too long. There are other demons who are far more ancient and powerful than your father."

Amon's nostrils flared. His temple throbbed. His aura, the silky coolness of it, was no longer calm. Ebony bands branched out of his biceps and shoulders, making Anger and Sadness dive.

I reached out to comfort Amon, grabbing his forearm. His skin was too hot to touch.

He tore away from me. "This is really fucking bad. If the demon council doesn't have Eugene Ravenblood to keep their heads level with what demons they let inside the shadow archives, just imagine what else might get in."

Eugene's eyes darkened. "I've encountered plenty of dark and devious demons in my time. Wendigos are just the beginning, and their kind is spreading. Pretty soon, this is going to be a big magical mess." He turned to face Amon. "Your mother had talents that could have put an end to all of this cannibalistic business, remember? That's what I was trying to prevent from being overwritten, but I fudged too much and got caught."

Before I could chime in, Amon's shadows coalesced around me. I was encased in his darkness as Eugene and his two ravens disappeared.

"*I will make sure you are safe from the Bone Threader. But right now, I need to spend some time alone with my father,*" Amon whispered to me as his tattoo parlor evaporated.

"*Amon, please don't shut me out,*" I whispered back.

Judging from the silence, I knew he already had. Solid ground met my feet as my bedroom manifested. A black feather was all I had left of the demon who I wished would share more with me about himself.

28
Amon

Organizing my thoughts wasn't going to happen this afternoon. I couldn't risk having Lucy near me, not after the chemistry between her magic and my own. My shadows were sure to take advantage of her with my mind distracted and my guard down. With the news that Dad had been fired from the demon council, I had a whole new set of problems regarding my inherited talents that the Bone Threader wanted.

I manifested in my parlor, finding my father sleeping. He was sitting on a stool, his back propped against the wall with his arms folded across his front. Chin tucked to his chest, he snored loudly. No use waking him now to talk. Dad was a broken man, even if he was too stubborn to realize it.

His loyal spirit familiars were wreaking havoc in my parlor. Ravens were notoriously intelligent creatures, their curiosity following them even after they had died. Grief found a new place to perch, joining Sadness, who has always been the more mischievous of the two.

"Come on, git," I growled, waving my hand at the ravens, who paid no attention to me.

Sadness swung his tail feathers sideways, knocking jars of pencils and paintbrushes over as he jumped off the shelf. He landed with an angry *squawk* on my drafting table, his tail feathers frilled to the max. He stabbed his beak into one of my spiral bound books, ripping a hole in the cover.

"Hey, quit it!" I bellowed, launching myself after the fucking familiar as he took off.

I grabbed the notebook and flipped through it, assessing the damage. He'd ripped a giant hole out of three pages of a sketch concept I'd abandoned years ago. My fingers itched to fix what Sadness had done, but paper was like skin. It bore scars and imperfections as beauty faded. Magic and ink were similar in so many ways. What we saw as permanent, the magic known as time would always make it fade.

Suddenly, I didn't have enough time. With the grimoire gone, and the Bone Threader preparing to use Lucy's magic to erase what remained of my family's records in the shadow archives, I had to find a way to preserve my mother's talents.

Her magic was what my father had fought for. It was as rare as Lucy's. It wasn't meant to be forgotten. No matter how much I tried to preserve it, I didn't think I could ever do it justice like my father wanted me to.

The ravens continued to make a mess out of my art supplies, sifting through them with their sharp, greedy talons.

"Give that to me," I barked at Anger, who clutched something I didn't want him to have.

He hobbled over to me and dropped a brown leather bundle on my table. He tilted his head to the side, intelligence shining in his soulful, ink-drop eyes.

"What do you want me to do?"

Anger snapped his beak at the twine that bound the medicine bundle I inherited from my mother.

When mom died, she gave me a gift. And I wasn't going to take it for granted any longer. If Dad lost his position in the demon council, that meant I would need to step up and practice what I, her firstborn son, had inherited from her.

A hollow feeling I hadn't experienced in years washed over me. Maybe the quote Lucy mentioned from C. S. Lewis was right about anger covering up one's grief. Without Dad working for the council any longer, the Bone Threader's bony fingers had the power to remove the Ravenblood family name from the shadow archives, permanently. If Dad had been fudging records like he'd admitted to, who knew how long it would be before the Bone Threader would make his move.

I fumbled the bundle in my hand. A small bead was fastened to the twine, decorated with a small black tree. Seeing the tree made me think of Lucy. What I had experienced from her magic was that it built like a storm. It started in wide open places, gathering moisture from the sea, before it warmed and became a billowing cloud full of lightning and thunder.

Working my fingers through the knot, I unraveled the sinew and poured the contents onto my table. The items scattered. Feathers. Bones. Quills. All were items that held medicinal purposes from a different time. Mom had given me her medicine bundle of art supplies right before she died.

I had opened the bundle before. I knew what was inside. Looking at items once sealed into a medicine bundle could bring bad medicine or magic onto the individual who gazed upon them. But until this moment, I hadn't withdrawn the items from the bundle, nor had I noticed everything.

The pigments were powdered, each held together in small leather bags that tied off at the top. The pigments my mother painted with were red ochre, blue, and black. I knew this, because she adorned all of her son's bedrooms with her paintings. These were the colors that made up a dream painting she gathered her visions from.

I grabbed the bags of pigment, weighing which to use. Black would come later. First, I needed to use the colorful pigments to flesh out the layers of her dreams. First, I added the red ochre pigment to a glass jar. After filling the jar with water, I grabbed one of the bones. I imagined they might belong to a rodent. I couldn't help but notice the similar shape and size of the Bone Threader's small, slender hands when he was disguised as a child.

Am I playing with wendigo fingers?

The thought sent a chill up my spine. I didn't need him creeping his way into one of Lucy's visions that she had of the tree of shadows. She'd already mentioned that she'd seen a monster in the branches, and she believed the Bone Threader had taken on Jeremy's identity. I didn't want to risk having that vision become more powerful than necessary.

Out of caution, I set the bone down and picked up a feather and a quill instead. The quill was from a porcupine. The feather was jet black. I suspected it belonged to a raven.

Which color should I paint with first?

I grabbed a spray bottle full of water and doused the pigment. Once the colors were saturated, I dipped the quill into the blue pigment and traced it across the parchment. The ink bled, then pooled, repeating the same movement as I worked it back and forth. Painting on paper was so different from skin. It was far less forgiving. Next, I dipped the feather into the red and repeated the same movements. The two colors mixed, turning into a purplish mess.

Shit. This isn't supposed to happen.

I flayed the feather across the pigment, hoping to smear the colors away from one another, but I only made it worse. I should have just painted in black to begin with.

"*What have you been up to*?"

I jumped as Dad's voice filled my head. My ghoul of a father stood by the front door, golden threads of the sun dancing over him. His features were oddly soft given all of the lines in his weathered face.

I saw real age in him. Dad was a few hundred years old, even though he refused to act it.

"Wow, you look like crap," he said as he approached.

"I feel it."

He stopped at my side. "Where the hell is Lucy?"

"I sent her back home."

"What? Why?" he questioned, scrutiny wrecking his expression. "I could have *sworn* the two of you were sending each other *I want to fuck you* vibes."

I shifted in my seat to face him. "Look, we need to talk about this shadow archive business and the fact that you are no longer in a position to defend it."

Dad's eyes flashed a dangerous shade of red before returning to black. "Or maybe we should discuss the fact that you decided to bring another witch to the shadow archives without first consulting with me."

I dropped the feather, smearing the pigment across the parchment. Energy crackled between us, the air practically snarling. My forearms burned. Even my shadows knew not to snap back at my father.

Dad's shoulders rose and fell as he sank down into the seat next to me. "I'm not mad at you."

My body relaxed. "You're not?"

"No. I know you would have only taken Lucy into the archives if you wanted to do what I've spent three hundred years trying to do for your mother. Preserving a witch's magic is easier said than done." His eyes meet mine. "The question is, why didn't you tell me about it?"

My stomach twisted. No more secrets. I had to tell him about my meeting with the Bone Threader. "Look. A few months ago, the Bone Threader confronted me about the Ravenblood family archive. He had discovered that the grimoire you locked Melrose's spirit into went missing, and threatened to devour our portion of the archive if I didn't find it."

Dad's brow furrowed. "I lost that book over three hundred years ago. Why would he just now start harassing you over it?"

I thought back to the boy patting his belly at the diner. "He complained about something giving him a stomach ache?"

Dad's face twisted. "What could possibly make a wendigo sick to his stomach? They're disgusting demons and can devour anything."

"Except death," I said, looking down at my painting. Death had always been the subject that mom had made beautiful.

"I guess our question is then, what could he have eaten that was dead?"

"No idea."

One of Dad's bushy eyebrows arched. "I think it has to do with the Separation of Magics Movement. The demon council has taken opposite sides on how to handle the way familiars have started to establish boundaries between witches and demons."

"How so?"

"Witches have a singular bloodline, where the magic of their ancestors is passed down from females only. Us Demon's, we have *two* bloodlines. A demon can inherit magic from both his father and his mother. You, my son, ended up inheriting the best of both worlds. Lucy's last name is Crow, isn't it?"

"Yes."

"Most witch and demon families have their last name formed around a species of familiar. Crows and ravens are a great way to illustrate just how similar goddess and shadow magic is." He gazed at my painting, where both Anger and Sadness hobbled about, inspecting the splotches of black ink that bled all over the parchment. "Crows appear as one. Ravens almost always show up in pairs. In your case, you have multiple shadows."

My tattoos darkened at father's words. My shadows formed according to my mother's magic. They all knew where they originated from. Instead of doubles as Dad had dictated, I had *multiple* shadows that branched as earthly symbols of feathers, mushrooms, and snakes across my forearms.

"We both know that female demons went extinct long ago because our shadow magic could not adapt to the greedy desires of some of our ancestors. Why us demons look to marry a witch is due to our dwindling bloodline."

"Are you saying the Bone Threader might be trying to separate our bloodlines?"

Dad's eyes darkened. "It sounds like he might be trying to do more than that. I've known him for a long time. This wendigo has tried to devour as many magical talents possessed by witches as he can. The fact that he is preying upon Lucy's magic to try and steal the talents your mother possessed? That's where I wonder if he's trying to destroy more than just the Ravenblood family archive." His gaze returned to me. "Why didn't you tell me that he was harassing you?"

"Why would I? You were overseas. I knew you were dealing with some disaster within the council, and I didn't want to bring you home."

"You also didn't know that your old man had been fudging records," he growled, his shoulders slumping over. "The only reason that fucking demon got control over the shadow archives in the first place, was due to the fact that your mother's magical talents threatened his own." Dad's gaze dropped to my mess of a painting. "Your mother used to write like you can paint. I know for a fact that you inherited many of her artistic talents."

"The Bone Threader knows that I inherited mom's talents. And to get them, he would have to kill me. So he unearthed the grimoire so Lucy could find it, using the opportunity to get a taste of her magic."

"And you walked right into his trap?"

I nodded.

Dad's shoulders stiffened. "He wanted your mother's talents, and now he's targeting Lucy? What for?"

I clenched my fist. "Shortly after Lucy discovered the grimoire, her own magic went haywire. That's why I brought her into the archives. I thought for sure that one of the elemental books would give us some clarity."

My father's massive hands fell upon my shoulders. I felt the scars and calluses of his rough fingers. "The elements are as elusive to a witch as they are to a demon. I've been too hard on you. I know I've been an ass since your mother. . ." his voice trailed away. "I've become a monster to you boys, not the father your Mom always wanted me to be to the three of you. Being my firstborn, I have been the hardest on you, Amon."

I didn't know if I should move, or run. Dad's never been this open with me. "What's gotten into you?"

"I think the real question is, has something gotten into you? Do you love Lucy?"

His words were so up front, it took my mind a moment to register. "It's so soon for me to know how I really feel about her."

"Your mother and I fell in love as fast as a wildfire. Even though that was over three hundred years ago, fire still works the same. But love isn't the same as magic. It can burn you up quicker than you can tame it if you aren't prepared to embrace it." He glanced up at the portraits on the wall. "The talents you inherited from your mother were meant to be shared. How? I don't know. All I can say is that

I've spent the past few hundred years wishing I could preserve what I remember of her."

I gazed down at my artwork. "What am I supposed to do? I can't abandon Mom's magic. And I can't force it on a witch who refuses to practice."

"Have you thought about asking your mother? She talks to Krim on a regular basis."

"Yeah well, she sure doesn't talk to me."

"She does. I just think that you choose not to listen to her sometimes."

I shook my head. Dad knew how Mom's choice of son to talk to had created some jealousy between Krim and I. Even if Mom did try and communicate with me, I couldn't understand what she was trying to say. Krim kept most of his discussions with her private.

"She was a remarkable witch in life, and even more remarkable in spirit," Dad said. "I know she's looking after all of you boys."

Dad's eyes met mine. "I think you need to tell Lucy how you feel about her. Make your feelings real. Stop hiding behind your shadows."

"I don't understand how my feelings for Lucy could fix our problem with the shadow archives."

Dad's hard weathered face softened. "Son, the magic in those grimoires belongs to witches just as much as it belongs to demons. We need to remind them of that. Many women are forced to live in shame because of their magical talents. Many don't ever realize they possess talents at all. Us demons, we're just viewed as nasty, bad, dark, malevolent, cocky beings. The world might not like us, but at least we are accepted for what we are."

I reflected on Dad's words. *Acceptance*. What a strange juxtaposition of what I'd always felt demons faced in the eyes of humanity. We were dark and had hidden agendas that didn't always coexist well with the human world.

But he was right. Our shadow magic was what it was, and we weren't persecuted for it. We were accepted for our darkness.

Dad shook his head. "I hated that your mother suppressed her magic. It wasn't until you were first born that she began to see her talents differently."

"How did you get her to share her talents with you?"

Dad chuckled. "I'm not going into those details. In fact, I wasn't the one who convinced her. I just put the ball in motion for who would eventually change her mind."

"Who are you talking about?"

"*You* were the one who convinced her to share her magic."

"How did I help her?"

"She realized she wanted to share who she was with her little boy, so one day he would be able to embrace to the fullest what he was. As the first born, you got the brunt of mom's magic. She was terrified to use it at times, but you were always there to make her laugh and cry and embrace the mistakes and imperfections that came with wielding it."

Emotion twisted my stomach. "Why didn't you ever tell me this?"

"You never asked. And talking about her is not something your old man is fond of doing. It makes me feel full of regret."

"What do you regret?"

"Not sharing with her what I was sooner. Not being vulnerable to her in a way that she was with me." He withdrew his hand from my shoulder and began to pick at a callus. "I know what it's like to be lonely. To feel like you've lost something special you will never find again." His gaze met mine. "You fight for her, even when the magics tell you not to. Even if those blasted little fuckers rise up and create another Earth Uprising, you do what is best for your witch. Do you understand?"

I nodded.

"Good, because witches have craved our magic for far longer than the earth has had soil. Sure, a witch derives her goddess magic from the earth, but even the earth came from a cavernous, dark void."

My shoulders tensed. I wanted to help Dad as much as I wanted to help Lucy. But doing both would be a challenge.

I glanced down at my painting. A liquid message formed on the parchment that sent my shadows clawing at my chest.

29
Lucy

I couldn't believe it. Amon sent me back to my bedroom like a child. *Fuck him.* He peered into my mind, then disappeared?

I patted my sides, my pockets, and found my phone. A text from mom lit up.

Call Me. I want to know how you are doing with Amon.

I wanted to throw my phone out the window. This was ridiculous! How was I supposed to understand my magic and save my library if he could call the shots on when he wanted to disappear? All because he wanted to have a private discussion with his father who apparently got fired from a demon council?

My stomach twisted. I didn't want to admit that this feeling might be jealousy. No man should have the power to disappear into the shadows.

Not a demon, my ex, nor my father.

A noise echoed from downstairs. It was probably one of Victoria's familiars knocking through her pots and pans. That, or a rogue hedgehog had found its way in.

I crept downstairs, careful not to step on the squeaky stair. Once on the landing, I peered around the wall, spotting a woman standing by my sister's bookshelf.

A curl of red hair unraveled from her shoulder as she thumbed over Victoria's naughty novel collection. "What's this? *Something Wicked This Witch Comes*? Oh," She turned over another title. "How about *Hex My Ex*? That sounds absolutely lovely."

"Melrose?" I asked. "What are you doing here?"

She continued flipping through the books, keeping her back turned to me. "I wanted to find you and thank you for what you did for me on Halloween. You see, it's not every day that another witch comes along who has the power to set the captive spirit of a witch free."

"Captive? What do you mean?"

Her lips pursed as her face became a transparent blur. "Didn't Amon tell you? After I died, that pompous ass of a father of his took it upon himself to lock my spirit away into that nasty book of shadows." She evaporated, taking on a transparent ghostly form as she hovered about the room. "Maybe if you weren't suppressing your magic, you would know what lived in those pages, and you wouldn't be trying to help Amon or his father with their hideous attempt to save their archive."

The scent of damp, stale earth suddenly filled my mouth and lungs. "Why did you give the grimoire to the Bone Threader?"

Melrose's face came dangerously close to me. "He has wanted that grimoire ever since Amon's father locked me inside it, then magically lost it. Now that you freed me, I have the power to dispose of it."

The smell of rot tinged my nose as Melrose drifted too close. I took a step back, my butt bumping into the bookshelf.

Melrose continued to encroach on me, her transparency wavering as she shifted between her solid and spirit form. "I can smell the other books on you. Amon has taken you to the shadow archives, hasn't he?" Melrose whispered, fury quaking her voice. "What I want to know is why he took you to such a dangerous place while you were alive."

Memories of the archive flashed before me. The grimoires emerging from the hollows in the wall. Amon's hard body pressed against me. The way his shadows became a sinuous cloak of bones and feathers as he encouraged me. "You also went into the archive when you were alive, did you not?"

"My reasons for entering the archive changed after I died. Only after I died, did Amon realize I had visited the archive to help find someone I lost."

"How did you die?"

Melrose's face twisted. "That, I cannot remember. When I became a spirit, my desire to learn the language of shadows became my only focus. The symbols inside of the grimoires can be used to translate many things related to magic."

"Could they tell you how you died?"

Melrose nodded. "I quickly learned that a witch has a much better chance of getting into the shadow archives after she has experienced death. Amon could not prevent me from getting into the archive, so Eugene locked my spirit into one of the grimoires I so desperately wanted."

I folded my arms. "The difference between you and I. I don't want to practice magic unless I have to. You seem to want to practice it for reasons you can't remember."

"Reasons a demon has stolen from me!" she screamed.

I clapped my hands over my ears as the wine glasses on the kitchen table shattered.

Melrose leveled her gaze with me, her face trembling. "A demon does not help a witch understand her magic unless his shadows have ulterior motives."

"What kind of motives?" I asked, lowering my hands.

The freckles on her nose crinkled. "Do you know what horrors live in those pages? Do you know why familiars work so hard to keep their witches safe from a demon's shadows?"

The symbols in her eyes mixed with rage—the same symbols I'd seen on Amon's arms when he'd been touching up his father's tattoo. "No, I don't know what the pages hold. The grimoire wouldn't open after I released you. And the books I saw in the archive also refused to open."

Melrose's smile became a wicked one. "They refuse to open, because the magic that binds them is trying to protect itself from the demon who created them."

"The Bone Threader?"

Victoria's kitchen fell away as Melrose clapped her hands and released a wave of surging magical energy toward me. Thick, suffocating clouds of dust and ash blew into my face.

Amon.

His name was all I could think as the ash clogged my nose and mouth. Magic bound my body, tugging me underground. The sound was deafening, like I was being dragged along the bottom of a riverbed, tumbling with the stones as the water forced me forward.

My foot gripped solid ground. My fingers scraped against damp stones as I dragged myself out of the rushing water. A giant black tree towered over me. I had been in this place before. I must be back in the Summoning.

The shadow archives were nearby. But all I could see was an ebony tree. The tree had a gravity of its own. I was pulled toward it as the branches lashed out in the wind above my head.

Silver wisps of light drifted between the branches. Spirits, dozens of them, were hovering about. But they were not familiars. They had human faces, some gnarled, some young. All were women. They were the spirits of other witches like Melrose.

One of the spirits was crouched over to inspect the river that brought me here. When she stood, her expression was half there. Her face had changed as the water came rushing toward me.

I knew this witch. I had seen her before. Amon had called her Changing Woman.

"I am not who you think I am," a voice filled my head. Her eyes met mine, warmth buried deep inside of them.

"Who are you?"

"I wish for you to give a message to my son. He likes to hide from his responsibilities, even though I gave him something to help him sort out the mess with his father."

I swallowed. "Are you Amon's mother?"

30
Amon

Go find the witch you love, my firstborn.

Mom's words burned into me with an urgency that made me sick. My father's face blurred as I was transported back to a memory from my childhood.

The sound of running water filled my ears. My mother sat next to me on the riverbed, a raven feather in hand, parchment folded across her lap as she studied the river. I sat next to her, eager for my painting lesson to start. I grabbed my own raven feather from my medicine bundle and unfold my roll of parchment across my lap to mimic her.

Mom's shoulders rose and fell as she slowed her breathing. Her hair was a mass of rebellious black strands that caught the yellow light of a thousand small creatures drifting in the breeze.

Familiars—hundreds of them—hovered in the air. They were disguised as fireflies, bats, and ravens. But in my mother's watchful eye, she knew they were really earth spirits. We were here to study them and make observations. My mother was a witch, but that didn't mean she wouldn't teach her demon son about the magic the earth spirits possessed.

I dipped my bare feet into the river. The icy water focused me.

"Do you remember what I said about the river and the land? Who moves who?" Mom asked.

"The river moves the stones," I replied.

My mother's hand came to my own, gently directing the feather over the parchment. "It would seem so, yes, but only physically. What the water does to the soil is something not all of us can visualize. That is what you are here to paint.

You are here to observe the invisible, and to be moved by it. A dream is what all of us feel, like the pebbles and stones that roll along the riverbed, invisible for us to see." Her chin lifted as she gazed across the river. "Look around you. Do you know what represents the dream?"

"Water?"

"Yes. Water brings clarity to our dreams. We are the stones, but the water is our clarity." She released my hand, and a great rush of water thundered in my ears. "Amon, you have inherited my magical talents. When you grow into a man, you must not hide from them, even when I am gone." Her eyes met mine, the light of a thousand earth spirits shimmering in them. "You must trust your shadows when you have forgotten how to trust yourself."

I shook my head, stirring from my childhood painting memory of mother by the stream. The memory was about to turn into a nightmare.

I had to find Lucy.

"Amon, what did you see?" Dad asked.

I rolled up my painting and stuffed it into my pocket. "No time to explain."

With my shadows gathering, I dissipated out of my parlor.

As soon as I manifested in Lucy's bedroom, my forearms burned. My shadows retreated, fear tingling through my veins. The feather I had given Lucy hovered in the air, taunting me. A witch had been here. She bewitched the space, marking the air with a shimmering afterglow of magic.

Fuck.

Melrose had been here. I knew her signs and scents, both of which clouded my nose. How could I have been so stupid as to leave Lucy alone?

I tore out of her bedroom, heading for the streets. There must be a trail of her magic, even just a fragment of her aura for me to follow.

The stocky figure of a demon made his way down the sidewalk. With his face concealed in reaper-like fashion, Krim's black aura flickered as he approached. Red eyes gleamed under his hood, both flashing as they landed on me.

He stopped a few paces from where I stood. "Zed tells me that Dad's back in town. Why the fuck didn't you say anything?"

"Why would I?"

Krim folded his beefy arms across his chest, sending tendrils of his shadows into the air. "Don't you think you should let your brother who owns a bar know when his alcoholic father decides to binge drink his entire drink collection?"

"Not when you kicked me out," I stammered, shoving past him.

He grabbed my shoulder and pinned me against the brick wall. "I kicked you out, because you decided to keep secrets from Zed and I about Lucy. You didn't tell us that she had magical talents like Mom."

I grabbed his hand and tore it away from me. "If it makes you feel any better, Lucy is missing. For all we know, Melrose has gone to feed her to the Bone Threader," I said, trying to hide the worry in my voice.

"If feeding him witches keeps him away from my bar, then so be it."

Fire ignited in my veins. "Krim, get the fuck away from me," I barked, ripping my arm away from him. His shadows held onto me. Something silver slid into his palm.

Krim launched his arm for my side.

I fell back, narrowly escaping the blade as it flew over my arm. I ducked, swinging my leg out, striking him behind his knees, which both buckled.

The blade flew into the air and landed straight in his forearm.

"You fucking stabbed me!" Krim bellowed, flailing his arm above his head.

"You shouldn't have brought a knife to a fight if you don't know how to use it," I barked, standing over him.

"Amon?" a female voice sounded from behind me.

I turned, finding a woman carrying a paper bag bulging with groceries.

Shit. This was not how I wanted Lucy's mother to find me, standing over my brother with his shadows pooling out of his forearm from a knife wound *I* made.

Cindy's eyes dropped to Krim before they met mine again with a new intensity. "Where is my daughter? I texted her not long ago and she hasn't replied."

My stomach wrenched. "I'm trying to find her."

"What do you mean, *trying to find her*?" Cindy stammered.

Krim's whimpering was the only sound that filled the silence.

Cindy rounded on me, her aura bursting into orange and yellow sparks. "Amon Ravenblood, I trusted you to protect her from this demon who I thought was threatening to devour her library."

What little shred of dignity I had left withered as Cindy's eyes bore into me. Her aura thickened, now aglow with blue sparks of electricity. A bag of carrots and two stalks of celery levitated out of the bag, caught fire, then disintegrated. "Where did you last see her?"

"She was at her sister's house."

"And before that?"

"My place."

Cindy's mouth turned upside down.

"I'm going to need stitches, you asshole," Krim grumbled as he climbed to his feet and tugged the knife out of his arm.

Cindy's shoulders shook as she rounded on him. "Shut it. It's just a scratch," she stammered, her voice trembling. With a wave of her hand, a box of Band-Aids came flying out of her bag. One unraveled itself, then slapped across the cut on Krim's forearm.

Krim's mouth snapped closed.

The Band-Aids returned to her bag as she squared her hips, facing us both. A few hairs sprung out of her tightly wound bun, frizzling out in her aura. "I will *not* have a demon come between me and my daughter, wendigo, or the entitled chemistry professor who bakes in his free time at Shadow Daddy's bar."

Krim squinted at Cindy. "How did you know that I work there?"

"You demons think you are such shady creatures. You work your day jobs at the tattoo parlor, the university, the bar, and as musicians. The truth is, the Crow family has long been involved with your kind. Us witches, we know that demons have other jobs, ones that channel your unique talents that deal with the afterlife."

Krim and I exchanged looks. *Point taken.*

She tucked her bag under her arm. "Now, are we going to find my daughter, or are we going to act like a bunch of dunderheads and twiddle our thumbs?"

I couldn't help but chuckle as Krim's reaper hood fell off. Cindy was right about the Band Aid. His cut had completely stopped bleeding, probably due to her magic.

Cindy glanced past us, catching something that made her eyes dilate. "I can always see my daughters' auras. Something is wrong, something *you* were supposed to prevent from happening to her," she scolded, her fearsome gaze returning to me. She tossed her arm up in the air, and a beam of light broke over our heads. "Goddess, show me where my middle daughter is currently."

The bushes next to the sidewalk trembled. Hedgehogs came scurrying onto the sidewalk.

Cindy turned on her heel, taking off toward the swarm of familiars. "This way."

Another figure approached. Dad caught up with me.

Krim turned to face the demon making his way toward us. "Go with her. I'll keep Dad busy."

The hedgehogs led us toward the library. By the time we arrived, my shadows were grumbling.

"*We know where Melrose took Lucy. Let us loose, and we will find her*," one of them suggested.

"*You don't need help from those stupid familiars, or her mother. You need to listen to your own mother and trust us.*"

"Amon, did you say something?" Cindy asked as she approached the library door and grabbed the handle.

She was knocked backward, her bag of groceries flying overhead.

I caught her before she landed in the bushes and helped her to her feet.

"What in the world?" she stammered.

"It's a shadow vortex," I replied. How did I know? The obnoxious way my shadows were behaving. They kept themselves concealed from Cindy, but I could see their ghoulish faces and flailing arms as they inspected the vortex.

"Well, it's nothing a witch can't handle," Cindy said, tossing her arms into the air. The atmosphere sizzled and cracked as electricity zapped overhead.

I threw out my arm, grabbing Cindy's magical burst before it hit the black mass of negative energy. "No. This shit can backfire. I'm going in. You stay here, got it?"

"Who has my daughter?" she asked, fury brimming in her eyes.

I could taste Melrose's floral scent on the back of my tongue. "The spirit of a witch your daughter released from a grimoire."

Before Cindy could stop me, I dipped inside the vortex. The energy suffocated me.

A web of thorns lined the entrance, each digging into my skin as I crouched into the claustrophobic space. By the time I fought through the entryway, I was almost out of breath. It felt like walking into a soggy, sea-urchin filled fishing net. Melrose had barricaded herself in here. The terrible web of a green vampire's magic was not kind to demons. I'd have to rely on my shadows to get through, or risk being shredded to pieces.

"*You should have fucked her when you had the chance. Now that other bitch is going to feed her magic to another demon,*" one of my shadows echoed into my ear.

"*If you didn't have us, Melrose would have shredded you to pieces,*" another chimed in.

"Help me find her," I demanded.

"*Oh, we will. And when we do, we will do what we want with her.*"

"*We will claim our prize and leave you with what's left of her.*"

Finally, the mass of vines released me as I tumbled through the tunnel. I landed on a solid damp surface that smelled of soil. The scent of water flooded my senses as I entered the Summoning.

"Well hello, Amon," a high-pitched female voice echoed around me. Melrose had her hands outstretched toward a mass of vines that grew up from the ground.

Lucy was bound by her vines, her body slumped over and lifeless.

Anger branched through me as I approached. "Let her go," I growled.

"So nice of you to join us. I was just about to share with Lucy about the truth behind your Daddy's grimoire."

"Lucy, stay with me," I said. She wasn't responsive.

Not good.

"What is it that you want?" I yelled at Melrose.

She lowered her hand, turning to face me. "I want Lucy to know what a demon's shadows are really capable of."

Lucy couldn't stay here. She suppressed her magic for so long, she had no defense against the negative energy inside of the Summoning that could rip her to shreds.

Melrose rounded on me. "Let's see if Lucy can survive what you did to me."

"*Read the landscape. That is where you will learn to trust your magic,*" my mother's words echoed in my ears. My forearms burned as my shadows coalesced, fighting to free themselves from my grip.

"*Trust us,*" one of them growled as he ripped out of my chest.

31
Lucy

As soon as the first rays of sunlight branched through my window, the dreams I'd experienced were brewing through me like a storm. I didn't remember being brought back to my room. I'd dreamed of so many places, I couldn't keep count. I'd been carried by a warm humid wind back toward the mountains, caught in the rain shadow where the sky met the earth.

Someone else had been in my dream—shadows. Their long, branching fingers reached over mountaintops from a world beyond. What they were searching for, I didn't know. But I felt their emptiness—their longing. They were searching for something invisible beneath the earth.

The fingers reached for moments when the first frost occurred. When the soil turned over as ice crystals formed and melted. As the fingers reached, their touch withered fallen leaves and brought new life to the landscape.

Those moments captured my magical surges. They also opened old wounds. I was left gasping for answers about what happened to my father.

I sat up in my bed and draped my legs over the side. Propping my elbows onto my knees, I leaned over, trying to nurse the throbbing headache as I remembered the details from my dream. A woman stood by the water. Her words were like silk, washing over me, "*I wish for you to give a message to my son.*"

Then, Amon appeared, concealed by a thousand ebony monsters.

My phone buzzed. Mom had texted me, again. I thumbed over her frantic messages asking where I was.

So had Grace.

Did the beans work?

I set my phone down. Something wasn't right. Melrose had been in my sister's house, thumbing through her collection of books. I'd seen magical symbols glinting in her eyes, the same symbols I'd seen from Amon's tattoos.

Then, Melrose had shared with me something very intriguing. She didn't remember how she died, or while she had been alive, what she had been seeking inside the shadow archives. All she could remember was that Amon's father had locked her spirit into the grimoire.

The magical symbols, were they a *language*?

Could I read it as Amon had suggested?

A roll of parchment sat on the edge of my bed. I ran my hand over the parchment, unrolling until an image appeared. It was a picture of the tree of shadows.

"Lucy?"

I jumped at Amon's voice. It was weaker than normal. "Where are you?"

"I'm trapped."

"Where?"

"Down here."

A splotch of black ink moved across the parchment, where it took the form of a feather.

"You can't be serious right now," I stammered.

The feather hovered about the parchment, mixing with the ink as other symbols appeared. "I'm as serious as the shadow spell you are holding."

My fingers grip the parchment. "You painted a spell?"

"I had to if I was to save you from Melrose." The feather turned into a serpent, a star, then a patch of mushrooms. "And right now, Melrose has me where she wants me."

"Trapped in your artwork?"

The feather bristled. "I inherited my mother's magical shadow painting talents when she passed away. It is both a gift, and a curse. Because this talent was once owned by a witch, only another witch can pull me out of here."

My hands shook, making the parchment tremble. "How?" I stammered as I tried to understand what was exactly going on.

"Lucy, you need to listen to me closely," Amon said. "You only have so much time before—"

Something moved in the room that was too big to be a hedgehog.

My body was forced backward, slamming against the wall. Coiling bands of ebony serpents came billowing out of the floorboards.

"*Finally...*" a sinister voice echoed in my head.

"*No, she's mine,*" another one growled.

My wrists were bound by thick black bands, forcing me against the wall.

"Hey back the fuck off!" I yelled.

"*Oh, she's a feisty one,*" one of them whispered behind me. "*Let's see just how feisty you are when we play.*"

Try as I might, I couldn't free myself from the restraints these shadows put on me. "Who are you?"

A hand caressed my hips, sliding down my ass. "*Amon has been doing his best to hide us,*" another replied. The voices were thick and gravely.

No, these things, they *couldn't* be part of Amon. There was a softness to him these entities did not possess.

Were these the shadows Melrose tried to warn me about?

"What do you want?" I demanded.

"*The question is, what do you want, Lucy Crow*?" A finger traced over my cheek. A shiver rippled up my spine as the hands began to venture lower. "*What does a witch who refuses to practice magic want from shadows like us*?"

"I didn't know you even existed until now," I shot back. "But if you must know, I want every witch, demon, and wendigo to leave my library alone!"

A growling chorus of laughter followed. "*Witches have long known about demonic shadows. The Bone Threader is a greedy demon. He has already tasted your magic. He will not stop devouring what is most important to you until he has consumed it.*" My head snapped back to the wall as the bands tightened. "*We must know. What did that witch say about us when she took you to the Summoning*?"

My throat constricted as a hand caressed my jugular. "She said Amon had another part of himself that I shouldn't trust."

Fingers traced down my neck, a thumb stroking a line across my clavicle. "*Do you believe her?*"

I stared into the ebony mass coalescing before me, wondering if Amon could hear this conversation I was having with his inner demons. Part of me wanted to fight. Another side of me wanted to close my eyes and fall into this devious part of him. The desire here was so thick, it threatened to suffocate me.

This darker side of Amon knew something about Melrose's death.

I turned my cheek away from the hand as fingers traced up toward my lips. "I want you to tell me what you remember of Melrose's death. I want you to pull Amon out of that painting and tell him what you have been keeping from him."

The hand became many, each with fingers tracing cold lines over my flesh. "*What is in it for us?*"

My fingers burned. "I will give you more than just a taste of my magic."

The hands caressing my throat pulled away. "*If we do, you must agree that we will be included, all of us.*"

I stared at the dominant form of the shadows, his eyes lurking inside of the ebony mass. I might as well be making a deal with the devil. "Deal. All of you, no less."

A growling laugh rumbled like thunder as the coiling blackness released me.

Slowly, the voices faded away, until Amon coalesced before me. His hair fell into his eyes as a crooked smile spread across his face. "Thank darkness that you are okay," he said, his voice barely a whisper. "I was worried sick about you." His hands worked through my hair, fingers gripping the back of my skull as his eyes found mine. "I knew you had talent, but I have never seen a witch convince my shadows to do what you just did. How did you convince them to let me out?"

"I told them that they needed to stop keeping secrets from you around Melrose's death."

His eyes met mine, onyx fire in them. "I think I'm the one who needs to stop keeping secrets."

His lips crashed against mine as he started kissing me. As his tongue and mouth traced a scorching line down my throat, something else was communicated with me. I knew that he'd been withholding. Not because he didn't feel something, but because he was afraid of what the hidden parts of himself might do to me.

I was fairly certain that Amon's shadows and I shared the same fears. Fears of being forgotten. Ignored. The fear of secrets we kept hidden.

When he pulled away, I shuddered. His kiss left me breathless. "Amon, I'm not afraid of you, or your shadows. I'd spent enough time running away from my own magic to know that I haven't been doing myself any favors, especially when it comes to relationships."

The mess with Jason blurred through me. Memories of blaming myself, all because I couldn't read him. That's where my magic stemmed from. To share. To make sense of. To *understand.* Those talents didn't come only from books in my library, or grimoires.

He traced his finger over my throat. "Did my shadows do this to you?"

I shivered in the huskiness of his voice. "They restrained me."

His brow slashed. "Where else did they touch you?"

Heat branched through my legs. I couldn't stop fantasizing about how badly I wish they had kept going. I shook my head. What was wrong with me?

"Show me, now," he commanded as his hands continued to inspect my arms.

"There might be something on my back," I said, turning away from him.

He lifted my shirt. Callused fingers grazed over my skin, raising gooseflesh. He traced over my shoulders, and each of my ribs, great gentleness in his caress.

"A demon's shadows can be dangerous," he whispered. "A witch should never turn her back to them."

My fingers were vibrating with magic I still didn't understand. What if I wasn't reading it correctly? If I turned away from it now, would I ever be able to face the hidden parts of myself?

I grabbed his hand, threading my fingers through his. "How dangerous?"

32
Amon

My cock twitched. *No.* It was already enough that my shadows had gotten this far. The fact that Lucy struck a bargain with them about secrets they'd kept from me for who knew how long was one thing. But I couldn't risk them harming her, not when I was this weak.

I squeezed her hand. "Come on. Your mom will be worried sick. She still thinks you are trapped in the Summoning."

Lucy pulled my arm, forcing me to spin and face her. Her eyes met mine, desire flickering in them. "You've taught me something. The truth is, a story doesn't have magic if it's not shared with someone else."

We both jumped as something buzzed on her bed that wasn't a phone.

"What the hell is this?" I asked, knowing all too well what witches used these magical wands for.

Lucy flushed so deeply, she almost matched the purple color of her cardigan. "Just a personal massager."

"Are you tense?" I asked, turning off the vibrating wand I wanted to crush. These electrical devices that witches relied on for pleasure were no match for what I had to offer. "I can make that tension go away."

Lucy's fingers caressed my chest, finding the raw spot where my shadows tore out of me.

Fuck. How every part of my being ached for her.

I tossed the wand aside. I was going to give her such a ride that she would never turn to one of them for pleasure again. Grabbing her wrists, I forced her back, pinning her to the bed. Her legs splayed open as I thrust into her.

"Fuck, Amon, yes!" she rasped into my ear. Our bodies became a mangled mess of spontaneity and passion with too many barriers of clothing. Dry humping was *not* my thing.

I pulled back, grabbing my belt and ripping it away from my waist.

Lucy tossed her shirt over her head as I ripped off my own.

"*She wants all of us*," my shadows growled.

"*Hold her down*," another demanded.

"No, she's mine," I barked. My inner demons had always been possessive assholes.

I wanted Lucy's slick pussy for myself.

Lowering myself between her legs, I kissed along her belly until I reached her inner thigh. "You are dripping for me."

I dove into her, lapping and sucking until she was quivering in my palms.

"Amon, don't stop," she whimpered, her hips gyrating as I devoured her.

I pulled away from her quivering body, trailing my tongue over the spots she wanted me to. She needed to know what she was really getting into with my appetite.

I lowered myself onto her, grabbing her wrists and pinning her against the bed. My hips bucked as I thrust my cock against her pussy. Her opening was so wet and tight. I teased her, slipping through her opening, then withdrew. I wanted to plow into her and take her now. If I did, my shadows wouldn't have the restraint when it came to their turn with her.

I took in her face, ecstasy dancing through her expression as I dominated her. She smiled up at me as I ground my hips into her.

She needed to come first, or my shadows would continue to try and establish their dominance.

The moment I released her wrists, her hands clawed for me. She grabbed my hair as I began kissing her neck, biting my way to her breasts. I sucked one of her nipples into a hard peak. Grabbing her other breast, I worked my thumb over her nipple until she moaned.

I pulled away, falling onto my back next to her. "Get on top of me," I demanded.

She sat next to me, grabbing my cock with greedy fingers. "My turn to tame the demon."

She stroked my hard length, the palm of her hand pulsing over the head. Her fingers were delicate and firm, finely tuned to reading what pleased me. I closed my eyes, focusing on the sensations. How badly I wanted to bury my cock into her slick pussy, pounding until my balls were slapping against her.

I opened my eyes, finding that she was giving me head. I grabbed a fistful of her hair as she lathered my cock with her mouth. Her fingers found my balls, which she began squeezing.

Fuck, this is amazing. My cock plunged into her throat as she continued to mouth fuck me.

She pulled her mouth away, wiping her lips with the back of her hand as a satisfied smirk crept up her face. Her leg swung over my center as she straddled my core. Her breasts were red from my rough touch.

"My turn," she said, lifting her hips as she found my cock and slid down my length, until I was buried deep inside of her.

She rode me, her hips undulating. Her hands worked over my chest, fingernails scratching over my tattoos as she found a rhythm. Lucy might be a librarian, but here on top of me, she was a creature from a dark fairytale. I wanted to drink her in and taste her magic before she devoured me.

As we synced our bodies, my shadows and her goddess merged into one. Feeling the rhythms of her magic and her body harmonize with me made me realize just how lonely I had become. But Lucy was a different creature that I couldn't remain withdrawn from. This orgasm had claws and teeth. Lucy's hips tightened as she ripped it out of me.

Our bodies shuddered as our release combined, forming something sacred and forbidden. She slumped over my body, breathing into my neck. Sweat beaded on her forehead. "That was insane."

She fell to my side, her fingers still clawing at my chest as she hit the pillow.

I reached my arm around her center, cuddling her. Her scent, a combination of fruity hair products and after sex, was simply intoxicating. We lay together in silence. Her breathing slowed to the point I wondered if she had drifted off to sleep.

I wiped her hair away from her forehead, kissing her tenderly. My shadows were quiet, for now. All I could hear was the murmur of her heart as her body formed against me.

She glanced up at me, her eyes glassy with pleasure. "Did your shadows tell you yet?"

"Tell me what?"

"How Melrose died. I told them that they must tell you as soon as they released you from the painting."

"Why are we talking about Melrose right now?" I asked, slightly annoyed. Hadn't I blown her mind? She sure blew me away.

Her fingers trailed down my front, tracing the length of my black strip of hair until she found the base of my cock. "Because her death is tied to what the Bone Threader wants. There is a certain demon I want to keep around my books."

I grabbed her wandering hand and brought her fingers to my lips, kissing each of them. "Only a few weeks ago you didn't want me anywhere near your library."

Lucy's eyes, still smoky from her first orgasm, found mine. "That was before I knew about these shadows you were hiding from me."

33
Lucy

Amon rose onto his knees, his flat stomach and chest heaving. I loved watching his tattoos dance over his skin, and how they merged with the dark strip of hair that ran from his chest to the thick base of his cock. He was already hard, ready to go again. He was also twice the size of what Jason ever had.

Thank the triple goddess I was on the pill, because I wasn't about to stop. I'd just rode his thick pulsing cock into an earth-shattering orgasm I could see happening again, and again, and *again.*

"*You haven't felt our cocks yet,*" a voice echoed into my head. "*We are bigger than him. You will be screaming before we—*"

"Fuck off," Amon growled, his voice hardening with his body as he grabbed my leg and began kissing the inside of my knee.

I shivered as he licked and bit my skin, sending a ripple of pleasure through me.

"Are you fighting with your shadows?" I asked, still breathless from my orgasm.

"They want you, but not as much as I do. A demon worships his witch with his shadows." His fingers dropped to my clit, where he teased my slick opening. "I hope you aren't afraid of serpents."

My back arched as he slipped two fingers inside of me. His artistic hands were all I'd been craving, and now I was being fondled by them.

So *this* was what it felt like to be wanted.

He curled his fingers, blending erotic pain with pleasure. "Eyes on me," he whispered, a cocky smile spreading across his face. "My shadows need to know who the dominant demon is."

My fantasies ran wild as I imagined what Amon was describing. Multiples of him, all wanting me, competing for me with the same ferocity reflecting in his eyes? I'd never had a single man, let alone multiples, want me this way in my entire life.

A half-gasp-half-whimper escaped me as his chest tattoos morphed into serpents. Their coiling bodies unfolded from his body as they wrapped around my legs. What kind of kinky shadow bondage was this?

His tattoos appeared as branches layering upon themselves like the tree of shadows amidst a terrible storm. One of the serpents slithered over my slick, joining his fingers as he pulsed them through my opening.

"Amon, please," I whispered.

"Make that noise again," he demanded. "Beg for it."

All I could manage was a whimper as the second serpent unfolded its tail over my clit. White flashes clouded my periphery as he brought me close to release.

"Good girl," he purred as he withdrew his fingers and the serpents from my opening. He hooked me under my knees and dragged me toward him.

I rested my legs on his shoulders as his cock pulsed across my entry. The shadow serpents uncoiled their tails over my clit, circling their smooth, silky scales over me. This was a position I'd always wanted, something I'd only read about in Victoria's witchy kama sutra collection that often involved the *devil's serpents.*

"Tell me what you like," he breathed, holding me steady. His cock slid over my clit as he continued to please me.

My body ached for another release, but he was in control. Fucking a demon was so much better than I imagined it to be. If this was what *one* of Amon felt like, what would it be like when I was with *all* of him?

My magic surged as larger, thicker serpents coiled down his arms. They formed into ribbons of silk, binding my wrists as he slid into me.

Amon groaned as my body accepted every inch of him.

He rocked me, pulsing in and out as his shadows and serpents coiled around me. The pressure was so intense, my vision began to blur.

What if I passed out?

"Darkness, Lucy. I fucking *need* you," he growled as he disappeared into his shadows.

My body lifted off my bed. As gravity fell away, Amon's shadows coiled around me, tethering my arms above my head. He continued to fuck me, pulsing between my legs until my back pressed firmly against the wall.

"Put your arms around me," he said as another shadow hand caressed my neck.

I sank into his solidness. My hips rolled as he bounced me. Goddess, the stars I saw. I was thrown into a fit of burning pleasure and ecstasy. The sheer force and rhythm his body made against mine was going to do one of two things—either light me on fire, or rip me apart.

"Lower me," I said, panting against his congealing shadows.

His stubble scraped against my chest, my neck, until his devilish smile appeared. "What, you don't like levitating while fucking?"

I grabbed a handful of his dark hair the moment I saw how far away from my bed I was. When he withdrew from between my legs, my body clenched around him. Part of me didn't want him to leave—the goddess in charge of my magic *also* wanted him.

Amon's smile turned into a smirk. He seemed to feel the way my magic had clung to him. As he slid out of me, rebellious blue and purple sparks erupted from my fingers.

My cheeks flamed as Amon lowered me down to the floor. We stood, panting. His hard body towered over me. I felt so small before him, so vulnerable and naked in ways I didn't want to retreat from. I was safe with him, even thought I knew the shadows branching out of his body wanted to do other devious things with me.

I set my head on his chest, listening for his heartbeat. The sound was crashing and relentless, breaking against his ribs. The melody made me think of the thunderstorms that were associated with my magic.

His lips pressed against my forehead, where I heard him inhale. His hands caressed my back, moving to my hair. He worked his fingers down my spine, tracing over me as I recovered my breath.

"How was that, too much?" he whispered.

"No, not too much," I breathed, not wanting to admit defeat.

I pulled away from his chest. His tattoos were cutting and angular, morphing and changing from bones to feathers. The mass of them coiled down his front, their darkness all funneling toward the base of his cock.

"You are so perfect, so soft," he said, nipping then kissing all down my neck. "Feel how hard you make me."

His hips ground into my front, his thick length bulging against my thighs.

I grabbed his cock. My touch made one of the serpents coiling around the base constrict.

Amon's chin shot up as he threw his head back. I grabbed his cock with both hands and pumped him. He set both of his hands onto the dresser behind me as I worked my palms along his length.

"Fuck," he growled, grinding into me. "Lucy, you have a magical touch, but I need to be inside of you."

"Not until you've tasted me again."

Shadows branched out of Amon's ribs, gripping me behind my knees. My ass slid onto the dresser as he bucked his hips.

I leaned back, propping my elbows onto the dresser as he pried my legs apart and dove between them. His tongue slid across my skin, licking and sucking as he devoured me. The ceiling became a blur of splotchy white lights as he brought me close to release. It wasn't one tongue, it was many. Teeth grazed my skin as Amon's inner demons feasted upon me.

My back arched as white-hot pleasure coursed through my body. Purple flashes of light blurred my vision as I was thrown into release. The euphoric rush lingered, filling my body with the gentle pulse of my magic.

"Welcome back to the world of the living, beautiful," he said, a crooked smile twisting his lips. He leaned into me, encouraging me to wrap my arms around him.

Woozy from my orgasm, Amon helped me down from the dresser. My feet wobbled as I regained my composure. The firmness of his touch told me that he wasn't done with me. His cock pressed against my belly.

He smiled wickedly. "Time for you to feel what it's like to be with all of me."

My stomach twisted. The thought of this multi-shadow orgasm was enough to make me see stars again.

"*Flip her over*," one of the gravely voices demanded.

Silky ribbons curled around my torso, forcing me from my dresser to the bed. Before I fell onto the mattress, I was pressed between two, no, *three*? There had to be more. Multiple dark figures were fighting to enter me.

"*Let's see how many of us she can take at once*."

"Amon, how many of you are there?" I breathed as I was quickly dominated by the hard masses of muscular shadow bodies. Their hands groped my ass and as they bent me over.

"Lucy?"

A familiar female voice called from downstairs.

"Shit," I stammered, my face crowded by my own sweaty hair.

Amon's shadows dispersed, leaving me panting on all fours on my mess of a bed. Grabbing my cardigan, I covered my front and I darted from my bedroom into the bathroom. After I shut the door, I turned on the tap. I just hoped that Victoria didn't see the aftermath of our devious lovemaking.

Victoria's footsteps thundered up the stairs as I jumped into the steam. "Lucy!"

"I'm in the shower!"

The door opened as Victoria made her way inside. "Mom said there is a shadow vortex by the library and that you had gone missing. I'm texting her that I found you right now."

"Texting her now!" Francine, her red tailed hawk, chimed in.

I lathered shampoo into my hair. *Fuck.* Red marks lined my wrists and torso from our serpentine bondage play. I couldn't let Victoria see any of it, or she would be all over me.

"Freshen up. Francine and I will be outside to hear where you've been. Mom is on her way over. She said she has something to share with us."

I rinsed off and wrapped myself in a towel.

The second I emerged from the steamy bathroom, Victoria and her hawk perched atop her shoulder gave me the stink eye. "You know, it wouldn't hurt for you to let Mom and your sisters know that you are okay."

"That was my fault."

"Well? Where have you been?"

"Fucking a demon!" Francine cried.

"Your bird lies," I stammered. I was still breathless from Amon. I bustled past my sister, trying to hide the marks on my neck and arms.

"Something is definitely going on," Victoria agreed with her hawk. "I could tell from the magic in the air. What's up with this magical vortex? And why are my wine glasses shattered into smithereens downstairs?"

"Smithereens!" Francine squawked.

As soon as I climbed into a fresh pair of clothing, the front door opened downstairs. My mother's aura blew through the house, filling the space with her protective magic. Victoria left me to dress as she descended the stairs.

I followed her, finding Mom in the foyer, both of her arms folded in front of her chest. Her bun was disheveled into a frizzy clump. Her eyes flickered with the fierceness of a protective lioness.

"Where in the *goddess's* name have you been?" Mom scolded me, her voice cracking with emotion. The air thickened with humidity as her brown eyes inspected my aura. "I have been worried sick. Do you have any idea how terrified I felt when I found Amon with his brother, and you weren't with him? There is a wendigo in town. I trusted him to protect you from it."

I wanted to sink down and hide. Mom's aura was dangerously thin, her energy dispersed like muggy air after a rainstorm. She closed the space between us, her hands hovering about, "Amon's aura is all over you." She paused, whisking away something invisible above my head. "Wait, am I seeing more than one? Where are all of these shadows coming from? The wendigo hasn't touched you, has it?"

Now I really wanted to hide. "No, the wendigo hasn't come anywhere close to me. I'm sorry I didn't reach out to you sooner. Amon and I have been searching for a book."

"Of course you have," mom warned in a dangerous tone. "Something else isn't adding up."

Victoria's mouth formed an *O* as her brows arched up. Even she knew that shit was about to get real. Mom's wrath rarely came out, but when it did, all of her daughters could feel the earthquake of energy from her aura. Growing up, all three of us had to deal with the seismic ripples of her discipline. The one thing she did not tolerate in the Crow household, was any form of lying, or cheating, involving the use of magic. I remembered a time when Grace and I were teenagers. We had been fighting over one of Mom's spices, both believing it would help us pass our history class. When Mom found out, we were both confined to our rooms without dinner privileges, forced to eat cold, bland oatmeal every evening with no sugar instead. Neither of us saw a hot meal for over a week, while Victoria bragged about eating Chinese takeout.

Victoria began to pick up the books Melrose had tossed about the room, stuffing them back onto her bookshelf.

Mom didn't let me out of her sight. She pulled me into a tight hug. Her scent of baking spices washed over me as I hugged her back. It felt like eons before she released me.

When she did, her aura thrashed over me. "Those grimoires have long been known to keep magic hostage. I didn't know they had the power to capture the spirits of witches too, until Amon told me. I was terrified that would happen to you."

"Mom, I'm sorry. I promise that I didn't mean to scare you."

A smile turned up the corners of her mouth before resuming back to a frown. The lines that framed her lips became more pronounced. The only thing that could make her look her age was fear about her daughters.

"Your father had a collection of books from an archive he said familiars had created, but demons had taken over. He said the books were so old, the spells inside of them had forgotten how they formed. Who could borrow the ancient texts was all regulated by—"

"—A demon council that witches don't like to talk about?"

Mom's brow furrowed. "Yes, how did you know about this said demon council?"

"Amon's father came to visit. He apparently got fired from the council."

"And why is that important?"

"I don't know. Amon wouldn't let me overhear the details, before he. . ." My mind was plagued with the hard, muscular bodies as Amon's shadows tried to dominate me moments before.

Thankfully, Mom looked away. She started helping Victoria with re-organizing her bookshelf. "Your father knew some of the shady individuals who worked for that council. The members were also heavily involved with the regulation of magical texts like grimoires."

"Amon took me to this shadow archive."

Mom dropped one of the books. "He took you there? Why?"

Victoria stopped beside me. "Girl, you've been keeping secrets. Mom and I know it."

Mom returned next to me. "I knew something strange was going on with your magic. But I never would have assumed that Amon brought you to an archive where these grimoires are all housed."

"Mom, she loves books. If a demon wants to impress a witch he's crushing on, I'm sure he'd try and woo her with what she likes," Victoria said, winking at me.

"Amon was trying to help me," I said, finding my mother's gaze. "He brought me to the shadow archive to try and remedy what was happening to my magic. The energy bursts were becoming dangerous. You both know I haven't practiced magic since. . ." My voice hushed.

"Since Dad passed?" Victoria said, setting her hand on my arm.

I start shaking. "It's not like me to be this way. I've never had issues with my magic flaring. Then a month ago, everything happened with Jason, and it was like this giant void came back into my life. I forgot what missing Dad really felt like."

Both Mom and Victoria's auras blended around me, forming a golden band of energy. Their magic felt like water, smoothing away the burning sensation Amon's shadows had brought to the surface.

"You could have said something, Lucy. Why didn't you say that you've been thinking about Dad recently?" Victoria asked. Her voice was soft and comforting.

"I didn't want to burden you," I said, emotion gripping my throat. "Look, I'm grateful for everything you both and Grace have done for me. But this problem with my magic is mine, not yours, got it? When and how I use magic is up to me. Not even Grubs should have a say on how I practice."

Both Mom and Victoria nodded.

"Speaking of Grubs," Mom chimed in, "I'm beginning to think that your familiar might also have his greedy little mouth parts involved with this shadow archive."

"Grubs? Why?"

Mom reached into her sweater pocket and pulled out a seed pod. "I stopped by Grace's greenhouse and I discovered this."

The seedpod had a symbol burned into its husk—a magical symbol I recognized from the grimoire. "This symbol is part of a spell all right. An ancient one."

"I can't read any of that gibberish," Victoria said, her brow pinching.

"Gibberish!" Francine squawked from atop the bookshelf.

"Do you think Amon can?" Mom asked.

"No, but his mother could," I replied as Francine's frilling feathers suddenly made me think of Eugene's two ravens. "Amon's mother was a witch. Her spirit has been communicating with me. She wants me to deliver a message to her son."

Mom's quizzical look intensified. "It all makes sense to me now. Your father was writing about the separation of the three magics." Her eyes found me again. "The symbols in the grimoires were something your father showed you when you were a child. They are bound to impact your magic if you were to rediscover them."

My stomach knotted. "He did? When?"

"I still remember him reading children's books to you, ones he would sprinkle the symbols into. He did it in a way that wasn't obvious, sometimes blending them with the illustrations and the characters without you knowing they were even there." Her voice became hushed with emotion. "He loved you to bits, Lucy. The way he read to you helped you to overcome your dyslexia."

A hazy blue figure appeared in my periphery. I swore I saw my father's outline in the chair as he waved at me.

I blinked, and his spirit was gone. The corners of my eyes stung. "How?"

"The symbols are at their core a language that binds all three magics," Mom answered.

I thought immediately of Melrose and what she had said about the symbols, and why she, too, had wanted them.

Suddenly, I might not need Amon's shadows to keep their end of the bargain. I might be able to help Melrose myself.

"The witch that was locked inside of the grimoire died a long time ago. Her spirit can't remember how she died, so she can't move on." I shivered, thinking about the deal I made with Amon's shadows. "I know in my gut that her death is tied to the wendigo."

Mom's face brightened as her aura brimmed with golden light. "Then you know what you must do. Your father has prepared you for this moment. If you can read these symbols, you can stop this vortex the wendigo has released into town." She turned on her heel. "Follow me."

Once around the corner, mom tore open the closet door. The scent of mothballs, as well as live moths, escaped into the air. "What household cleaning appliance can a witch rely on these days?" Mom asked as she began to shift through the coats.

A witch didn't dig through a closet like this unless she was preparing to go airborne. Mom rarely flew. The last time I took to the skies with her, I was probably in middle school, when she frequently had to travel quickly across town to rescue one of her daughters from something they wanted no part of. Mom was the one witch in the Crow family who possessed the talent to spontaneously levitate with her will alone.

I, on the other hand, couldn't fly without her help. She was looking for an item to bewitch so I could tag along with her.

She pulled out an item, holding it over her head like a trophy. "Not a broom, but how about purple polka dots and octopuses?"

The umbrella flew open with a swift *pop*! sending the moths scattering.

"Not playing Marry Poppins today," I replied.

"Victoria, where did you put the sun hat I lent you?" Mom asked my sister.

"The one that looked like a mushroom? I gave it to Grace, remember?"

Mom thrust the umbrella into my hand. "Octopus Marry Poppins will have to do for now." She grabbed my other hand and tugged me out the front door. We stood in the garden, the lilacs curling in my mother's magic. A few bees buzzed about, completely out of season. Her magic could summon springtime, even amidst autumn.

Mom kicked up her heels and levitated off the ground. I fumbled with the umbrella as I knew her magic would soon sweep me up. It flopped open as the wind took me into her magical wake. My feet dangled beneath me as she raised her arm, guiding both of us up. Trees and rooftops became my focus as we hovered in the air. Darkness cloaked my periphery the higher we went.

Shit.

I'd been spotted by Amon's shadows.

As soon as they saw me, they withdrew behind the grove of trees below. I clutched onto the umbrella, grateful they weren't slithering lustfully after me like they had in my bedroom.

I could feel their silky bodies coiling between my legs, warming me from the inside. The sensation was enough to make me want to rip out of my skin. The marks they left on my arms burned as the town below began to glow.

"My goddess, what is this?" Mom asked, her voice carried away by the wind whipping her hair out of its bun.

"I can read it," I said. There were symbols bleeding all around town. They bled through the trees, the rooftops, softening and hardening like Amon's painting.

"*I have a message I want you to deliver to my son.*"

This was the message Amon's mother wanted me to give to him. It was right here, written all over town. All I needed to do was trust in my magic.

34
Amon

It took all of my strength to rip my shadows away from Lucy's body when her sister showed up. The air smelled of burning rubber as I entered my tattoo parlor. Jars of ink hovered in the air, bewitched with the seductive aura Lucy left.

I had a problem. Having shadow-twisting sex with Lucy had only made it worse. My tattoos had rediscovered themselves, threading together like they were meeting each other for the first time. But I knew it was a warning for the mess to come. My tattoos were an expression of my soul, and right now they were doing something they hadn't done for over a century.

They weren't arguing—they were *talking* with one another.

They were discussing what happened between Lucy and I like a soap opera. While I could only catch bits and pieces of their cryptic discussion, the vocalization was overwhelming. It would take a whole lot of willpower not to give in to their control.

"*She's a firecracker!*"

"*What a witch!*"

"*She took those serpents like a pro!*"

"Stop it," I hissed.

"*We were only getting started! Imagine what she might do when we release the anaconda!*" one of them bellowed, his voice growling as it blew past me. My hair parted as my shadows began roaring with one another. "*Come on. We all know how much you wanted us to have a go at her.*"

I grabbed one of the bands of silk before he escaped my grasp. "Apparently you've been keeping secrets from me. Lucy said you agreed to tell her how Melrose died. Well?"

"*We didn't get our end of the bargain*," he growled back at me.

My fingers disappeared into the ebony mass of my shadow. "I don't care what you get. She's mine, not yours."

A greedy smile spread across his twisting, vaporous face. "*A witch's word is a demon's pleasure. It's time you show her your true self, Hidden One.*"

My shadow dispersed in a plume of black smoke, leaving me feeling hollow.

Shit.

My shadows had me cornered.

I gazed around my shop, Where was Dad, anyway? Krim was supposed to distract him when I took off to find Lucy.

Anger and Sadness had rummaged through my art supplies. What had they done with my mother's medicine bundle?

One of the portraits morphed, darkening until the face became concealed beneath a cloak of darkness. Krim's head manifested, his eyes glowing red behind the shadows draping over his face. His mouth snapped open as a snarl escaped his lips. "Dude. I've been trying to get a hold of you. Turn on your fucking phone. Get to my bar, now."

"Where is Dad?" I snapped at him.

His eyes flashed, redness burning in them. "No idea. But I think Lucy's little bookworm might have left something we can work with."

My stomach twisted.

Grubs.

I thought he was gone.

What had that bastard little bookworm done?

Moments later, I manifested inside of Shadow Daddy's. The air was thicker here than it was in my tattoo parlor. It was noon, and Krim had taken time off from his teaching duties at the university. Not a good sign. Even though it was the middle of the day, all of the shades were drawn.

Krim wasn't behind the bar where he usually worked out some horribly-gone-wrong baking experiment. Other figures lurked in the room, coalescing near the pool table. Their auras were concealed, preventing me from making a reading on them. The energy was so thickly negative, one could cut it with a knife, sending vortexes and ley lines haywire.

Krim's shadow was there among the others, but he was smaller than he usually appeared. He wasn't tucked behind the bar, but was out in the open like me.

I approached the bar, stopping by my younger brother. "What's up with all of the shady vibes in here?" I asked, knowing Shadow Daddy's had always done well to attract restless spirits. I sucked in a breath, choking. The nasty humid air thickened by the second.

Krim folded his arms across his chest, keeping his reaper hood drawn over his face. His gaze found me. Something I couldn't quite read flickered in his bloodshot irises. "The spirits are trying to figure out what to do with the bookworm."

The mass of shadows morphed as my youngest brother stepped out of the darkness. The silver spikes of Zed's leather jacket oozed with something damp. A burlap sack hung from his fist, the bottom bulging as it swung in front of him.

Zed separated himself from the shadows, standing in front of Krim and I. "That little bastard bookworm has gone and ate something that killed him all right." He folded the sack open and poured the contents out, filling the space with the musky scent of earth.

A shriveled body of what had been Lucy's familiar fell onto the pile of dirt. It rolled until it stopped at my foot, where I finally got a good look at him. His body resembled an elongated raisin.

Part of me was happy the little dick was gone. Another part of me knew that somehow, this was a really bad sign.

"Is he dead?" Krim asked, squinting so hard at the dirt that his hood fell into his face.

"Familiars don't die," I corrected. "Their magic is all about recycling, isn't it? Don't their spirits resurrect themselves shortly after. . .*this*?"

"*No. They like to burrow into your skin first.*"

I slapped my wrist, hoping to muffle my shadows before they latched onto the negative energy spewing out of the shadow vortex growing before us.

"Who said that?" Krim asked.

"Me," I said, which was partially correct. My shadows might have voices of their own, but I could easily disguise them if necessary.

I could feel their arms and fingers waiting to branch out of me. They were flirting with the ball of black energy that had started to spin.

"Well, this one apparently *did* die," Zed grumbled, wiping a bead of sweat trickling down his face. "When he did, he opened some kind of shadow portal to the Summoning, hence all of this spirit business."

I glanced at the dirt, watching as the shadows seemed to devour what spilled on the floor. Like sand pouring through an hourglass, the pile began to disappear, until only the shriveled body of Lucy's familiar remained.

"Whatever he munched on, that was it. That little grubby thing went and feasted on his last treat."

The three of us brothers turned to face the female figure forming in the corner of the bar. The scent of roses filled the room, masking the aroma of damp earth as she closed in on us.

"Melrose, what are you doing here?" I asked, taking a stance in front of my brothers.

Her green eyes settled onto me, a dangerous flicker in them. She tossed something forward, where it landed with a dusty *thud* on the ground. "Don't you want to see what was making the Bone Threader sick to his stomach?"

It took me a moment to figure out what was now fuming on the ground. The grimoire smoked and hissed, tendrils of green vapor escaping from its soggy pages.

"He couldn't devour it?" I asked.

"No," Melrose said. "Apparently, some other familiar took a bite out of it first."

We all stared at the shriveled raisin on the ground. I couldn't believe it. I was actually grateful for Lucy's grouchy bookworm. He just might have saved my family's archives by preventing the Bone Threader from devouring my parents' grimoire.

The ground trembled, quaking as a plume of dirt and smoke manifested. The boy I'd met at Greasy's Dinner emerged, flexing his fingers as his eyes fell to me. His fingers gripped the side of his face as he peeled the identity of the boy away.

The wendigo's true form emerged—a spirit made of soil, bone, and decay. "Today is the day I devour every last one of you and turn you into binding paste," The Bone Threader barked. His bony fingers morphed into claws.

I ducked as he swung his arm and knocked Krim's alcohol selection to the ground, shattering the liquor bottles. I hit the ground as his claws sliced their way over my arms, gouging through me. One-by-one, each of my shadows was ripped out of my skin, leaving behind nothing but my hollow body.

35

Lucy

"There!" I cried as the wind whipped past my airborne mother and I. Panic pulsed through me. As quickly as I'd seen the black shadows coalescing over town, they disappeared again. I needed to stop Amon's shadows from turning on him.

I tunneled through the air, diving for the ground as quickly as my mother's magic would allow.

"Lucy, wait!" Mom cried as we dipped toward the garden. "What did you see?"

"Didn't you see the mass of shadows hovering over the street?" I stammered.

Mom's hand came to my shoulder. "No, I didn't see anything."

My stomach twisted. The Bone Threader was doing something horrible to him.

A gust of wind ripped past us, tearing me away from Mom before I met the trees. I was hurled through the air, bits of bark catching my hair. My feet hit the ground, scraping over damp pavement.

"Lucy."

I turned to face the silky male voice echoing behind me.

Amon stood on the sidewalk differently than he had before. No black shadows coalesced in his wake, nor did he have that crooked grin of his that I'd grown fond of.

My breath caught. Something was wrong with him. He didn't seem to be himself. His skin was porcelain white, not the warm honey brown color I was used to. His eyes weren't dark. They lit up in an unnatural way. When I gazed into them, I felt empty.

The scent of electricity filled my nose as his irises flickered with red and blue sparks. My periphery darkened as the tattoos on Amon's arms became bands of colorful texture. The markings brought me back to my visions of the tree of shadows.

He turned away from me.

"Amon, wait, where are you going?" I grabbed for his arm, but my hand moved through him.

He wasn't solid, just emptiness.

"I've lost myself," he whispered, his voice fading with his form.

"Listen, I think I know how to defeat the Bone Threader. His power is tied to Melrose's death."

Amon's eyes found mine, great hollowness drifting in them. "I'm trying to find my missing shadow before the Bone Threader does."

"Amon, wait!"

He faded away. I must have been hallucinating. A woman wearing a mushroom hat was staring at me.

"Lucy?" What is going on?"

I blinked a few times, until I finally registered who I was seeing. Grace stood on the sidewalk, her giant floppy mushroom hat flapping in the breeze. "I just got back in town. Victoria texted me. She said that Mom took you flying?"

"Yeah. There have been some issues with a shadow vortex."

"There are sinkholes everywhere. What is going on?"

"I need to practice."

Grace's mouth dropped open. "You want to practice your magic? Why?"

"I don't want to, I *need* to. Amon's life and my library depend on it. A wendigo is going to devour our town if we don't stop it."

"There you are," Mom said, hovering above us. "You should see what's going on at your greenhouse, Grace. A very dangerous demon is in town the Crow coven must contend with."

Grace's face turned white.

Mom waved her hand, sending a whirlwind of leaves around us.

Moments later, the whirlwind of Mom's magic settled the three of us outside of Grace's greenhouse. Exactly what I didn't want to see was making its way toward us.

A wave of tiny jumping spiders came sprung out of the walls, each making a little *ratta-tat-tat*! as they landed on the leaf litter outside.

"Nothing spooks my jumping spiders," Grace said, horror ringing in her tone. She tore ahead of us, her mushroom hat flying off as she raced through the door. Mom and I followed, treading carefully as to not step on any of Grace's frightened eight-legged familiars.

The greenhouse groaned as the enchantments used to keep the rickety wooden beams together shook. Something had obviously disrupted the magic Grace bewitched the faltering structure with.

A creature jumped onto my shoe, then up my leg, landing on my arm. A pair of shiny ink-drop eyes sparkled in the dim light as the eight-legged creature began to dance atop my arm.

I scrambled backward, my butt knocking into one of the raised garden beds. My back slammed into something woody and solid.

"Grace, since when have you been growing trees in your greenhouse?" Mom asked as she walked to my side.

Grace's brow knitted as she squinted past me. "Well, this definitely wasn't here when I left a week ago."

I staggered to my feet, turning to find the tree my Mom and sister were ogling. I recognized the slick texture of the ebony bark—the same hollowness I'd seen moving behind Amon's eyes.

I stopped next to my sister. The tree of shadows was sprouting right out of Grace's compost pile where the two of us had performed one of her green magic rituals. "When did this start sprouting?"

Grace's mouth opened and closed. "There was a tiny sprout in the dirt this morning when I arrived home. I never imagined it would grow this much in just a few hours."

Branches twisted like vines as the tree spiraled up out of the ground.

"The screaming death beans come from *shadow trees*?" I clarified.

"I guess so. I've studied species of medicinal spirit plants for a long time, but never have I seen one actually grow. They are able to connect the physical world and the worlds of the paranormal."

I squinted at the tree's gnarled roots. Symbols decorated them—the same symbols I'd seen in Amon's tattoos when we visited the shadow archives—the place where he'd encouraged me to read them. I still didn't know what they meant. The symbols morphed between serpents and feathers, eventually turning into bulging mushrooms.

The trunk made a nasty cracking sound, sending wood splinters flying into the air.

"How do we stop this thing from growing?" Grace asked, backing away from the dangerous bark.

I stared at the gnarled wood of the tree where the symbols were fast appearing. I needed to figure out how to read them and reverse this rebellious magic.

One of the branches snapped through one of the ceiling panels, shattering the glass.

"Well hello there, Lucy Crow," A female voice sounded from behind the tree.

I turned, facing the woman who had manifested beside the trunk. Her hair curled unnaturally at her sides, branching out like vines.

"I know what she is," Grace growled. "Get out of my greenhouse, you nasty green vampire!"

Melrose's lips curled, widening her thin mouth. "I'm not here for your nasty little beans, my dear. I want your older sister to help me seal a demon away in the stomach of a wendigo for good."

Grace's magic burned from her fingertips, making the stems and leaves on some of her plants tendril. Even a few mushrooms bowed their bulbous heads, straightening as little puffs of spores issued from their caps. "You're not stealing my sister's magic, you witchy bitch!"

The mushrooms unleashed a plume of spores that quickly condensed into a cloud nobody with allergies would want to mess with. The sight brought back so many memories. I remembered watching Grace summon spores when we were kids, after some other child tried to steal her shovel and pail from the sandbox.

Melrose dipped behind the tree, vines following her cackling cries. "Mushrooms are no match for vines my dear!"

But Grace had other tricks up her sleeves that involved her eight-legged familiars. They huddled together by the cactus, their shiny ink-drop eyes catching daylight streaming through the shattered windows.

While Grace had Melrose preoccupied, I darted for the compost pile, where Mom was busy sorting through banana peels and other decomposing organic objects.

"Oh, deary me. What will the Crow sisters do when their magic has all been absorbed by the shadow tree?" Melrose cackled as she thrust her arms out, coiling her wrists as she chanted an incantation, "From the earth, the sky, and the wind. Shadows from beyond, I ask that you—"

Screeeeech!

Melrose was knocked backward, her hair catching in the branches of the tree.

Victoria's red tailed hawk swooped down through the ceiling, gripping the vines and ripping them to shreds.

Victoria emerged in the greenhouse, a nasty scowl upon her face. "You all decided to light up your magic without inviting me to the party?"

Another spirit emerged from the tree—a young boy. He climbed down from one of the branches, landing onto the ground. He was dressed in clothing that didn't seem like it was from this time.

"Stop that stupid bird!" Melrose shrieked as Francine swooped overhead. The hawk's wings clipped the ceiling as she maneuvered and dove once again for Melrose.

Melrose jumped, landing in a pile of dirt, sending a plume of soil into the air.

This boy held something in his hands.

My stomach hollowed as he unfolded his fingers. "Grubs?"

36
Amon

There were more shadows than I could handle, each branching out of me like thick dark sheets. They moved like black water. Smooth on the surface, and violent underneath. It was just the Bone Threader and I now, our shadows a spiraling vortex of tunneling darkness. The energy here was thick with other restless spirits. We were lost somewhere in the Summoning.

A hand clawed for my face. Fingers grazed my cheek, tearing my skin.

I ducked as another sharp bony finger swiped in front of me, grabbing a fistful of my hair.

"Where is she?" the Bone Threader breathed, sending his hot, humid breath into my face.

Staggering backward, I hit the solid surface of another demon. One of my shadows reached his arms around my center and restrained me. He tried to use me as a shield to protect himself from being ripped to pieces.

"What are you doing?" I yelled at the Bone Threader, who became a rippling mass of ebony shadows and glistening white bone. His face was a mask of the past victims he devoured—all spirits who had no home.

"I'm not letting you go until you bring me Lucy," he growled, his voice thick with hunger.

"Fuck you. I'm not letting you near her," I bit out, trying in vain to free myself from my shadows as they tried to hide from the Bone Threader.

His arm extended, fingers long and thin, flexing as he approached me. The cold tip of his finger traced along my cheek until it curled near my chin. "You think you could show her what your nightmare of a past could reveal for her magic?"

I pulled my cheek away. "You tricked Lucy into using her magic. She thought she was doing you a service by helping you to read."

The Bone Threader smiled, his wide mouth grimacing. "Too bad I was the demon who got the first taste of it. That means I will be the one who decides what to do with it."

He disappeared again. His fingers clawed over my back and arms, ripping away my shirt to expose all of me. My shadows elongated. Some towered over me, others crouched, their bodies bent unnaturally.

The Bone Threader's hollow eyes glowed red. "You know this has always been about your mother's death. Why you were the one to inherit her talents is due to the fact that part of you refuses to let her go."

"You will *not* devour my mother's talents. Not through me, or through Lucy."

The Bone Threader's bony fingers grazed my chest. "We have both tasted their magic. You have what I need. Release their magic to me now, and I will make sure both Lucy and your mother's spirits go quietly." He dragged his finger over my chest, tearing yet another shadow out of my skin. Two of them had their ebony bands wrapped around me. "Don't you want to know what your missing shadow has seen regarding your mother? Us demons, we are complicated beings with many faces and memories."

He was right. I didn't know the entire truth behind my mother's death. My father had long kept that story a secret, trying to protect his boys from the mess of it.

My knees buckled, and I slipped through his grip.

Kicking my leg, I swung for him.

Two more of my shadows were on me before I could think. They grabbed my arms and linked them behind my back.

The air ripped open, revealing a small silhouette. A boy appeared, his jet-black hair and white face concealed by the thickening aura of the Summoning.

"Every demon has a shadow for every stage of his life," The Bone Threader whispered. "Which one of you should I devour first?"

The mass of my shadows retreated, except for one hovering aura. He stood to my right, his hand outstretched for me.

Seeing him here, a light shining in the dark, I was no longer alone. All of this time, was this my missing shadow that would make me whole?

"You need to leave," I demanded to the silver light flickering between my towering shadows. Despite how large and monstrous they had become, he was not afraid of them.

He shifted closer to me. This shadow, however small, refused to leave my side.

All but one of my shadows retreated from the Bone Threader's fingers as they branched atop us.

I looked into the face of the small shadow, barely recognizing who he was. I'd spent so long battling the bigger, darker sides of myself. Yet this one had strengths I overlooked.

He was my childhood shadow. How I wish I could retain that braver part of myself. I had become such a coward as an adult.

He threw his hands out, light branching through his small fingers.

The scent of water filled my nose.

I blinked, suddenly returning to a spot by the river from my childhood.

My mother stood by the water. Her eyes lit up, one blue, the other red. "Go find them and bring them to me, my son. Today, I will share the magic behind my talents."

The black roots of the tree I sat next to began to glow. Glow worms—dozens of them—were inching their way up the trunk and into the branches.

I followed them, my bare feet digging into the bark as I scrambled up the roots. I made the movements over and over, becoming acquainted with the familiars who lived in the ancient tree. Each branch I grabbed or placed my foot upon became an old friend.

As the branches thinned near the top, I discovered what my mother had requested of me to find. The worms left small cocoons behind in the branches, which I collected, in a small bag. These were the colors of my mother's pigments.

As time fractured around this memory of mine, so did the branches of the tree. Another journey climbing, I wasn't alone. A small boy stood beneath me, his face gazing up.

"Jeremy!" a small girl's voice cried from the forest. "Don't climb any higher! You will fall!"

"Go away!" I called back to the boy, but he refused, and followed me up.

"Melrose!" he cried. "I can see the familiars up there! I can climb to the top!"

The boy was Melrose's brother.

"No, turn back! It's not safe!" I called down to him.

But the boy was already half-way up the tree.

His small white fingers grip against the branch my foot was on.

Snap!

The tree was encompassed in mist as I descended.

By the time my feet hit the ground, the sound of trickling water was all I could hear. I returned to the spot where I remembered my mother standing many times, only finding a single black feather.

Crouching to the ground, I retrieved the feather, tears burning my eyes. My mother was gone. She left me her medicine bundle.

A hand came to my shoulder, the pressure protective and warm. "You were always fond of climbing trees, Amon. Chasing the birds up into the branches. You were always one with the ravens."

My throat closed. The memory vanished. My knees buckled as I fell to the ground. "Melrose's brother died, because of *me*?"

The Bone Threader smiled greedily. "Your mother's spirit refuses to leave the Summoning because of this memory. Unless you give me what remains of her magic, her spirit will always belong to me."

My childhood shadow-shelf began to walk toward the Bone Threader.

"No, stop! He'll tear you to pieces!" I cried out.

The Bone Threader flexed his fingers. "Come play with me, Hidden One. Return to the shadows. I happen to know there is another witch who has the same magic possessed by your mother, and I am about to devour it."

"Leave Lucy out of this! I'm the one you want!" I yelled.

His laughter echoed, ricocheting off of me. My ribs buckled as the reverberation thundered around us. My child shadow stopped, turning to face me. My mother's reflection shone in his eyes. She stood next to the tree of shadows, her aura hovering like a raven's wings as they took flight.

"Amon," she said, her soft voice caressing me. "You must not fear what has happened to me. You must trust yourself. The lives of your brothers and your father depend on it."

I blinked, and my mother was gone.

My childhood shadow's eyes changed. One was red, the other blue.

Anger surged through me.

No.

I won't let the Bone Threader destroy what's left of my family.

If this is what he wanted, to consume what was left of my shadows, then so be it.

The Bone Threader's mouth extended, ripping upward into the sky. With a great terrible gnash, his jaws clamped down, swallowing every last shadow of mine in sight.

37
Lucy

The greenhouse groaned as magic from both of my sisters and my mother spiraled out of control. I was the only witch who had yet to join in with an attempt on trying to tame the tree of shadows. Branches twisted and bark splintered as it continued to unfold out of the earth.

"*Lucy, listen to me. The tree of shadows has earth magic that your bookworm has been feasting on*," Amon's voice filled my head.

"*Where are you*?"

"*Don't worry, I'll find my way out. Focus on finding your familiar*."

I searched the room. The boy that had been holding onto Grubs has vanished. But the tree, an ebony mass of spiraling bark that looked like something out of *Jack And The Beanstalk*, had quadrupled in size. Hundreds of little bookworms glistened up in the branches. Their wriggling bodies illuminated the ebony bark, making it shimmer with colorful iridescence.

A vine whipped across my ankles, knocking me off my feet.

"Lucy, look out!" my mother cried, her yellow bands of protective magic reaching for me.

A branch snapped, falling inches from where I was, all of which flailed violently in the magical vortex.

Melrose tossed her hands into the air, sending splinters and thorns flying. The light from the glowing worms illuminated her face as her gaze dropped to me. Her mouth twisted as her pupils dilated.

"Jeremy!" she cried.

The boy who had Grubs in his hands appeared by the tree's roots. I knew this spirit. He was the same child I had tutored.

"Jeremy? That's your name?" I asked.

He turned to me, ignoring Melrose. He reached his hand down and helped me to stand.

"Don't touch him!" Melrose cried, vines exploding out of the earth toward me. She crouched, extending both of her hands. "It's me, it's your sister."

Jeremy didn't respond. He was too interested in what the bookworms were leaving behind. Cocoons, dozens of them, rained down from the tree.

I thought back to the tree in my vision, where I'd been in the water. I'd seen someone fall out of the branches—a small boy. But prior to that, I'd seen a hand reach out of the water.

It all made sense now.

I climbed to my feet, a newfound energy surging through me. The energy pulsed, a lifeblood of water that was curious about the witch who had discovered the truth behind the death of another witch.

Amon's words poured through me. "*We can hide truths from ourselves, even in death. The grimoires have magic that helps to decipher truth often lost by spirits.*"

I approached Melrose, brushing her vines away. "All this time, the Bone Threader has kept you in the dark about what happened to you by that tree." Lightning flashed in my mind's eye as the ground flooded. "You can't remember how you died, because it happened very quickly."

Melrose rounded on me, anger burning in her eyes. "Do you think I am stupid?"

"Think about it. You haunted Amon for years after you couldn't find your brother. Why couldn't you find him? Because *you* were lost. You were already dead by the time you began searching for him."

Melrose scoffed, tossing her hands into the air. "I died *before* him? That's insane! You are lying!"

"Shadow magic doesn't lie. It reveals the pieces of ourselves we ignore. Remember the rain—the thunderstorms? You died in a flash flood the day you went searching for him."

"No, I don't believe this. Amon had been there. He saw everything!"

"You are right, *part* of him had been there, but it's not who you remember. Amon has been missing one of his shadows ever since you died."

"No, that's not true! Amon did this, he. . ."

"Sister, stop fighting," Jeremy said, holding out his hand. "All I wanted to do was climb that tree, because I had found a friend."

"Jeremy, is this true?" Melrose asked, falling to her knees. "Who were you following? Who was this friend?"

Jeremy smiled. "A boy my age who called himself Amon."

A great weight lifted from me as Jeremy grabbed his sister's hand and tugged her to her feet. He walked with her toward the hollow of the tree. With the two restless spirits now reunited, maybe at long last, we could all find some peace.

Water poured out of the roots, making the tree sway violently.

"My greenhouse!" Grace cried as the tree collapsed, blowing the structure into smithereens.

38
Amon

The air was thick enough to suffocate me. As soon as I hit a solid surface, I tumbled forward. I squinted into the dark, feeling stupid as I grasped for something to tell me where I had fallen.

But there was nothing. I was surrounded by an endless void. Was this a different part of the Summoning?

"Amon?" a gravelly voice called from my right.

"Who's there?" I replied.

A groan followed. "Can't you recognize the sound of your father's voice?"

I crawled toward Dad's sarcastic question until my hands met something solid. "Where the fuck are we?"

Greenish-yellow light illuminated my father's ghoulish features.

"Inside of bone boy," Dad replied, shaking his head to remove his greasy hair out of his face. "You ever wonder what the process looks like for him to turn demons into grimoires? Well, welcome to the fresh hole of hell where it all gets started."

"If Amon hadn't been flirting with that librarian witch, none of us would have to be here in the first place."

I jumped at the new voice to my left. "Krim?"

"Yeah, I'm here. I found Dad shortly after you took off with Lucy."

I caught the yellow outline of his thick neck muscles flexing not far from where Dad was. "Who else is here?"

"Zed's not saying much. He's pretty fucking pissed about everything," Krim replied as he cracked his neck.

Dirt flew into my face.

"Zed, are you seriously digging?" I stammered, shielding my eyes.

"Hey, I've dug a lot of graves in my life. But I don't think I'm going to find anything that—"

A terrible sound of metal on bone filled the Bone Threader's stomach.

"Got something!" Zed cried.

A hot blast of air burst into my face. The smell was a horrible mixture of sewer gas and rot.

I thrust my hand out, gripping sticky bones. His ribs were sharp and angular, cutting into my skin as I felt my way around our enclosure.

The burst of air stopped.

"*Any last words, Ravenbloods*?" The Bone Threader grumbled around us.

"Leave my sons alone, you fucking scab of a demon!" Dad barked.

Purple streaks exploded out of the dark. Anger and Sadness, complete with onyx wings, ripped out of the ground, burning with ash and smoke that was hot enough to burn flesh from the bone.

A dark chuckle followed as my father's purple cinders died. "*You can't burn your way out of me, Eugene.*"

Dad held his hand out, purple flames billowing as his ravens hissed and shrieked into smoldering ash. "He's won, Amon. He's always been ahead of the game."

One of the ravens darted past my face, his wing clipping me on the cheek.

"Stupid bird!" I yelled, angry in my own certainty that Anger had clipped me.

Something glinted in the dark on the ground. I crouched down, finding my mother's medicine bundle had opened. One of Dad's ravens must have taken it from my tattoo parlor. I didn't remember a *crystal* being inside of it.

Lucy said her father's love of nature inspired her to write her book about a witch named Crystal. The story began to coil through me like her magic had when we were in the shadow archives—magic she had suppressed since her father passed.

Here it was here, a shimmering crystal light in the dark belly of a wendigo. Suddenly, Lucy's children's book had a purpose.

"What is this?" The Bone Threader barked, his terrible voice echoing around me.

"Where did your mother's bundle of art supplies come from?" Dad asked as he slid beside me.

"Your angry raven stole it from my place," I replied.

Krim and Zed huddled around the crystal that started to glow between us. The light emitting from it branched across our bodies, casting shadows on the cavernous walls of the Bone Threader's stomach.

Suddenly, I had an idea.

I grabbed the crystal and held it over our heads.

"Shit, that's fucking bright!" Zed grumbled, shielding his eyes.

"Guys, we are going to make this wendigo really sick to his stomach," I said, squinting into the light.

"How?" Krim asked as he slapped his hands over his face to prevent himself from being blinded.

"Get closer to me. I'm going to count to three. When I do, I need all of you to release your most terrifying shadows, got it? We are going to impersonate death."

Zed and Krim nodded. Dad just stared at me, confusion wrecking his expression.

"One," I said, and the crystal pulsed in my hand. "Two—"

"I'm breaking out the Nematodes!" Zed cried.

"Amon, stop!" Dad cried as he grabbed my arm.

"Three!"

The crystal exploded into a shimmering ball of white. The shadows from my brothers and my fathers ripped upward, carried by the light.

I dove as the Bone Threader's ribcage came crashing down on me. I would feed him what he wanted. I sucked in a breath as I threw the crystal into the void of his stomach, surrendering what was left of my shadows.

39
Lucy

The following days became weeks as what should be normalcy fell upon town. Despite Grace blaming me for summoning a giant spirit tree that destroyed her greenhouse, I was getting by. The good news was that my library reopened.

With the sinkholes gone, I threw myself into work, finding my rhythm with my shelving routine. Grubs, on the other hand, was still missing. He might not be perched atop the bookshelf inspecting my every move, but I could still ask him questions. "*Where is Amon*?"

Nothing but silence, along with some muffled munching, followed. I usually embraced the quiet of the winter months as they approached, when Grubs had gone into chrysalis, preparing to emerge sometime in spring. But this year, the silence was too much. My mind was full of magical symbols and shadows that danced in a breeze full of raven feathers.

I should have known Amon would disappear as soon as Melrose and her brother departed. Having him around was too good to be true. His shadows were bound to a world of spirits, while I was tethered to a world of books.

After work, I found myself over at Mom's place. I'd spent many an evening over here, as Alba left for the Caribbean for the holidays. She wanted to see bronze men wearing banana hammocks in real life, not just behind the television.

Mom glanced up from her baking experiment, a smudge of white flour on her crimson cheeks. "Lucy, you look like you've seen a ghost."

Mom wasn't lying. Since I met Amon, all I wanted to read were books about the paranormal. I didn't have the grimoire any longer, or Amon to harass me. But the symbols inside had burned so deeply into my memory, I didn't think they were something I could ever forget.

Not in the way I had read them on him. Amon had forever changed the way I looked at my magic.

A bamboo spoon scraped across her porcelain bowl as Mom mixed another batch of her famous muffins. All three of us sisters were planning to get together with her for Thanksgiving. "Maybe your demon friends have all fled back to their demon council. Any word on Amon?"

"No, and Grubs refuses to tell me anything about what happened to him."

Mom's mouth twisted as she formed a reply. "Don't worry. He'll show up. A demon is bound to lose one of his shadows eventually, especially a creative one like Amon."

That afternoon, I tugged on my winter coat complete with a scarf and made my way down the sidewalk, taking in the usual sights and smells of the neighborhood. The crisp autumn air burned my lungs, followed by the white puffs of my breath. Sinkholes were repaired, new asphalt and concrete applied. Some areas had been left barren to Grace's liking, which she has volunteered through the City Council to start up a branch of community gardens.

All of the exposed earth left me feeling vulnerable. Ever since the tree of shadows bloomed out of the greenhouse, my magic refused to return into dormancy. While this new energy caused dandelion stems to curl as I walked by, all of the Ravenbloods disappeared from my life.

I found myself walking past Shadow Daddy's bar. Another bartender took over, one who was far less attractive than Amon's demon brother. My next stop was Amon's tattoo parlor. I stopped outside the window, blowing across the glass until a patch of condensation emerged. The blinds were drawn over the grimy windows. I couldn't see if the demon portraits were still inside. The shop had been closed for weeks. Staying the night in his flat again seemed like a fantasy now.

I traced my finger over the condensation patch, drawing a raven feather with a heart around it before I continued walking down the street. Returning to Victoria's, I found the gardens were well on their way in their winter transition. Frost lined the pathway, layering icy crystals upon the withered stems of the lilac bushes.

I followed the path, finding a pile of rocks that were disturbed. The hedgehogs were busy messing with the foliage, prepping their dens for winter. They did this in both Mom and Victoria's gardens, and I'd become quite accustomed to tripping over the rocks they displaced every year.

One of the stones wasn't like the others. A smoky chunk of quartz sat on the path, a dazzling sample of crystal. The ebony imperfections inside reminded me of Amon's feathers, each and every one of them perfectly sculpted. All I could see were the symbols on his beautiful naked body.

Those times were long gone. He came as quickly as the wendigo did, disappearing back into the shadows.

40
Amon

The crystal I had discovered in the Bone Threader's stomach was not just a crystal—it was an artistic tool from my mother's medicine bundle. The magic locked inside had the earthly power created by familiars, which she was very connected to, even in death. In his greed to devour her magic, the Bone Threader had accidently bitten off more than he could chew. The crystal had sprung upon him as quickly as Dad, my brothers and I all purged out of his stomach.

I sat in my tattoo parlor, pondering what to do with what remains of the wendigo. I shook the crystal, and he raised his fist at me. He was forever trapped, until I decided how to return his spirit back to the Summoning. Maybe I would turn his greedy hide into a grimoire.

There were *two* things a wendigo could not cannibalize. One being death, the other being the colorful pigments that brought a painting to life. This crystal had been my mother's tool for grinding up bookworm cocoons to create her pigments.

For the past couple of weeks, I'd been working on a piece of artwork, painted with a crow feather. I'd put the final details on it this morning. There was a certain witch I knew who would be able to read it better than any of my shadows.

Lucy's grouchy bookworm was no longer a worm, but a vibrant glowing ball of light that refused to leave my shoulder. He inched close to my ear, whispering unsolicited opinions about the colors I was *borrowing* from his kind to finish my painting.

"*Stop adding details and show it to her already,*" he griped.

I set down the feather. Once the ink was dry, I knew who I needed to finally share this painting with.

I coalesced inside of the public library, my senses finely attuned to the witch I was searching for. Lucy's aura lit up the bookshelves in a bluish-purple glow, offsetting the others.

She was tucked behind the shelves, crouched down near the bottom. A patch of skin showed on her lower back, a blank canvas I desired to mark.

She rose from the ground, turning to face me. Her eyes went wide as her mouth dropped open.

Before I could take a step toward her, she leapt into the air, wrapping her arms around me.

"Amon," she whispered as I was enveloped by her sweet, intoxicating scent, "where have you been?"

I breathed her in, feeling whole again. I didn't want to let her go. Not now, not *ever*.

She unraveled her arms from my neck but kept her belly pressed flat against me. "My mom and my sisters said you would show up. I didn't believe them."

"I had to sort some things out with the Bone Threader."

She slammed her fist into my shoulder. "Why couldn't you just tell me that? The last I saw you, your shadows. . ." Her voice trailed away, but an undertone of curiosity lingered as she grabbed my arm, rolling up my sleeve. "Where are your tattoos?"

"My shadows are whole again, thanks to you," I said as I took her hand and brought it to my lips. She flushed crimson, and I knew exactly where I wanted to take this.

Lowering her hand, I trailed my fingers through her hair, removing a strand away from her face. "Can you forgive me?"

"Only if you keep doing that," she breathed, her voice full of desire.

Being away from her had only made each of my shadows want her even more. I pressed my face against her neck, not wanting anything else but this moment.

"*All right, break it up. There will be no pinning one another to the bookshelves in the public library.*"

Grubs appeared as a glowing purple ball of light that hovered between us. Lucy waved her hand, swatting him away as her lips crashed against mine.

Her taste reminded me why I couldn't live alone without her any longer.

She pulled away, but her arms and hips stayed firmly pressed against me.

"*Fine, be that way. Don't come running to me if his shadows decide to misbehave again,*" Grubs scolded as he landed on a nearby bookshelf. He was no longer a grubby little bookworm, but a brilliant blue and red moth. "*You've never seen colors like this on me, have you*?" he asked, shimmying in place. His wings flipped up and down as he displayed his new appearance.

Lucy squinted at him. "No, I have not. Why are you so colorful?"

"*Show it to her, demon boy.*"

"Show me what?" Lucy asked, unraveling herself from me.

I reached into my bag and tugged out the parchment, unraveling it for Lucy to see.

Her fingers trembled over the paper edges as she took it into her hands. "What in the world?" Her eyes continued to work over my painting of a giant black tree. Raven and crow feathers drifted between the branches, illuminated by a full moon in the distance. "Your shadows, they aren't just magic, they are a work of *art*." She traced her fingers over the splotches of color, finding the places with the most contrast. "This is absolutely gorgeous, Amon. You have a real gift, you know that?" she said, her eyes finding me.

Pride swelled in my chest. "That is a real compliment coming from you."

She dug her hand into her cardigan, pulling out her phone.

"What are you doing?"

"I need to make a call." The phone rang twice before someone picked up. "Alyssa? Yeah. I've got some good news. I wanted to let you know. I found myself an awesome illustrator for my book."

41
Lucy

It had only been a month before Amon painted at least a dozen concept illustrations for Crystal's first picture book, which according to Alyssa, would be ready for print by summer. After my shift at the library, I found myself over at Amon's tattoo parlor. White clouds of condensation puffed with each of my breaths. With winter upon us, the days were short and crisp. A few shimmering stars emerged across the darkening sky as I arrived.

Warm air enveloped me as I entered his shop. The portraits on the wall all eyed me as I sauntered inside. The room wasn't dingy with monochromatic black and white images. Amon was a night owl. From the look of his space, he was getting his creative spark on for the evening.

Easels were propped everywhere, all of them a mess of brilliant color. He'd taken his artwork to another level with a new symbol.

My breath caught. Paintings of the night sky covered his space. Great sweeping movements of what could be water or starlight flowed like a waterfall between each piece. At first glance, it would appear that he had painted an ocean with how liquid the pieces appeared, each brimming with raw tranquility.

A shadow descended, the soft edges of his wings encompassing me. "There is my favorite librarian."

I relaxed as his stubble grazed my cheek. I shivered as his ink-splotched hands came to my waist, pressing firmly against me.

"I need your opinion on something," he whispered, his long fingers removing the scarf from around my neck, where he placed a sensual kiss just behind my ear.

"I need your opinion as well," I said as I turned to face him. "Alyssa said marketing my children's book is going to be difficult, even with a badass artist like yourself."

One of his brows arched. "How come?"

"Her motto has always been that smut sells. Everything else you have to rely on luck, or magic."

He brushed a strand of hair away from my cheek. "Well then, it's a good thing that the author of this children's book is dating a demon who does wild and wicked things to her magic."

His voice lowered, sending a shiver up my spine. All I could see was Amon's body etched like a work of art, covered in shadow symbols.

Grubs was napping in the corner, his wings a constant shimmer between iridescent blue and green. For some strange reason, he'd taken a liking to Amon's paintings.

Amon shifted me toward his art desk, where his pigments were scattered everywhere. He grabbed one of the pigment bundles. "I'm trying to figure out what I want to do with this." He held up one of his sketches he'd done of Crystal.

"I like her hat. You really have the witch vibe going for her."

He shook his head. "Something isn't right. All I can seem to do is get outlines. Every time I try to blend colors for her character, they turn into a mess."

I glanced over at the starlit ocean he'd created, then back to his sketch. "I have a simple solution. Why not turn it into a coloring book? That way the kids who read her story can pick what color they want for her adventures." I glanced down at his other sketches, completely transfixed with the serpents. "Maybe you could have her befriend some creatures too, and not just crystals."

A feral growl erupted from his chest. "You know there are many creatures that a demon conceals within his shadows."

"Yes, I know," I replied, wishing desperately we could pick up where we left off before my sister performed coitus interruptus a few weeks ago.

Amon maneuvered to my front, the muscles in his forearms tensing. "We have a couple of techniques to play with. Hold out your hand."

I did so, and he lathered my skin with a feather in what felt like liquid silk. A symbol appeared, which instantly tugged at my magic. Bands of ink bled across my palm. The sensation began in my fingers, then branched up my arm.

"Feathers?" I asked. "Is that all you've got?"

Amon chuckled. "Not impressed I take it?"

"No, I like it."

"But you don't *love* it."

The ink dispersed, leaving my skin shimmering with purple iridescence.

Amon ran his fingers over the iridescence, making it brighten. "It's okay for you to tell me what you like and what you don't. I'm not going to settle for less in the art my shadows create for Lucy Crow."

His words sounded like a challenge. "What's option number two?"

"Hmmmm." A purr escaped his lips that made my insides quiver; "That will require something I have yet to show you about my own talents. It involves creating a new symbol."

I searched his eyes. "Like a tattoo?"

"It's more than a tattoo. It's a magical bond that states you are mine, and that I belong to you."

The sheer idea of this magical bonding concept was something Alyssa should be texting me about in her latest binge read from some dark fantasy romance series. But here I was, living an actual scenario so many women escaped into books trying to live out a fantasy.

Amon might not have been some dark fae lord with pointy ears and a court of his own. But he had a studio full of easels and art he was creating for our own story. Amon was mine, and I was his. I wouldn't have it any other way. I refused to return to a life of hiding behind bookshelves, unless he was going to be there pinning me against them.

I traced my finger along his jaw, savoring his skin as it became rough with stubble. "Is this symbol permanent? Once you give it to me, is there no removing it?"

"The mark will remain with you forever, even after you die. Our magic will be bound together, and eventually recorded in the shadow archives."

I shivered. "How do I get this tattoo that bonds our magic?"

He leaned forward, his scent of ink and rainstorms washing over me. "I don't give tattoos to a witch the same way I would give to my old man." His fingers grazed down my back. "It starts with shadows, and ends with a goddess's light."

His tattoo parlor faded away as Amon's cloak of darkness enveloped me. Crisp night air burned my nose as I emerged in a new place. "Where are we?"

"Where the magic between demons and witches becomes one. We are in the heart of the Summoning, right outside of the shadow archives."

I glanced around the space searching for what I remembered of the confined walls, creeping vines, and the decay. We weren't in some abandoned tunnel in the earth at all, but up in the canopy of a tree. I had seen this tree from all angles, from the roots, to the bark, and now up here in the open air.

Starlight branched over us, the shimmering silver catching Amon's hard features. He stepped behind me, looping his arms around my front as he embraced me.

Resting on the branches in front of us was a single book, its binding knotted and worn from age. I crouched to touch the spine, running my fingers along the bumpy length. "I was wondering where the grimoire went." The cover didn't refuse my touch as I lifted it open. "Where are the pages? Have they all been ripped out?"

"The grimoire is returning to the tree of shadows."

"I don't understand." The remaining pages turned to dust beneath my fingers.

Amon held out his hand. A crystal no bigger than a small orange sat at the center of his palm. "My mother placed her and my father's bonded magic into this crystal before she died, then she gave it to me. For three hundred years, it remained hidden, right under my nose. The Bone Threader couldn't find it, and neither could Melrose." He let out a sigh. "I never knew it was inside of the art bundle, until recently. Apparently it was used to grind up pigments used for her vision paintings."

"So even if Melrose *could* open the book, she never would have found the magic she wanted, would she?"

He fumbled the crystal in his hand. "Not without this. This crystal is what housed the magic to open it. You were able to open the grimoire and free Melrose's spirit because you possess magical talents similar to my mother's."

"Why put the ability to open the grimoire into a crystal?"

His gaze returned to the grimoire, its cover flickering with dull, yellow light. "I told you that my parents wrote this book together when I was a boy. Back then, it was a custom ritual for a demon and a witch to bond their magics together inside of crystals." His voice rang soft, a tone of loneliness echoing in it. "I never would have thought that pieces from my mother's medicine bundle had also been sealed inside of it." The crystal danced in front of me. "This is yours."

"Shouldn't you give it to your father?"

His eyes met mine, flecks of starlight shimmering in their ebony depths. "No. He requested that to honor my mother's magic, that I give the crystal to a witch who possessed talents like hers. I mean, you *did* write a story about a witch named Crystal. I think that sort of speaks for itself."

My throat closed. *Me*? I felt like I was stealing something from another witch, a very powerful one that Amon lost one of his shadows over. I took the crystal from Amon. The smooth transparent edges were cool against my skin. My magic pulsed, emanating like a star.

Lights emerged from the branches like ghosts. My magic guided the lights out into the night. The tree became a display of liquid light as it spread into the air, drifting up and out to join with the moon and clouds.

The stars appeared a little bit brighter by the time the magic settled itself.

"What just happened?" I asked, huddling next to him.

"You've released magic tied to the witches and demons devoured by the Bone Threader."

The bark of the tree went dark again, leaving Amon and I to gaze out at the burning silver stars dancing in the night. The crystal was no longer in my hand. It also dispersed with the stars.

His lips came to the cusp of my ear. "I think it's time we claim this tree as our own." His hands fell to my waist, where his fingers traced circles along the small of my back.

"Does this act involve claiming me?" I whispered.

"Very much so." His fingers dipped into my leggings, diving into my panties. "Like this?"

"Lower."

His fingers found my slick. "Tell me to stop."

"I don't think I will," I breathed, arching my back as he flicked his experienced artistic fingers over me. "I think I'm ready to be worshiped by more than serpents."

I felt him harden. He began grinding against me as his fingers explored my clit. "Amon, this is fucking hot."

"It's about to get hotter." He grabbed me, his hands lifting me up into the limbs of the tree. His hands came to my wrists, pinning me.

"Undress me, please," I moaned.

A crooked grin spread across his face. "I like it when you beg." He tugged my shirt over my head, taking my bra with it.

I peeled off my leggings as his fingers grip my panties, ripping them in half. My breath was ragged as he traced a scorching line down my neck. He dragged his teeth over my skin, nipping at each of my breasts.

His clothing has already dissolved, leaving me with his muscular starlit body. Bands of shadows branched away from his arms and through his hair. He lay back on the tree, his cock bouncing as he hoisted me onto his lap.

I straddled him, not wanting to wait any longer for his thick penetration.

He bucked his hips, forcing me forward. My breasts smothered his face as he took one into one of his wide hands, the other into his mouth. His sucking and nipping continued as he explored my skin and neck. "You are mine, Lucy Crow. Don't ever forget that."

I grabbed his cock, sliding the palm of my hand down the back of his length. I'd waited for this moment for so long, I could scream. I lowered myself onto him, his body hard beneath me. His hard length slipped through the tightness of my opening.

A grunt erupted from his chest as I found a rhythm with him. I rocked my hips as we created an undulation as violent as a stormy sea.

Amon grabbed both of my hands, supporting me. "Our bodies are so perfect for each other. This perfect little pussy—I can feel how much you want me buried inside of you."

He rocked me, sending my body rippling into a fit of pleasure. I was so close to release when he stopped. I sank down, accepting every glorious inch of him. He continued with this movement and motion, bringing me so close I could taste my magic crying out to be released.

Everything I wanted my demon to do to me, he was doing. His face and chest with the tattoos branching out of his skin blurred in front of me.

"Sweetheart, this is only the foreplay," he teased. He pulled my hand, forcing me to fall to his side as he slid out of me. His other hand guided me to flip over so I was lying on my back, the thick haze of my near-orgasm brimming through me.

"*Slow down. She can't handle all of us at once.*"

"*Yes she can, she's a witch.*"

While the ebony mass folded in on itself, Amon's hands came to mine over my head, pinning me to the tree. He bucked his hips, plunging into me.

Surrendering to this moment was in no way a fantasy. This was real, not from some smutty romance book from Victoria's book collection.

"Take me. Take all of me, baby," he groaned as he pumped into me.

I rolled my hips as his stomach pressed against my belly. The way he could stretch and touch places I thought were untouchable, he could reach.

"Lucy, you are so perfect for us," Amon grunted, his voice a rasp of pleasure and urgency.

He bucked his hips again, this time with enough force that made me see stars. "You will take all of me, or my shadows will devour you."

I couldn't tell if his words were a tease, or real. All I heard was *me* and *devour*, which I was not about to stop from happening.

The black bands from his arms snaked down his wrist and coiled onto mine.

"*All of us, together, as one.*"

Amon towered over me, a monster of darkness. Yet I'd seen another side of him that wasn't scary at all. I'd seen a man who lost is mother as a child, and an artist.

Maybe his shadows wanted the same thing I wanted—a simple way to express myself.

A hand grabbed my shoulder and flipped me over onto my belly. Fingers traced along my spine, tracing circles around the small of my back as Amon's hard body pressed against my ass.

He gripped my hips in his callused hands as he entered me again. The sheer force and pressure of him was exactly what I needed. As Amon pounded me, a hand grabbed my hair. Another grabbed my ass. Teeth grazed my skin as another hand grabbed my leg.

"*Now it's our turn.*"

Shadows became hands as Amon's darkness coalesced around me. The hard shadow bodies merged into one dark form that pinned me between it and Amon. I was jostled between the two as Amon and his shadow selves entered me.

I will not pass out.

My body stretched as I surrendered to the shadows. Bands of ebony branched out of Amon's body as our climax exploded.

I fell next to him in what remained of the tree. The bark our bodies touched had shadow symbols engraved in it. As we finished, I glanced at the mark his shadows had left on me. It branched all the way up from my legs to my torso, where it stopped below my breast.

The light faded, and our magic bound together in one gorgeous symbol. A crow and a raven intertwined, their beaks and feathers shimmering in the starlit night.

"Do you like it?" he asked, his voice husky.

"I think the symbols are perfect for the Crow and Ravenblood archive."

He grabbed my fingers, kissing them. "Lucy Crow, I hope you write enough books to fill your own library. I hope you'll have me illustrate them, too."

I shivered as I was reminded about what a demon's shadows could do. I couldn't wait to see what our magic and love would be capable of when it came to the world of books.

A Sneak Peek at Grace's book: A Witch's Forbidden Bloom!

It wasn't like I always wanted a giant dead tree taking up the place where my greenhouse had once been, but here I was. The tree of shadows wasn't the only thing that winter hadn't forced into dormancy. A couple of months had passed, and with my grades dwindling, I needed to study. Spring semester would soon be upon me, and I had zero motivation to spend another five months with my nose buried in a textbook.

I plopped down on one of my overturned pots and glared at the gnarled mass of the dead tree. The aroma the bark put off was a mixture of mildew and something slightly spicy. Its splotchy black bark made me think of Halloween. Where there was death, there was life, according to my botany texts. I also knew that this was no normal species of tree. I'd studied spirit species for as long as I could remember. Dad had loads of books in his private library that talked about the species of flora planted by familiars. These species thrived in an alternate dimension where other familiar spirits mingled, dimensions my sister Lucy had experience with seeing. Their fruits, seeds, petals, and anything a witch could harvest was forbidden for her to combine with her magic.

Unless, of course, you were a green witch with a mushroom fetish like me.

Having a wendigo burrow through our small Midwestern town presented me with an incredible opportunity. I never imagined that I would have a physical spirit tree decomposing right here in the heart of my greenhouse. With its appearance came the destruction of what I'd spent the past three years pouring my own enchantments into. I had stayed up all night, my eyes damp from crying over how I was to get rid of it. By morning, however, something else had appeared on the slimy, knotted wood of the tree's roots.

Mushrooms—hundreds of them—had gotten to work decomposing the tree. By spring, this tree would hopefully be gone, returned to its original realm of magic. But I would be left with something forbidden—my own spirit ingredients I could use to experiment with my own green magic.

I'd spent my evenings taking photos of the bizarre mushrooms, hoping to capture the bioluminescent lights before they faded. Like the lights, my grades in college were also fading. Plants didn't need homework to survive. All they needed was sunlight, water, and a bunch of dead things to grow in for them to live on.

I'd practiced green witchcraft for as long as I could remember. My first experiments occurred when I was a tiny girl in the sandbox, finding snails and roly polys, which I made homes for out of Victoria's rain boots. Boy, did I remember her screaming the moment she squished five of them between her toes.

My magic had always been green in nature. Green magic tapped into the goddess in ways that were forbidden. Unless, of course, a witch was in the company of a demon.

One demon in particular has made my life a hell of sorts. He was the owner of Shadow Daddy's bar, and one of Amon's brothers. Professor Krim Ravenblood has always made my blood boil. He taught the class I loathed the most—organic chemistry.

Spring couldn't come quickly enough. Next semester, I was going to pass that stupid chemistry class and graduate. I had a plan for the mushrooms growing on the tree. It was only a matter of time before I was flirting with Professor Ravenblood over a piping hot cup of forbidden mushroom tea.

Acknowledgements

I've always loved paranormal stories, and this book quickly became a ghostly visitor in my brain while I was drafting the second book in a fantasy series that also dealt with spirits. So I decided to give it a shot and see where it took me. My hope is that the result is something my readers will enjoy and connect with. I could not have created this book without the help of many others. I wanted to acknowledge a few prominent influences in my life that continue to encourage me on this writing journey.

My mom and brother who have always supported my random creative endeavors, whether it be panting, drawing, or writing.

My father who is no longer with us, but still encourages me to write in spirit.

My husband Bill, for supporting me on this journey and for making me laugh with your feedback on my first drafts.

My critique group, who has put up with my stories for the past seven years. Carly, Debbie, and Ed, you've helped me to craft my character's voices as well as find my own author voice.

My amazing editor Sarah, my beta readers, and my street team for cheering me on when I had lots of doubts.

My readers, because you are what brings the written word to life.

My taiko group, Sun Mountain Taiko, for drumming with me and driving the rhythm behind my stories.

My local library, where I work in the family and children's department. To my fellow library staff who provide energy and enthusiasm for reading, art, and the community. Your energy is contagious!

The park where I work, providing me with the opportunity to connect others with nature. I'm so blessed to have the Colorado outdoors in my backyard.

Upcoming Release

A Witch's Forbidden Bloom will release in 2025.
Visit Amanda's website at www.amandacaseybooks.com to follow along with her writing adventures.

www.ingramcontent.com/pod-product-compliance
Lightning Source LLC
Chambersburg PA
CBHW020500310726
48979CB00016B/2733/J
* 9 7 8 1 9 6 5 3 7 5 0 0 6 *